What the critics are saying...

5 Angels and a Recommended Read "*Enchanted Rogues* is a delightful anthology filled to the brim with mischief and mayhem, hot love scenes, and romantic endings." ~ *Jennifer, Fallen Angel Reviews*

5 Coffee Cups "All three stories in this anthology will leave any reader gasping for more and wondering when her Prince Charming will come along to sweep her off her feet." ~ *Sheryl, Coffee Time Romance*

4 1/2 Unicorns "*Enchanted Rogues* is a fun read full of magic, love, and hot sex." ~ *Lyonene, Enchanted In Romance*

"Each of the three stories within *Enchanted Rogues* is imaginative and filled with erotic action." ~ *Susan, The Road to Romance*

"*Enchanted Rogues* takes us on one adventure after another. This is one book you will want to revisit, no matter what time of year it is." ~ *Janean, Romance Junkies*

Lynn LaFleur
Titania Ladley
Lani Aames

Enchanted Rogues

An Ellora's Cave Romantica Publication

www.ellorascave.com

Enchanted Rogues

ISBN #1419952366

Edited by: Raelene Gorlinsky, Briana St. James,
Pamela Campbell
Cover art by: Syneca

Electronic book Publication: February, 2005
Trade paperback Publication: August, 2005

Warning:

The following material contains graphic sexual content meant for mature readers. *Enchanted Rogues* has been rated *E-rotic* by a minimum of three independent reviewers.

Ellora's Cave Publishing offers three levels of Romantica™ reading entertainment: S (S-ensuous), E (E-rotic), and X (X-treme).

S-*ensuous* love scenes are explicit and leave nothing to the imagination.

E-*rotic* love scenes are explicit, leave nothing to the imagination, and are high in volume per the overall word count. In addition, some E-rated titles might contain fantasy material that some readers find objectionable, such as bondage, submission, same sex encounters, forced seductions, etc. E-rated titles are the most graphic titles we carry; it is common, for instance, for an author to use words such as "fucking", "cock", "pussy", etc., within their work of literature.

X-*treme* titles differ from E-rated titles only in plot premise and storyline execution. Unlike E-rated titles, stories designated with the letter X tend to contain controversial subject matter not for the faint of heart.

Contents

Mirage

Lynn LaFleur

Trademarks Acknowledgement

The author acknowledges the trademarked status and trademark owners of the following wordmarks mentioned in this work of fiction:

Equal: Merisant Company
Windex: The Drackett Chemical Company

Chapter One

Kaci Montgomery folded her arms across her stomach and stared out the window. A soft mist fell, blurring the scene on the other side of the glass. How appropriate. A gray weather day perfectly matched the gray feeling inside this room.

A glance at her watch showed her she'd been waiting almost half an hour for her friend. Hannah Ives had shown Kaci into her plush office, then excused herself and said she'd be back in a few moments. That few moments had stretched into a lot longer. If Kaci didn't want to get this over with, she'd walk out the door right now and not look back.

Closing her eyes, Kaci tilted her head back and released a deep breath. She didn't want to hear what Hannah had to tell her. Her beloved great-grandmother was gone and nothing would bring her back. Whatever Nana had left in her will didn't matter to Kaci. She'd gladly give it up, plus all her own possessions, to have her great-grandmother back.

The sound of a door opening made Kaci turn away from the window. Hannah breezed into the room.

"I'm sorry for making you wait. I'm training a new assistant and things are a bit…confused."

"I understand."

Hannah motioned toward the leather chairs before her desk. "Please sit down. Would you like something to drink?"

"No, I'm fine. I just want to get this over with."

A look of sympathy crossed Hannah's face. "I'm sure you do. I know how much you loved your great-grandmother."

Hannah sat in one of the chairs and Kaci sat next to her. She had known Hannah since high school. Hannah had been the wild one, the party girl, the one everyone knew would end up in jail or hooked on drugs. She surprised everyone by going to college, graduating in the top twenty-five of her class, and becoming an attorney.

"You were out of town when I read the will to your father, stepmother and brother."

"And I'll bet my dear stepmother was *thrilled* with all that money and property that Nana left to my dad."

Hannah wiggled her mouth back and forth, as if trying to decide exactly what to say. "She seemed…pleased."

Kaci snorted. She'd never understand why her father couldn't see the witch he married the way she and her brother did. "And my mother?"

"She didn't come."

"No surprise there." Kaci sat back in her chair and crossed her legs. "She and Mauri aren't exactly friends."

"Your great-grandmother didn't forget your mother. She loved her very much, and left her a nice settlement."

That pleased Kaci. Her mother had put up with her father's affairs for years. He'd always come crawling back to her, begging her forgiveness, which she always gave. When he became involved with Mauri, she finally told him to go to hell and left him. It had taken her until her two children were grown and on their own before she started living her own life. Kaci was happy for her. Not only had her mother been successful with her art, she'd felt satisfied with her life for the first time in years. "I'm glad."

"Now, as for you." Hannah leaned forward and picked up a folder thick with papers from her desk. "Do you want me to read the entire will to you, or simply hit the highlights?"

Kaci pushed the hair back from her face with a shaky hand. She was trying so hard not to cry. Losing her great-grandmother had to be one of the hardest things she'd ever endured, even harder than when her parents had separated. She didn't know how much longer she could hold back the tears. "I don't... Whatever she left me... Hannah, it doesn't matter."

"You may change your mind when you see it." She squeezed Kaci's hand, then opened the folder and withdrew several sheets. "Your great-grandmother was quite wealthy, as you know. Since your father's parents died several years ago, she left all the hotels to him. I'm sure he'll want you to stay on as manager of The Seattle Montgomery, but he's the official owner now."

Kaci had expected that her father would inherit the hotels. It made sense that they would pass down to him. He'd been running the company for years, anyway.

"Your brother inherited her house on Mercer Island and received a generous settlement." Hannah looked at Kaci and arched one eyebrow. "Although not as generous as yours. I can certainly tell who was your great-grandmother's favorite." She continued to sort through the papers until she found the one she'd apparently been seeking. "There's a gold and diamond necklace, a Celtic trinity knot. It's lovely and *very* old." Hannah passed the sheet to Kaci. "Here's the appraisal."

Kaci's mouth dropped open at the sight of all the zeroes. "Are you sure this is right?"

"Absolutely. That necklace is centuries old. It's been in your family for many generations."

"I couldn't possibly wear something worth this much money."

"The best place for it is in your safety deposit box at the bank, or the safe at the hotel. It's in my safe now. I'll get it for you when we're through." Sorting through the papers again, Hannah withdrew another sheet and passed it to Kaci. "She left you $250,000.00 now and another $250,000.00 in trust for when you turn forty."

Kaci gulped.

"She left you several acres of land in Ireland and here in Washington, near Mount Baker. And a mirror."

Kaci's mind whirled from Hannah's words about money and properties, so it took her a moment to comprehend that last sentence. "Mirror?"

"Yes. Another antique, apparently. I don't have an appraisal on it, but your father said he remembers it from the description. It hung in the foyer of his parents' home in Ireland for many years. He didn't know what had happened to it."

"Nana was always on me about going to Ireland and studying my ancestry. I never did it. I never saw my grandparents' home. They died when I was four, so I barely remember them." Kaci flipped through the sheets Hannah had handed her, but the words and figures blurred. "What do I do now with these?"

"I'll take care of everything I can for you. You'll have to talk to your accountant about your inheritance, check on the taxes and any forms you may have to file."

"Yes, I'm sure the government will want their chunk."

"For now, Kaci, go back home to the hotel and get some rest. I know all this has been hard on you."

"There have definitely been times in my life when I've slept better."

Hannah squeezed her hand once again. "I'll get the necklace for you from my safe. The mirror will be delivered to your suite this afternoon or tomorrow. Also, I have an envelope in the safe for you from your great-grandmother. I assume it's a personal note."

Kaci watched Hannah rise and round her desk. A beautiful landscape hung on the wall directly behind her desk. She swung the painting away from the wall to expose a large safe. A few flicks of her fingers and the door silently swung open. Hannah withdrew an envelope and square box, then shut the safe and replaced the painting.

"This necklace is exquisite, Kaci. Do you know the history behind it?"

Kaci shook her head.

"Maybe your great-grandmother told you in her letter."

"Maybe." Accepting the box and envelope from Hannah, Kaci held them against her chest a moment before she put them in her purse.

"Are you all right?" Hannah asked softly.

Kaci nodded. "I will be. Time heals all wounds, right?"

"Some wounds take longer to heal than others."

"Yes, they do." Kaci gathered up her purse and stood. "Thank you for everything, Hannah."

"You're very welcome." Hannah hugged her. "I'll talk to you in a day or so, as soon as I get some of the paperwork done, okay?"

"Okay."

*****

Kaci slid her key card into the slot and waited for the green light. A soft click, a flash of green, and she pushed down the handle. Stepping inside, she flipped up the light switch. Muted light filled the living room. Kaci slipped off her shoes and leaned back against the door. Her gaze immediately went to the large window directly in front of her. The wall of glass faced west, giving her an incredible view of Puget Sound and the Olympic Range. Gray clouds filled the sky today, but on a clear day, the sunset over the Olympics literally took her breath. All the comforts of living in the large suite on the twenty-third floor of the hotel pleased her, but she loved the view most of all. It never failed to calm her, no matter how upset she might be.

Not even the incredible view had made her feel better this past week.

Her mood definitely called for a glass of wine. She needed the artificial courage before she opened the envelope from Nana.

Kaci poured herself a glass of Chardonnay and carried it to the couch. After taking a large sip, she set the glass on the coffee table and opened her purse. She removed the small box first and lifted the lid.

Kaci gasped.

It was stunning. Approximately the size of a nickel, the three diamond-encrusted gold knots intertwined with each other. A delicate gold chain, a bit dull, passed through the top knot. Kaci touched it with the tip of her finger. It felt…warm.

It definitely belonged in her safe. Wearing something this valuable would be stupid and irresponsible.

Yet she wanted to. She wanted to feel the necklace against her skin. Surely trying it on here in her suite would be safe.

Carefully, Kaci lifted the necklace from its black velvet nest. She located the small clasp and opened it. Her hands trembled as she placed the necklace around her neck and fastened it.

Warmth flowed from the gold knots. Kaci touched them with the tips of her fingers. A feeling of contentment, of serenity, washed over her. Her ancestors had worn this very necklace. It made her feel closer to them, to her Irish heritage.

Nana would've liked that.

Kaci sipped her wine then drew her great-grandmother's envelope from her purse. She touched the scrawled "Kaci" written on it. A tender smile touched her lips. Nana's hands had become so shaky and painful in the last year she could barely write, yet she'd ignored that pain to write this.

The ringing of her doorbell stopped Kaci from opening the envelope. Laying it on the table, she rose and went to the door. A glance through the peephole showed two of her employees with a large, slim crate on a rolling cart.

The mirror.

Kaci opened the door and stood to the side so they could enter. "Hi, guys."

"Hi, Ms. Montgomery," Sal said, smiling. His name fit him perfectly. He looked Italian, with dark hair, dark eyes, and olive skin wrinkled from too much time in the sun. "Delivery for you. Where do you want it?"

An excellent question. Kaci had been expecting the mirror, but she hadn't expected it to be taller than she. Perhaps it was simply packed in a larger box to protect it. "The bedroom, I guess."

She led the way to her bedroom and watched them open the large crate. As the plywood and protective wrapping fell away, she saw that the mirror definitely needed a crate that large to hold it. A thick, ornate silver frame surrounded the glass. Kaci guessed it to be at least six feet tall and three feet wide, and in desperate need of a good cleaning.

She had no idea where to put it.

"Do you want this hung up?" Sal asked.

"No, not yet. Just lean it against the wall for now."

"Will do."

The guys secured the mirror and Kaci walked them to the door. Once they were gone, she returned to the couch. She forgot about the mirror for now and picked up the envelope from Nana. After taking a deep breath to calm her racing heart, she slipped her finger beneath the flap.

My darling Kaci,

If you're reading this note, it means I've passed on.

I had a wonderful, incredible, exciting life. My only regret is not having more time with my darling Barry. Ah, what a man. We had 65 glorious years together, and I loved every one of them. If every woman could marry a man as considerate and loving as your great-grandfather, there wouldn't be any divorces.

I want that kind of happiness for you, Kaci. I've watched you fall in love and have your heart broken more than once. Whenever you were hurt, I was devastated. You were the most wonderful thing in my life, the one who brought me the greatest joy. There simply are not words to describe how very much you meant to me.

I lost my son and daughter-in-law many years ago. I hope you never know the pain of losing a child. Having you close to me made losing Riley easier to bear. If I hadn't already treasured you, that alone would have made me love you.

I know you are saddened by my death. I don't want that. Remember my life, and all our times together, and be happy that I'm finally with Barry again. True love never dies, Kaci. Sometimes it has to be put on hold, but it's always there, in your heart.

I want you to experience the kind of love I had with my husband. That's why I left you the necklace and mirror in my will. They've both been in the Montgomery family since the late 1500s. Together, they'll help you find the love of your life. Trust me on this, my darling. That necklace and mirror led me to my Barry. They'll help you too.

You'll meet him on St. Patrick's Day. Appropriate for us Irish, don't you think?

Your name means brave, Kaci. Never forget that. You're a strong, independent woman, and I was always so proud of you for that. But you need love, as does everyone. Don't turn your back on the gift when it's presented to you.

Until we meet again,

Nana

Tears streamed down Kaci's cheeks as she carefully folded the letter and replaced it in the envelope. The large sum of money her great-grandmother left her didn't mean nearly as much to Kaci as this hand-written note.

Oh, Nana, if only it were true. If only the necklace and mirror could actually bring me the love of my life. But I know that won't happen. I've given up on love.

Kaci laid the envelope on the coffee table. The tight lump in her throat refused to go away. Past experience had taught her that once she started crying, she wouldn't be able to stop for hours.

She had way too much to do to give in to a bout of self-pity.

The first thing she should do was decide where to put that huge mirror. It should be here, in the living room, so any visitor could see it. She certainly didn't have many visitors who saw her bedroom. Kaci couldn't remember the last time she'd made love. After her last disastrous relationship ended, she'd sworn off men forever...although she wouldn't mind one visiting her—and her bed—every now and then.

Kaci rose from the couch, picked up her wine glass, and headed for her bedroom. She sipped her Chardonnay as she turned in a slow circle at the end of the bed, studying the spacious room for a possible place to put the mirror. It either had to hang on the wall, or it needed some kind of brace put on the back so it could stand on its own. While all Montgomery hotels were built with the finest materials possible, she had no idea if any of the walls would hold such a large and heavy item.

Maybe it really would be better in the living room. She could call Sal and a couple of the other maintenance guys back to hang it for her.

Stepping closer to the mirror, she studied the ornate frame. She couldn't make out a definite pattern in the swirls and curls of silver, but some kind of design existed. Kaci set her glass on her desk and returned to the mirror. She peered closer, trying to make out the pattern. It almost looked like...

Kaci's eyes widened. Surely she hadn't seen what she thought she'd seen.

Once more stepping close to the mirror, Kaci studied the design. It looked like a couple entwined. No, it looked like *several* couples entwined, in many different positions. Her great-grandmother had left her an X-rated mirror!

Kaci covered her mouth with one hand to hold back her laughter. Nana had often told her stories of their wild family. Apparently, those stories had been true.

"My ancestors were perverts. You never told me *that* part, Nana." She chuckled again. "So much for hanging this in the living room."

It was the first time Kaci had laughed in two weeks, and it felt wonderful. The long work hours, along with Nana's death, had made laughter impossible. Normally a cheerful person, the lack of joy lately had been hard on Kaci. She didn't like feeling sad.

No more. Nana didn't want her to be sad.

First things first. She had no silver polish, but she did have glass cleaner. At least she could clean the mirror.

Another benefit of being the manager of The Seattle Montgomery included never having to do any cleaning in her suite. Still, Kaci liked to have a collection of her own supplies. She returned to her bedroom with a small bottle of Windex and a lint-free cloth. Beginning at the top, she sprayed a generous amount of cleaner on the mirror and began wiping it off.

The accumulated dirt and film melted away, letting her see the beauty of the mirror. Her family had obviously taken exceptional care of it over the centuries.

Centuries. Kaci had a hard time accepting that this mirror was hundreds of years old.

As she cleaned the spot directly in front of her, her gaze fell to the reflection of the necklace around her neck. She'd forgotten all about putting on the necklace before she read Nana's letter. The light from the small lamp on her desk shone on the piece of jewelry. The sparkle of the diamonds took her breath, they were so lovely. Kaci touched the necklace, awed by its beauty.

Warmth radiated through her fingers and up her arm. The mirror seemed to shift, blur, before her. She blinked to clear her vision. It didn't help. Instead, the blurred effect intensified. Something began to form.

Eyes. Vivid blue eyes, surrounded by dark eyelashes.

Kaci gasped. She stumbled back and sat down hard on the end of her bed. Grasping the bedspread with both hands, she stared at the mirror, trying to see again what she thought she'd seen.

Nothing.

You did not *see blue eyes, Kaci. Your eyes are green. The Windex made the mirror blurry, that's all.*

Kaci took a deep breath and released it slowly, hoping it would make her heart stop pounding. It had to be a combination of the glass cleaner and a reflection from the lamp. That's the only explanation that made any sense.

Another few moments passed before Kaci felt as if her legs would work again. She rose and crossed the floor to her desk. Picking up her wine glass, she drained it in one gulp.

"Oh, Nana. What have you done to me?"

* * * * *

Ryne Wilkinson drew the razor down his right cheek, removing whiskers and the heavy shaving cream. He watched the razor as he swished it beneath the running water in the sink. When he raised his gaze to the mirror again, he saw her.

The first time he'd seen her, almost two months ago, it scared the hell out of him. Once he'd stopped panting for breath, he'd decided he was either dreaming or going crazy. He would've accepted either option for an explanation of seeing a woman hovering in mid-air.

He never knew when she would appear. He had no way to *make* her appear. She just…arrived without any notice. Sometimes she appeared in the air, sometimes in a mirror, sometimes in his dreams. He hadn't been able to make out her face at first, but over time he'd been able to see her clearly. Shoulder-length blonde hair, big green eyes, a peaches-and-cream complexion, an oval face. Her body…ah, her body. She always wore some kind of gauzy thing, a cross between a dress and pantsuit. That didn't hinder him from knowing she had a voluptuous body with full breasts and wide hips.

He wished she'd turn around so he could see her ass.

No longer afraid of the vision, he remained still and stared at it. She stood underneath a large evergreen tree. Her eyes were closed, her face tilted up to the sky. Her hair flowed around her face, as if a gentle breeze touched it.

She opened her eyes, looked directly at him…and smiled.

The vision faded.

Ryne waited, knowing what would happen next. Within a few seconds of the vision, he would have another visitor.

Right on cue, the fairy appeared with a faint *pop*.

"A lovely lass, isn't she?" the fairy asked him in a beautiful Irish accent.

"Lovely."

Ryne watched Shae float in front of the mirror a moment before she came to rest on top of his hair dryer. It must have been too warm from its recent use. She quickly darted away from it, rubbing her bottom.

Struggling not to laugh, Ryne asked, "Too toasty for your tush?"

"Aye."

She floated up to within six inches of his face. No more than four inches tall, Shae had short red hair and ivory skin. A few freckles were scattered across her turned-up nose. Her green wings matched the green leotard that covered her tiny body.

Ryne thought she was adorable.

"She's the lass of your dreams, Master Ryne."

"So you keep telling me. What you *don't* tell me is how to find her."

"I cannot do everything here. You must find her on your own."

"And how do you suggest I do that?"

Shae floated closer and touched his chest, over his heart, with one finger. "Start here."

With that comment, she disappeared.

Ryne looked back in the mirror where he'd seen the blonde and sighed. He didn't know why he'd begun to have the visions, or why a pointy-eared fairy decided to pop into his life. One thing he *did* know—the beautiful blonde was out there somewhere, waiting for him.

He would find her…no matter what it took.

Chapter Two

Kaci flipped through the pile of applications on her desk. Although The Seattle Montgomery had the lowest turnover rate in the chain, new employees still had to be hired. New wait staff in the main dining room was at the top of her list.

The Montgomery hotels were known for their generous wages and benefits, which meant Kaci never had a lack of applications for jobs. She began sorting them into several stacks—wait staff, maintenance, housekeeping, clerical, and managerial.

Tapping her pen against her teeth, Kaci studied the five applications she had for assistant managers. She had three working for her already, but wanted to add one more. Preferably a woman, since she had two male and one female assistants currently employed.

Kaci laid down her pen and leaned back in her chair with the forms. She pushed her hair behind one ear. Her finger passed over the gold chain around her neck.

After laying the applications in her lap, Kaci touched the necklace. She hadn't taken it off since she put it on last night, because she couldn't. No matter how hard she'd tried, she couldn't get the clasp to open. The short chain wouldn't fit over her head, so she'd worn it to bed.

She still hadn't been able to unfasten the clasp this morning. Despite hating to get it wet, she had no choice but to shower while wearing the necklace.

Not even soap on the stubborn clasp had helped her open it.

A soft rap on her office door made Kaci look up. Her brother Kaylen stood in the doorway.

"Hiya, sis," he said with a grin.

Kaci squealed and jumped up from her chair. She met him halfway across the room and flew into his arms. Kaylen lifted her off the floor and turned her in a circle.

Once back on her feet, Kaci cupped Kaylen's cheeks in her hands. She smiled into a pair of green eyes identical to her own. "What are you doing here?"

"Visiting my baby sister."

"Baby sister. You're all of ten minutes older than me."

"And I'll never let you forget that."

Holding his hand, Kaci led her twin to the plush loveseat beneath the windows and pulled him down beside her. "Seriously, what are you doing here?"

"I didn't get to see you when Nana's will was read. And you sounded kinda down when you called me last night, so I decided to hop on my plane and fly up here this morning." He touched Kaci's cheek. "I guess you know Nana left me her house on Mercer Island."

Kaci nodded. "Hannah told me."

Kaylen pushed his thick blond hair back from his forehead. "I love that house, Kac, but I don't need it. I live in the hotel, just like you. I love it in San Francisco. I doubt I'll ever live in Washington again."

Kaylen managed The San Francisco Montgomery, and did his job very well. The hotel had barely been meeting expenses until Kaylen took over the management. Now, reservations had to be made weeks in advance, and their father had planned major, expensive renovations for this fall. "What are you going to do with the house?"

"Sell it, I guess. Unless you want it."

"Me?" she squeaked.

"Call me sentimental, but I know Nana would've wanted it to stay in the family." Kaylen frowned. "I sure as hell don't want Mauri to get her hands on it. She was so sure Nana was going to leave that house to Dad. You should've seen her face when Hannah said the house belonged to me. Talk about not being a happy camper."

Kaci bit her bottom lip to keep from smiling. She liked the idea of Mauri feeling jealous and unhappy.

"Do you want it, Kac?"

"Kaylen, I'm like you. I live here in the hotel. I don't need the house. But you're right. Nana wouldn't want it sold."

"So what do I do with it?"

"Do you have to make a decision now? There's no reason why you have to sell it immediately, is there?"

"No. Paying for the upkeep isn't a problem with the inheritance Nana left me. I just hate to see that beautiful old house vacant." He turned to face her and stretched his arm along the back of the loveseat. "That house is perfect for a family, Kac. Right on the water, huge backyard, four bedrooms, giant kitchen—"

"You sound like a real estate agent."

"Just telling it like it is."

"Well, if you're trying to tell me *I'm* the one who should have the family in that house, you can hold your breath. It takes a man to have a family. I've been burned enough by members of your sex, thank you very much."

Kaylen tilted his head. "You're much too young to be so cynical."

"What about you? I haven't received an engraved invitation to *your* wedding."

"Ah, but I'm not cynical, just damn picky. I haven't met the woman worthy of me yet."

The devilish light in his eyes made Kaci laugh. No matter how low she might be, her brother could always make her laugh. "So no prospects?"

"None. But it's sure fun looking." His gaze dropped to her neck. "Speaking of looking, that's quite a necklace you're wearing. Is that the one Nana left you?"

Nodding, Kaci touched the jeweled knot. "I have the mirror too, in my suite. Want to see it?"

"Lead the way."

Kaylen stood with his hands behind his back while he studied the mirror. "Looks like our ancestors were a rowdy bunch." Eyes twinkling, he looked at Kaci. "Now I know where I got the wild blood running through my veins."

"You're getting into territory I don't need to know, bro."

Kaylen gave her a devilish grin then returned his attention to the mirror. His grin faded. "It's beautiful, sis. Nana done good leaving it to you."

"I haven't decided where to put it yet." Kaci fingered the knot of her necklace and slid it back and forth over the chain. "I like it in here, but maybe it should be…"

Her voice trailed off when she saw the glass blur. Breath hitching in her throat, she watched the blue eyes form. This time, black eyebrows appeared above the eyes. Mesmerized, she watched as a straight nose materialized beneath the eyes.

Kaci grabbed Kaylen's arm with both hands. "Do you see that?"

"See what?"

"The eyes in the mirror."

Kaylen frowned. "What are you talking about, sis? What eyes?"

The image shifted and disappeared.

She gestured toward the mirror. "They were right there! Blue eyes, with dark eyebrows. Didn't you see them?"

Taking her upper arms, Kaylen turned Kaci to face him. "Kaci, there weren't any blue eyes in the mirror. You saw some kind of mirage, maybe a reflection from your curtains."

Kaci stared into Kaylen's face. His eyes were filled with worry and concern. She shifted her gaze to the windows that were covered with sky blue drapes the exact color of the eyes in the mirror. Perhaps that's what happened. Perhaps it *had* been a trick of the light.

"Kaci?"

Her brother's anxious tone made Kaci look at him again. Not wanting to worry Kaylen, she forced a smile. "You're right. It must have been a mirage."

He didn't look convinced. "Are you sure you're okay?"

"I promise you, I'm fine. No, I take that back. I'm hungry." She slipped her arm through his. "Let's go to the waterfront and you can buy me lunch."

"How come I always have to buy?"

"Because you're the oldest."

"I knew that would come back to haunt me." He tweaked her nose. "Okay, lunch is on me. Then we'll come back here and talk until midnight, just like we used to. How's that?"

"Sounds perfect to me."

* * * * *

Phoenix, Kansas City, Denver, Salt Lake City, Seattle. Ryne sat back in his chair and studied the list he held in his hand. He blew out a heavy breath. Five cities in less than three weeks. He'd done it in the past—he'd done *more* than five cities in less than three weeks in the past—but his heart wasn't in this trip.

The traveling would be more fun if he had someone with him.

Ryne tossed the legal pad on his desk. Spinning his chair around, he stared at Los Angeles sprawled out before him. He had a busy, successful business. He had good friends, lived in a great condo. He had a number of women to date, and the dates usually ended with sex.

He had no reason to feel so restless.

It was *her* fault. Ever since he'd started seeing the vision, he'd been consumed with finding the real woman. He looked into every woman's face he passed on the street, in the supermarket, in stores, in restaurants. No luck. Either she didn't live in the Los Angeles area, or he simply hadn't found her yet.

Or she didn't exist.

He suspected the latter. He'd seen this vision, this perfect woman, yet he would never be able to find her.

Turning his chair back to face his desk, Ryne reached into his pants pocket and removed the gold charm. He turned it over in his palm, studying the three entwined knots. He wasn't sure why he'd bought it, but as soon as he saw it in the pawnshop window, he had to have it.

Ryne never even *looked* in pawnshop windows. He'd passed one on his last trip to Miami two months ago. Curiosity had made him stop and gaze at the array of jewelry spread out before him. Something about the charm called to him. Without questioning his feeling, he'd bought the charm for twenty dollars.

Research on the Internet had shown him the charm looked like a Celtic trinity knot from Ireland. His ancestors came from the Emerald Isle. Perhaps a bit of that Irish blood had drawn him to it.

Something that only cost him twenty dollars in a pawnshop couldn't be an antique, even though it did look old. That didn't matter to him. He didn't care if it was only worth fifty cents. He cared that he'd felt compelled to have the charm, enough so he'd carried it ever since he bought it.

Propping his elbow on the desk, Ryne brought the charm closer to his face. "Is it a coincidence that I first saw *her* a couple of days after I bought you? Are you supposed to help me find her? If so, how?"

"You have so many questions, Master Ryne."

Startled by Shae's voice, Ryne moved his hand so he could see his desk. She sat on his stapler.

The tiny fairy had appeared to him the same day he'd seen *her* for the first time. Seeing Shae right after the blonde had disappeared shot his blood pressure right back to the top of the gauge. After two months, Shae's appearance no longer surprised him.

"Yeah, I have a lot of questions. Do you have any answers?"

"I have told you how to find her."

"You told me to listen to my heart. That doesn't tell me how or where to find her. Is she close? Does she live here in L.A., or somewhere in Southern California?"

Shae tapped her chin with one finger. "Does it matter where the lass lives?"

"Hell, yes, it matters. I've tried a long-distance relationship. Twice. They don't work. It's hard enough to make a relationship work without adding miles to it."

"But if she is the one meant for you, it cannot matter where she lives."

Blowing out a heavy breath, Ryne leaned back in his chair. He didn't know how personal he could get with the fairy, how much she would understand. "Shae, a couple needs to be close. They need to spend time together, get to know each other."

"Ah, you're talking about sex."

A strangled laugh escaped before Ryne could stop it. He didn't realize fairies even *knew* about sex. Of course, until a couple of months ago, he didn't realize fairies even existed.

Shae frowned. "And what do you find amusing?"

"Nothing."

She flew over to Ryne and landed on his left knee. "You are mistaken if you believe fairies know nothing of sex. Where do you think we come from?"

"Mushrooms?" he asked with a shrug.

Shae scowled. Ryne chuckled at her fierce look. He touched the tip of her nose. "Just kidding, Shae."

Her scowl relaxed into a grin. "You are forgiven."

"Thank you. Now, back to my problem." He opened his palm so she could see the charm. "What does this have to do with her? Is this supposed to help me meet her?"

"Aye."

When she said nothing else, Ryne prompted, "How?"

"You will know when it is time."

Before he could question her further, she disappeared. Ryne sighed in frustration. He had no more information now than before he ever spoke to Shae.

The charm was somehow the key. That much he knew.

The first leg of his trip began in three hours. Ryne jiggled the charm in his palm then stood and slipped it back in his pocket.

Chapter Three

The waterfall cascaded over the rocks, forming a deep pool at the base of the cliff. She stood beneath the spray in the waist-deep water, her head tilted back so the spray could flow through her hair. Paradise.

A cool hand on her stomach made her smile. He had come up behind her without her knowledge.

"I love to see the water flow over your body," he whispered into her ear.

She turned to face him and lifted her lips for his kiss. It started out soft, tender. He sipped at her lips, as if drinking from a glass of the finest wine. His kisses affected her more than wine, making her light-headed and dizzy with desire.

His tongue came into play as the kisses deepened. Sighing, she wrapped her arms around his neck and pressed her nude body to his. His cock, hard and full, branded her belly. She loved the feel of him touching her almost as much as the feel of him inside her.

Almost.

His hands ran up and down her back in a slow caress. They dipped down to her buttocks, squeezed, lifted, then traveled up her back again. The water made both of them slippery. She rubbed against him like a cat seeking to be petted.

He cradled her face in his hands and stared into her eyes. "You are trying to tempt me."

"Yes, I am."

A hint of a grin lifted the left side of his mouth. "Ah, so you admit it."

"I admit I want you."

"And I you." He kissed her again, long and deeply. "Come lie with me."

She nodded. Taking her hand, he led her toward the bank. When her feet touched the earth, he swept her into his arms and carried her to the blanket he had placed beneath the trees. He lowered her to the blanket and lay beside her.

A breeze blew over her wet skin. Goose bumps skittered across her flesh and her nipples tightened into hard beads.

"Are you cold, my love?" he asked, circling one nipple with his fingertip.

She shook her head. "I can never be cold when I am with you."

"Then why are these hard?"

He tweaked the nipple between his thumb and forefinger. Her breath hitched and she arched her back. "They are hard because of you. Do you not like them this way?"

"I love *them this way." To prove his words, he bent his head and swiped his tongue across one tip, then the other, before returning to the first one. He drew it into his mouth and suckled it.*

She touched his head as pleasure flooded her body and moisture gathered between her thighs. "That feels so good."

"To me also." He continued to circle the peaks with that lone fingertip. "They are not the only thing hard." He shifted, brushing her hip with his cock.

"I noticed."

"Do you have a suggestion what I should do with it?"

She let her hand glide down his body until she grasped him firmly. "Oh, yes."

Instead of pushing her to her back and entering her, as she expected him to do, he lay on his back and pulled her on top of him. "Take me, my love."

She lowered herself onto his hard shaft, moaning when they became one. He held her hips tightly, yet didn't move, letting her decide the pace, the intensity, of their lovemaking. She preferred it slow at first, a gentle build-up to that glorious, breath-stealing ending. As the pleasure rose in her body, she quickened the pace. Still, he didn't move, although she could tell by the tenseness in his body that he wanted to.

So close. That incredible feeling was so close. She threw back her head and rode him harder, took him deeper. There. Oh, yes, right there –

A loud knock on her bedroom door made Kaci jump. She swallowed the scream before it could escape her throat.

"Hey, lazy ass, are you gonna stay in bed all day?"

Disoriented, Kaci looked around the room. She blinked at the hazy sunlight filtering through the sheers on her windows. No waterfall. No trees. No lush green grass. No handsome hunk making love to her. Nothing but her bedroom and her brother beating on the door.

"Your timing stinks, bro," she muttered.

"Hey, Kac, you awake?"

"How could I be asleep with all that noise?" Kaci said louder.

"I'm hungry. Let's go to the restaurant for brunch."

She didn't care anything about food. She wanted to go back to the dream, where he looked at her, touched her, like she was the most precious thing in the world. She wanted to feel that glorious cock pounding into her body. She wanted –

"Yo, Kac."

"Okay, okay. Give me a few minutes to get ready."

"I'll start coffee while you take your few minutes. And make it a *few*, sis."

"Yeah, yeah."

Kaci sat up and pushed her tousled hair back from her face. She never had erotic dreams. At least, she couldn't remember having erotic dreams. This one seemed so *real*, as if it were really happening.

Or had happened in a previous life.

"Overactive hormones can be a curse."

Blowing out a deep breath, Kaci leaned back on a pile of pillows. The mirror leaned against the wall at the end of her bed.

She looked at the frame before her gaze focused on the glass. She wrinkled her nose at her appearance.

"A brush would help a lot, Kac."

She shifted to get more comfortable. The necklace's diamonds sparkled in the sunlight. She still hadn't been able to remove it last night. She'd asked Kaylen to help her, but he hadn't been able to loosen the clasp either. She touched the charm. Warmth flowed into her fingertips and up her arm.

The mirror began to blur. Kaci held her breath and remained perfectly still, waiting for an image to appear. Last night, she'd tried to convince herself she'd seen a mirage in the mirror, a trick of light. She didn't believe that. Seeing those blue eyes twice, combined with the dream about a man with those same blue eyes, proved to her that she hadn't seen a mirage.

The eyes appeared first, as usual. Kaci swallowed when the thick, black brows came into view. A straight nose came next, then full, sensuous lips. The rest of his face filled in slowly—firm chin, high cheekbones, forehead. Black hair tumbled over that forehead and past his tan shoulders.

His *bare* tan shoulders.

He looked exactly like the man in her dream. She licked her lips.

What an absolutely edible hunk.

The vision grew to include all of his broad shoulders. Still clutching the charm, Kaci pushed aside the covers with her other hand and rose to her knees to get closer to the mirror. She could see his strong, muscled arms, his large hands, his thick fingers.

Oh, my.

She saw a wide chest with a generous sprinkling of dark hair that tapered down his flat stomach. She followed the vision as it spread downward to expose more of his body. The hair grew wider, thicker—

"Kac!"

A squeaky scream erupted before she could stop it. She jerked, fell on her butt, and bounced twice. When her heart returned to her chest instead of lodging in her throat, she looked back at the mirror.

He was gone.

Damn it, Kaylen, your timing is really lousy.

"Are you up, or do I have to bring in some cold water?"

"I'm up!" she yelled. "I'll be ready in fifteen minutes.

Kaci stared longingly at the mirror. She could still see him in her mind, although the dream image was a bit fuzzy. She'd hoped to see *all* of him in the mirror, to compare him to the dream version. Her twin's interruption dashed that hope.

Kaylen had told her last night he would fly back to San Francisco this afternoon. For the first time ever, she was actually anxious for her brother to leave so she could get back to the mirror. Somehow, it was the key to get to *him*.

She wouldn't give up until she discovered how to use that key.

*****

Kaci jumped when Kaylen waved his hand in front of her face. "What?"

"Just making sure you're still here."

Warmth seeped into her cheeks when she realized she hadn't been listening to her twin. "I'm sorry, Kaylen. My mind is wandering today."

"I noticed. Want to tell me why?"

She watched her brother shovel another forkful of scrambled eggs into his mouth. It had always amazed her how much he could eat and still stay so trim. "How do you pack away so much food and never gain any weight?"

"You're changing the subject." He washed down his food with a gulp of orange juice. "What's going on?"

Picking up her fork, she speared a piece of waffle and swished it through the blackberry syrup on her plate. She couldn't admit thoughts of the man in the mirror filled her mind. Her brother would pack her off to the nearest mental health facility. "I was just going over tomorrow's schedule in my head. There's always so much to do around here."

"Tell me about it. But this is your day off, and your handsome, charming brother is here to take your mind off your troubles."

Kaci chuckled. "You left out modest."

"That too." Coffee mug in hand, he sat back in his chair. "Is that all that's bothering you, the hotel?"

"And I miss Nana."

"There's a lot of that going around." Kaylen sipped from his mug. "Hannah told me Nana left you a personal note."

"She did."

"She left me one too." He gestured toward her throat. "Did you know there was a man's charm that matched the one on your necklace?"

Kaci touched the jeweled knot. "No, I didn't."

"It was a bit bigger, about the size of a quarter, and didn't have any diamonds on it like yours. It was stolen from our great-great grandfather in the mid 1800s. Or maybe there needs to be three or four greats in there. Anyway, he immigrated to New York when he was in his early twenties, and was robbed shortly after he arrived. He never recovered the charm."

"I wonder what happened to it?"

"It was probably lost years ago, or sold to someone for a tenth of its worth. It may have been stolen by someone who simply wanted to sell it so he could feed his family."

"That's true." Kaci slid the charm back and forth over the chain. "I guess we'll never see it again."

"I think the chances of that are higher than the odds of winning the lottery." He set his mug on the table. "As much as I hate to say this, sis, I'd better get going. I have two conventions booked starting tomorrow."

"I have one next week, two the next, and two the week after that."

Kaylen winced. "Ouch. No wonder you look tired."

Kaci's mouth dropped open at his insult. "Hey!"

"I'm not being an ass, Kac. Running this place is a huge responsibility. Losing Nana didn't help. I know how close you two were."

The mention of losing Nana brought a lump to Kaci's throat. "Yes, we were. I really miss her."

"Maybe you should think about a vacation. Come to San Francisco and let me pamper you." He snapped his fingers. "Better yet, go someplace you've always wanted to go to but figured you never would. Be bold, be brave, be daring."

Kaci chuckled. "Bold, brave, and daring, huh?"

"Absolutely," Kaylen said with a grin.

"I can't do anything until at least April. There's too much going on around here in March."

"So go in April. Pick somewhere exotic and exciting."

"How about somewhere relaxing and quiet?"

"If that's what you need. Just do whatever will make you feel good." Kaylen glanced at his watch. "It'll make me feel good to get to my plane. Take me to the airport?"

"You bet."

*****

Kaci stood with her head tilted back and let the warm water cascade over her body. She'd hoped the shower would help end her frustration. So far, it didn't seem to be working.

She'd wasted no time in hurrying to her bedroom as soon as she got back from taking her brother to the airport. Saying goodbye to Kaylen was always hard. Today, she'd practically pushed him onto his plane so she could get back home to the mirror.

She longed to see *him* again.

The mirror hadn't cooperated. Kaci had sat on the end of her bed for over twenty minutes, staring into the glass. Nothing. No blurring. No shifting of the glass. No image of a man's eyes, or any other part of him.

She'd *really* wanted to see other parts of him.

Kaci turned off the water and pushed back her wet hair. *Something* made him materialize. Maybe her wishing him to appear didn't work.

Well, that's obvious, Kac, since he didn't appear when you wanted him to.

Sliding open the glass door, Kaci stepped out of the shower stall and reached for a towel. She used an edge of the blue terry cloth to wipe steam from the mirror above the sink. Her gaze immediately fell on the necklace. The soft lights surrounding the mirror made the diamonds in the knots sparkle.

It hit her with the force of a slap in the face. The charm. Every time she'd seen him in the mirror, she'd been touching the charm.

Kaci dropped the towel on the counter and dashed into the bedroom. She skidded to a halt and fell to her knees two feet in front of the mirror. Taking a breath to calm her racing heart, she raised her left hand and touched the charm.

Warmth tickled her fingertips and whooshed up her arm. A moment later, the mirror began to blur. A waterfall appeared.

A chill raced down her spine. It looked like the waterfall in her dream.

Kaci wrapped her fingers around the charm to be sure the image didn't fade. She had no intention of letting go of the necklace or moving until she saw *him*.

The flowing water fell over rocks surrounded by thick ferns and large-leafed green plants. It could be a scene from the tropics, or from a rain forest. She inched closer to the mirror, not wanting to miss anything.

It was almost as if she were watching a movie. The "camera" moved down the waterfall, until she could see a crystal pool.

Just like in her dream.

A man's torso came into view. Kaci clutched the charm tighter.

More of the scenery appeared to her, as did more of him. He stood beneath the waterfall, head tilted back, fingers combing through his long, black hair. A pool of clear water lapped at his groin. She saw a hint of black pubic hair above the water. His skin was tan everywhere she could see.

She wondered if it was tan where she *couldn't* see.

He lowered his head and wiped the droplets from his face. Kaci watched him move through the water toward its edge. She swallowed hard as the water became more shallow. The rest of his body came into view—his thick, flaccid cock, strong thighs, well-shaped calves, and long feet.

Oh, my.

The image of him from her dream was fuzzy, unclear, as if looking through a camera lens that wasn't focused correctly. This image was sharp and clear…so clear she would swear she could touch that incredible body.

Heat engulfed her at the sight of all that masculine beauty. Her heartbeat sped up, her breathing deepened. Her clit began a slow throbbing. Kaci slowly slid her right hand down her stomach to between her thighs. It didn't surprise her to discover the cream moistening her feminine lips.

He walked across lush, green grass to a brown blanket spread beneath a large tree. Dropping to his knees, he pushed his wet hair behind his shoulders then ran his hands down his torso. His eyes closed as he cupped his cock in one hand, his balls in the other. His cock quickly rose to attention with his stroking. Over and over, he moved his hand slowly up and down his hard flesh.

Kaci's breathing became choppy. She pushed two fingers inside her pussy, wishing desperately it could be his cock filling her instead. Her thumb flicked over her clit, massaging it to the same rhythm that he massaged his balls.

His eyes closed, his head tilted back, his stroking became faster. Kaci could tell he was on the verge of a climax. She pulled her fingers from her body and rubbed her clit faster, wanting to come at the same time as he.

His hips jerked. Kaci held her breath. A moment later, his cum flowed out the head and ran over his hand. His shoulders slumped a bit. He lowered his head and watched himself as he rubbed his cum over his cock.

Then he raised his head and looked straight into her eyes.

The orgasm grabbed her by the throat and galloped through her body. Kaci closed her eyes and moaned. Shoving two fingers back inside her pussy, she rode out the waves of pleasure.

When she opened her eyes, he was gone.

"No!"

She'd released the charm in the throes of her climax. Kaci quickly wrapped her fingers around it again. The image didn't reappear.

Tears of disappointment flooded her eyes. She'd just experienced the most powerful orgasm she'd had in years, and it came from her imagination instead of a live man.

Slowly rising on shaky legs, Kaci braced herself against the end of the bed. She knew believing in something so unbelievable had to be insane. Yet, she couldn't deny what she'd envisioned, or what she'd experienced. She'd seen him in the mirror, and it hadn't been a mirage. Her climax certainly hadn't been a product of her imagination.

Don't turn your back on the gift when it's presented to you.

Nana's words from her letter flowed through Kaci's mind. *Is this him, Nana? Is this man supposed to be the love of my life? If so, how do I meet him? Where do I meet him?*

She didn't understand what was happening to her. Long hours and stress had to be the reason for these strange visions. She'd never meet the real man. And even if she did, her heart had been broken into tiny pieces twice. She wasn't sure if she'd be willing to try for thirds.

Chapter Four

Ryne checked his ticket once again to verify when his flight left tomorrow. Seattle was his last stop before returning to Los Angeles. He'd visited the Emerald City two years ago, but planned to check out The Seattle Montgomery on this trip. It had been renovated a year ago, as had other hotels in the chain.

He was very impressed with all the improvements here at The Denver Montgomery. The Montgomery family had updated the guest and conference rooms with new décor and all the latest electronic equipment, yet had kept the old-fashioned feel of the hotel. With the reasonable convention rates the hotel offered, plus all the amenities including a full spa and workout area, Ryne would have no trouble suggesting it to his clients.

Tossing his ticket on the nightstand, Ryne unbuttoned his shirt, slipped off his shoes, and sat on the bed. He should be tired since it was almost midnight, yet his mind churned with everything he had to do when he got back home. Visits to the hotel were only the start of his job. He had to take the information back to his office, have his staff input everything into computers, and prepare packets for his clients who planned to hold conferences. Many hours of work awaited him when he returned to Los Angeles.

Thinking about all that work wouldn't let him rest. Sleep wouldn't be possible until he turned off his brain.

Deciding a late night movie should hypnotize him so he could sleep, Ryne picked up the TV remote and pointed it at the set. His finger froze on the power button when she appeared in the glass.

He hadn't seen her for several days, and had begun to think she'd disappeared for good. Her face filled the television screen, those huge green eyes looking right at him.

Ryne stuffed a pillow behind his back and leaned against the headboard, prepared to watch her for as long as she remained.

A coy smile touched her lips. Closing her eyes, she tilted her head back. She touched her chin with one fingertip then slowly drew that fingertip down her neck. As her finger moved, more of her body came into view. A long, ivory neck, creamy shoulders, the slope of her breasts.

He'd never seen so much of her skin since she'd always been wearing that gauzy outfit. Ryne sat up a bit straighter. He wondered how far she'd take that finger…

She took it all the way to the tip of her round, ivory breast.

Ryne swallowed. He'd seen his share of adult movies and pictures of nude women in magazines. He'd read some very hot sex scenes in books. They'd enticed him, but he wasn't a young boy who got a hard-on from just a peek of a nipple.

His cock immediately came to attention at the sight of that hard pink nipple in the center of her full breast.

"Damn," he muttered. Shifting on the bed, he tugged on the crotch of his pants, trying to get his shorts positioned so they didn't cut into his erection. The tugging didn't help. Ryne unzipped his pants and pulled his cock from his shorts. It sprang up, full and hard, against his belly.

Ignoring the part of his body that had a mind of its own, he returned his attention to the TV screen. The blonde cupped both breasts in her hands and rubbed her nipples with her thumbs. Her eyes were still closed, her head still tilted back. The rapturous expression on her face proved she was enjoying her own touch.

Ryne's breathing deepened. His heartbeat increased. He wrapped his hand around his cock and slowly pumped it while he watched her.

He wondered how far she'd go.

More of her body came into view as she slid her hands down her stomach. Ryne increased the speed of his strokes when she touched her blonde curls. Her fingertips ruffled those curls a moment before gliding between her thighs. She pushed two fingers inside her pussy.

"God," Ryne muttered. This was more erotic than any adult movie he'd ever watched. He arched his hips and stroked his cock faster.

Her entire body was exposed to him now. She knelt on a pale blue bedspread, her legs spread wide. She looked delicious. Large breasts, broad hips, shapely thighs, a rounded stomach…everything he wanted in a woman's body. He'd dated women who were model thin, but much preferred a full-figured woman. He liked cupping heavy breasts and cradling wide hips in his hands. He loved to hold onto a plump ass as he drove his cock inside a woman.

A light sheen of perspiration covered her skin. Eyes closed, she moved her hips as she pumped her fingers faster into her pussy and played with her clit. Faster, deeper, until her body trembled and her mouth fell open in ecstasy.

A moment passed before she opened her eyes and looked at him. Withdrawing her hand from her pussy, she dragged her tongue up her skin from wrist to fingertips.

"Oh, *fuck*!" The orgasm sped through his body, grabbed his balls. Groaning loudly, Ryne tossed his head back and gripped his cock as cum ran over his hand.

When he could think clearly again, he looked back at the television. She had disappeared.

Ryne removed his shirt and wiped off his hand. After he'd cleaned his softening penis, he slipped it back into his shorts and zipped his pants.

"Okay, Shae, you can come out now."

She materialized on his right knee, cheeks flaming and wings fluttering madly.

Ryne chuckled at her obvious discomfort. "Did I embarrass you?"

That sharp little chin of hers jutted forward. "Of course not. 'Tis silly of you to think so."

"You said you knew all about sex. Don't fairies pleasure themselves?"

Shae cleared her throat. "I do not wish to continue this conversation."

"Fine. Then let's talk about what *I* want to talk about. When do I meet her?"

"I have told you—"

"I know what you've told me, but I'm tired of waiting." Having to take care of himself instead of making love to *her* made Ryne's anger rise. He'd had enough of the fairy's playing. "I've been seeing her, and *you*, for months. I want to meet her *now*."

"I cannot make her appear out of thin air."

"Why not? *You* do."

She flew up to within six inches of his face. "I am a fairy, Master Ryne, not a wizard. You will meet her when the time is right."

"Damn it, Shae, I'm tired of this. I've had a long, hard trip and the last thing I need is games. Is she real or not?"

"Aye, she's real. And that's all I can say."

Shae vanished with a loud *pop*, leaving Ryne even more frustrated and angry. Cursing violently at Shae and fate in general, he rose from the bed and stormed into the bathroom to take a shower.

A cold one.

*****

Kaci hurried into her suite and shut the door firmly behind her. She didn't hesitate, but headed straight for her bedroom. After dropping her purse and briefcase on the bed, she faced the mirror. She'd looked into it every day, touched the charm, and waited for him to appear.

The scene was always different. She'd watched him pleasure himself. She'd seen him sitting at a table, eating with other men. She hadn't been able to see their faces, but their gestures and the intense expression on his face had shown her their conversation had been serious. He'd engaged in a sword fight twice with other men. Kaci had cheered for him, urging him to win the battle. He had, both times.

She'd watched him sleeping, bathing, walking through a meadow. She never knew what she'd see when she looked into the mirror.

Her heart pounded as she wrapped her fingers around the charm.

He appeared instantly. Slowly, Kaci lowered herself to the bed. She watched him gallop toward her on a black horse, his dark hair whipping in the wind. As always, his clothes seemed to come from King Arthur's time, minus the armor.

He looked incredibly sexy in the ancient clothing.

Kaci tightened her grip on the charm, not wanting to risk losing him yet. She'd learned from her previous visions that he only appeared once per day. When she released the necklace, he disappeared and didn't reappear, no matter how many times she touched the charm.

Leaning low over his horse's neck, he urged the black steed to run even faster. The horse practically flew over the tall grass. Kaci watched, entranced, as the horse skidded to a stop beneath a grouping of large trees. He dismounted and strode quickly across the ground.

Kaci had not noticed the woman before now. She wore a long blue gown and sat on the grass beneath one of the trees. Her back was to Kaci, so she couldn't see the woman's face. Blonde curls tumbled over her shoulders, almost to her waist. Something about the way the woman tilted her head looked familiar to Kaci, but she didn't understand why.

He dropped to his knees, cupped her face in his hands, and kissed her. Kaci's mouth went dry at the hungry way he moved his lips over the woman's. It had been years since a man had kissed her like that. Or maybe a man had *never* kissed her like that, as if he didn't want to stop.

Kaci sighed.

He stood and jerked off his tunic. The rest of his clothes quickly followed, until he was gloriously nude. And aroused.

The woman slid her hands up his thighs to his groin. She wrapped her fingers around his hard penis then touched it with her tongue. Kaci could easily imagine herself in the woman's place. She saw herself cradling that luscious cock, tickling the slit, circling the head with her lips. It had been much too long since she'd licked the perspiration from a man's skin...

Her clit began to tingle.

He knelt once more between the blonde's spread legs. His hands traveled under her gown, gathering the flowing material as he moved higher up her legs. When it bunched around her hips, she reclined on the grass and lifted her buttocks. He followed her down, gripped her waist, and thrust inside her.

Kaci moaned and shifted on the bed. She still couldn't see the woman's face since his head lay on her shoulder closest to Kaci, but her movements clearly showed she was in the throes of ecstasy. She clasped him tightly, placed her feet flat on the ground, and met each hard thrust.

An unfamiliar feeling traveled through Kaci's body while she observed the lovers. It took her a moment to recognize it as jealousy. It should be *her* in his arms, beneath him, feeling his hard cock sliding in and out of her body. Tightening her grip on the charm, she watched the woman grab fistfuls of his hair and pull his mouth back to hers.

Now Kaci could see her face. She gasped.

My God! It's me!

His body shuddered, his hips thrust twice, before he lay still. The woman caressed up and down his spine until he lifted his head. He smiled at her then kissed her again, softly. Rising to his knees, he took her hands and helped her to a sitting position. He grasped the hem of her gown and pulled it over her head. Now nude, she rose to her knees also and turned so her back touched his chest.

It couldn't be possible. Kaci squeezed her eyes closed for a moment before opening them again. Other than for the waist-length hair, the woman in the mirror could be her twin, right down to the small birthmark on her left hip.

He cupped her breast with one hand, her mound with the other. Seeing his hands on Kaci's look-alike seemed even more intimate than watching them make love.

Kaci's pussy clenched, her clit throbbed with the need for release. She wanted *his* hands on her, his lips covering hers, his cock in her pussy. She didn't want to bring herself to an orgasm. Making herself come seemed so…sterile.

Sighing heavily, Kaci released the charm. The image in the mirror disappeared.

Nana's letter said she'd meet the man of her dreams on St. Patrick's Day. Unfortunately, Nana hadn't said what *year* she'd meet this special man. Tomorrow was March 17th. Her hectic schedule didn't include meeting any men tomorrow. And even if it did, she doubted they'd look anything like the man in the mirror.

The man who had captured her heart.

Kaci crawled up on the bed. Ignoring the insistent demands of her body, she pulled a pillow from beneath the bedspread and hugged it to her chest. She'd never felt more alone than she did right now.

Chapter Five

Ryne walked up to the reception desk. Withdrawing his business card from his shirt pocket, he handed it to the lovely redhead behind the desk. "Hi, Deborah," he said with a smile, after reading her name tag. "I'm Ryne Wilkinson from Wilkinson Conference Services. I have an appointment with Ms. Hobbs."

The redhead—who appeared to be in her early to mid twenties—gave him a one-hundred-watt smile. Ryne chuckled to himself. There were polite smiles of greeting, and come-hither smiles of flirting. Deborah's smile definitely fit in the latter category. "Welcome to The Seattle Montgomery, Mr. Wilkinson. I'll let Ms. Montgomery know you're here."

Ryne frowned. He would've sworn he had an appointment with Daria Hobbs. "Ms. Montgomery?"

"The owner's daughter and the manager of this hotel. Ms. Hobbs is ill today, so Ms. Montgomery is taking her appointments. Would you like to have a seat in the lobby while I call her?"

No, he didn't want to have a seat in the lobby. He wanted this damn visit over with so he could head for home. Less than three hours of sleep last night combined with a bumpy plane ride had left him grumpy and in no mood to deal with the daughter of the owner, who was probably a spoiled rich kid and knew nothing about running a hotel. Instead, he smiled at the redhead again. After all, it wasn't the young woman's fault that he had a four-inch fairy in his life slowly driving him crazy. "Thank you. That would be fine."

Ryne returned to the luxurious lobby. Spotting an overstuffed chair in the corner next to a window, he headed that direction. A small table holding a lamp sat next to the chair. If he had to wait for God knew how long, he could at least get some work done.

He'd barely opened his briefcase when the redhead came up to him. "Mr. Wilkinson?"

"Yes?"

"Ms. Montgomery is in a meeting with the head chef right now. She said she shouldn't be much longer and asked that I take you to her office."

Ryne thought it considerate of the manager to offer. Maybe she actually had a brain. "Thank you."

Her smile spread from ear to ear. "My pleasure."

He followed Deborah to the bank of elevators. Once inside the small space, she inserted a key card in the elevator panel and pressed the button labeled "5".

"All the business offices are on the fifth floor. I'm sure you'll be comfortable in Ms. Montgomery's office while you wait."

"Thank you, Deborah."

She glanced at him often while they rode to the fifth floor. She obviously found him attractive. Ryne was flattered by her attention, and thought about asking her out to dinner. It'd been weeks since he'd been on a date, or made love with a woman.

That thought quickly fled from his mind. *She* filled his mind so completely, he couldn't even consider being intimate with another woman.

I'm really tired of this, Shae. How much longer do I have to wait to meet her?

Soon, Master Ryne, Shae's voice sounded in his head. *Very soon. I promise.*

The elevator doors opened. Deborah smiled at him again before exiting. "This way, please."

Ryne followed her down a short hall to an oak door with a brass nameplate that simply said, "Kaci Montgomery,

Manager." Deborah used her key card again, opened the door, and gestured for him to go inside. He stepped into a spacious office, decorated in the same pastel and jewel tones as the rest of the hotel.

"Please make yourself comfortable, Mr. Wilkinson. Would you like a cup of coffee or cold drink?"

"No, I'm fine. Thanks."

She shifted from one foot to the other, as if she knew she should leave but didn't want to. "Well, if you need anything, *anything* at all, just press '8' on the phone. That'll connect you directly to the reception desk. I'll be happy to help you."

Ryne gave her his most charming smile. "Thank you again, Deborah. You've been very helpful."

A delightful blush colored her cheeks. It made Ryne think that Deborah didn't receive nearly enough compliments from men.

She left the room, closing the door behind her. Ryne turned a slow circle, studying the décor. The manager's desk faced the large windows. She had a nice view of the Olympic Range. Several paintings and photographs hung on the walls, all of the Western Washington area as far as he could tell. Putty-colored lateral file cabinets lined one full wall. A deep blue loveseat sat beneath the windows, and matching armchairs sat on either side. Coffee and end tables made of oak and glass completed the arrangement. The room felt more like a living room than an office.

Since Ryne had to wait for the manager, he decided he might as well get comfortable and do some work. He sat on the loveseat, opened his briefcase, and spread paperwork over the coffee table.

He had no idea how much time passed while he compared the amenities of the different hotels he'd visited on this trip when he heard the door open. He looked up...and his heart ceased beating.

She stopped inside the doorway, her hand still on the doorknob. Her eyes widened and her mouth slackened. Ryne slowly, slowly rose to his feet. He watched her gaze quickly travel over his face and body, a disbelieving look in her eyes. He knew exactly how she felt. He didn't believe who he was seeing.

She stood before him…the woman of his visions.

A slight shake of her head set her shoulder-length blonde curls in motion. She cleared her throat and closed the door. Stepping forward, she held out her hand. "I'm sorry to keep you waiting, Mr. Wilkinson."

He'd never heard her voice in his visions, but she sounded exactly how she looked—soft, feminine, sexy. Ryne accepted her hand. "No problem, Ms. Montgomery."

"Kaci, please."

"And I'm Ryne."

"Ryne," she said softly.

My God, he could come just listening to her voice. All the blood in his body rushed to his cock. Still holding her hand, he took one step forward. "I'm happy to meet you."

She wore a long-sleeved, green turtleneck and dark gray slacks, not the gauzy outfit she always wore in his visions. He wasn't the least bit disappointed. While not tight, the sweater flowed over her generous breasts. Ryne had to tell himself not to ogle them, and especially not to touch them.

Even though he desperately wanted to.

Kaci released his hand and stepped back. Her heart pounded, a thin layer of perspiration coated her body despite the cool temperature in the room. *He* stood before her, alive and real, and every bit as gorgeous as the mirage in the mirror. His dark hair was different—barely touching his shoulders and with a hint of curl instead of chest-length and straight—and his clothing was naturally different. His shoulders were just as broad, his body still husky, his eyes blue and intense.

She had no complaints about the modern version.

"Deborah told you my conference coordinator is out today. Daria has the flu. I hope my substituting for her won't be a problem."

"No, not at all," he said, his voice husky.

Oh, my. The way he looked at her, as if he wanted to devour her right here in her office, made butterflies dance around in her stomach.

He slipped his hands into the front pockets of his baggy navy pants. The action drew her attention to his groin. The enticing bulge there made her quickly look away again.

"Where would you like to begin?" she asked after swallowing.

His gaze dipped to her breasts for a moment. Kaci could feel her nipples hardening. She had to fight the urge to cover her breasts with her arms to hide that sign of her reaction to him.

"Actually, I could use a cup of coffee. How about if we start there?"

Casual would be good. Casual would help her get her hormones back under control. "Would you like to have an early lunch, or a late breakfast?" She folded her hands across her stomach. "To be honest, I haven't eaten yet today and I'm hungry."

"Food sounds good. I want to check out your dining facilities anyway."

He turned back to the coffee table, giving Kaci an excellent view of his bottom.

Oh, my.

She snapped out of her trance when he began to gather up the papers he'd strewn across the table. "You can leave those there if you want. My office is secure."

"I wasn't worried about the security. I didn't want to leave a mess."

"No problem. Just leave your stuff there and you can get it when we're finished."

"Okay." He picked up a clipboard holding a pale blue legal pad. When he turned back to her, he smiled. "Lead the way to the coffee."

I'd rather show you to my suite. Instead of saying what she'd been thinking, Kaci returned his smile. "Coffee it is."

*****

He smelled so good! His after-shave wasn't overpowering, but enough to entice Kaci to bury her nose in his neck. He stood next to her in the elevator...not close enough to touch her, but close enough so she was keenly aware of him.

She couldn't believe her mirage stood less than two feet away from her.

"How many restaurants does your hotel have?" Ryne asked.

Kaci breathed a bit easier. Talking about the hotel would be a safe subject. "Four. We have a twenty-four-hour coffee shop on the first floor. That's where we're going now. We also have a family-style seafood restaurant and a buffet on the second floor. Our steakhouse is on the twenty-fifth floor. The steakhouse is only open for dinner, but we serve a wonderful brunch there on Saturday and Sunday. I'll show you the other restaurants after we eat."

"So your guests won't go hungry, will they?"

His eyes twinkled with humor, making Kaci smile. "No, they definitely won't go hungry."

The elevator doors swished open. Ryne touched the small of her back as they exited. Once outside the small area, he dropped his hand from her.

She wanted to ask him to touch her again, and not stop touching her for the next week.

Kaci remained silent as she led Ryne to the coffee shop. A quick scan of the room showed her an empty table in the corner. Waving to Blair, the hostess, Kaci continued to the corner so she and Ryne could have privacy.

He held her chair while she sat then took the chair across from her. They'd no sooner pulled their chairs up to the table when Jan appeared, coffee pot in hand.

"Good morning, Ms. Montgomery."

She smiled at the fifty-something waitress. Jan had worked at The Seattle Montgomery for as long as Kaci could remember. "Good morning, Jan."

"Coffee?"

"Yes, please, for both of us. I'd also like a glass of orange juice." She looked at the handsome man seated across from her. "Ryne?"

"Sounds good."

"Do you want to look at a menu?" Jan asked while pouring Kaci's coffee.

Kaci laughed. "Hardly. I'll have the two-egg ham and cheese omelet and home fries."

Jan grinned. "Your usual." She turned to Ryne and filled his coffee cup. "And you, sir? Do you need a menu?"

He glanced at Kaci before returning his attention to the waitress. "I'll have what she's having, except make mine a three-egg omelet."

"You got it. I'll be right back with your cream, Ms. Montgomery."

"Thank you, Jan."

Kaci watched Ryne choose a packet of Equal from the ceramic container on the table and add it to his coffee. Even that simple action made her heart flutter.

"Your employees seem to like you," Ryne said while stirring his coffee.

"I'm very lucky."

"Do any of them call you by your first name?"

"Not in public." Kaci leaned forward and folded her arms on the table. "I've never demanded it, but they all call me 'Ms.

Montgomery' when other people are present. In private, I'm Kaci."

"That shows a lot of respect."

Kaci shrugged. "Like I said, I'm lucky."

"No, I'd say you're very skilled at hiring employees." Ryne sipped his coffee. "Mmm, very good."

Kaci grinned. "Well, Seattle is known for its coffee."

"True." Returning his cup to the table, he withdrew a pen from his shirt pocket and turned the clipboard toward him. "So, Ms. Montgomery, tell me why I should recommend The Seattle Montgomery to my clients."

"We're located in one of the most beautiful cities in the world. There are numerous local attractions and easy transportation to get to them. I've already told you about the restaurants in the hotel. We also have a full shopping center on the second floor. If you can think of an item, you can buy it here. It's all about convenience for our guests.

"Our conference center is almost 60,000 square feet and can seat 3,000 for a banquet. We have four ballrooms, the largest almost 40,000 square feet and able to seat 4,500 theater-style or 2,600 in a classroom setting. The conference area foyer has another 25,000 square feet for a reception or additional seating. We have spacious meeting rooms on the fourth floor, plus a complete spa and workout area."

He made several notes on his legal pad. Laying down his pen, he pushed the clipboard aside and leaned back in his chair. "You're very passionate about your hotel." A sultry, hungry look filled his eyes. "What else are you passionate about?"

Her eyes widened. Ryne wondered if he'd stepped where he shouldn't have by making a remark that personal, when her expression changed. A sensual, provocative look filled those gorgeous green eyes. Her lids slid half closed. He watched her gaze travel oh so slowly over his face, shoulders and chest.

"I'm passionate about a *lot* of things," she said softly.

"Such as?"

Jan appeared with a small ceramic pitcher of cream. "Here you go, Ms. Montgomery."

The seductive light disappeared from Kaci's eyes. She cleared her throat then smiled at the waitress. "Thanks, Jan."

Ryne waited until Kaci had added cream to her coffee before he spoke again. "An example?"

"Of what?" she asked without looking at him.

"The things you're passionate about."

Kaci's gaze snapped up to meet his. At first, he didn't think she'd answer him. She looked into his eyes while she sipped her coffee and returned the mug to the table. Holding the mug with both hands, she leaned forward slightly. "Art. Music. Books. Washington. My family."

So she wanted to stick to neutral subjects. He'd go along with that for now. It would give him the chance to learn more about her. "Okay, let's go down your list. What kind of art do you like?"

"I actually prefer photographs over paintings, but there's a local artist whose work I admire very much. He's nowhere near famous, but his work is as beautiful as Thomas Kinkade's, at least to me. I love the paintings he does of thatch-roofed houses. They remind me of Ireland."

"You're from Ireland?"

"My family is. They came to America in the 1800s."

Discovering they shared the same heritage pleased him. "So did mine."

She smiled. "Really? You're Irish too?"

"With a last name like Wilkinson, you have to ask?" He took a large sip of his coffee. "What kind of music do you like?"

"Some rock, some pop, some classical, but mostly soft instrumentals. I'm crazy about the saxophone."

"You must like Kenny G."

Kaci grinned. "Seattle's his hometown. Of course I like his music."

"Of course," Ryne said, returning her grin. "Books?"

"Biographies. Non-fiction. Mysteries. Women's fiction. I have a huge collection of cookbooks." She glanced down a moment before looking directly into his eyes. "Erotic romance."

Ryne raised his eyebrows. "Erotic romance?"

"The story of two people falling in love, including love scenes that leave the bedroom door wide open."

So much for sticking to neutral subjects. "Sounds...intriguing. Do you have some of them?"

She nodded. "Dozens. My erotic romance collection is even bigger than my cookbook collection."

"So that would mean cooking is your second passion, while making love is your first?"

She didn't answer his question for several seconds. That smoky, sensuous look once more filled her eyes. "It...could mean that, yes."

Intensely curious, Ryne would've questioned her further if Jan hadn't returned with their breakfast. He had to put his curiosity on hold, at least until after they ate.

He watched Kaci cut off a bite of her omelet and pop it into her mouth. He'd never thought of eating as particularly sexy. She made it so. She chewed her bite slowly, swallowed, then licked any traces of egg from her upper lip. Ryne groaned silently. He thought about what that pink tongue would feel like on his body, especially sliding up and down his hard cock...

To keep from getting a full-blown erection in public, Ryne decided to turn their conversation back to business. "This is my first trip to Seattle, so I only know what I've seen on TV," he said while cutting off a piece of his own omelet. "Tell me about some of the local attractions."

"Oh, wow, there are so many, I'm not sure where to start. We have some excellent brochures in the lobby about the area. I'll make sure you get them."

"How about hitting the highlights for me?"

She swallowed her bite of home fries. "The highlights. Well, there's the magnificent scenery. You can look in any direction and see beauty. There are four national parks in the area—Mount Rainier, North Cascades, Mount Saint Helens, and Olympic. We have professional sports teams and horse racing. There's the waterfront, beautiful gardens, the symphony, the opera, great shopping, restaurants, clubs, galleries. The list is practically endless."

He listened closely as she described the different attractions. All the places she'd mentioned sounded intriguing. He could easily imagine himself visiting them with Kaci by his side to act as tour director.

By the time they finished their breakfast, he was totally captivated by the lovely blonde sitting across from him.

"Would you like to see the conference area?" Kaci asked as she wiped her hands on her napkin.

He'd like to see her naked body draped across his bed. Later. They would be together later, in every way a man and woman could be together. For now, he had work to do. "Yes, please."

*****

What would've normally taken two hours to accomplish took over twice as long. Kaci dawdled while showing Ryne the amenities of her hotel, wanting to be with him as long as possible. He didn't seem to mind. He sometimes asked the same question more than once, as if he, too, wanted to draw out their time together.

She showed him the conference area, the meeting rooms, the spa, the shopping center, the restaurants on the second floor. When she reached the point where she had nothing left to show him, she reluctantly led him back to her office so he could collect his briefcase.

Once inside her private space, she stood next to her desk and watched him gather up his paperwork and replace it in his briefcase. Other than for those few moments at breakfast when they'd flirted a bit, he'd been all business. Ryne owned the largest, most successful convention planning business in the States. Kaci easily understood why. His questions had been thorough, his intelligence obvious. She couldn't help but be impressed.

And aroused simply looking into those incredible blue eyes.

Ryne faced her, briefcase in hand. "I'd like to see some of those brochures you mentioned. You said they're in the lobby?"

"Yes, we have a large display rack close to the registration desk."

"Then I'll pick some up as I check in."

"You haven't checked in yet?"

"No, not yet. Your employee Deborah brought me here to wait for you." He shifted his briefcase to his other hand. "I think the only thing I didn't get to see is your steakhouse."

"No, we didn't make it that far, did we?"

"I want to unpack and clean up a bit then I'd like to check out your restaurant. Will you have dinner with me?"

She'd take any chance to be with him. "Of course. But..." She stopped, unsure if she had the nerve to ask him the question she wanted to ask.

"But?" he said, tilting his head slightly.

Go for it, Kaci. You've already told him about your erotic romance collection. That isn't the type of thing you tell a guy you just met. Don't wimp out now. "The view at the restaurant is gorgeous and I do want you to see it. But I could arrange for dinner from the steakhouse be served someplace where we'd be more comfortable and have more privacy to talk."

"And that would be where?"

Kaci swallowed the lump of nervousness in her throat. "My suite."

His gaze passed over her face, lingering on her lips a long moment, before he looked back into her eyes. "I'd like that."

Kaci turned to her desk. Picking up a pen, she jotted down her suite number on a notepad. "Is seven all right?"

"Perfect."

She turned back and handed him the small piece of paper. Ryne took it and slipped the paper in his shirt pocket. "Then I'll see you at seven."

He gave her a devastating smile before he left. Alone again, Kaci slumped against her desk. She laid her hand over her racing heart. *Wow. What a hunk.* Not only was he intelligent, successful and courteous, but he was so yummy.

She wondered if he was a good kisser.

He would come to her suite at seven. If she had anything to say about it, he wouldn't be leaving after dinner.

Chapter Six

After solving several problems that no one else seemed able to solve, Kaci finally managed to escape to her suite shortly after five. She headed straight for her bedroom and the mirror. Now that she'd met Ryne, she had no idea what—or whom—she would see, but she couldn't contain her curiosity. Reaching inside her turtleneck, she withdrew the necklace and wrapped her fingers around the charm.

The mirror shifted, blurred, until an image began to form. She drew in a sharp breath when she saw Ryne in his hotel room. He must have recently showered for his hair was wet, his body damp. A towel hung low on his hips. He stood by the bed, his cell phone to his ear. His stance gave her the perfect view of the front of his body.

A light covering of dark hair swirled across his chest and down his flat stomach to disappear inside the towel. The same dark hair was sprinkled over his strong legs. His shoulders looked as broad as a doorway, his arms strong and muscular. A man didn't get a body like that sitting behind a desk all the time. He obviously exercised regularly.

Whatever he did worked really well.

Oh, yeah. Definitely yummy.

He finished his telephone conversation and laid his cell on the nightstand. Before Kaci had any idea what he was about to do, he whipped off his towel and tossed it on the bed.

Her breath hitched. Even flaccid, his cock looked long, thick and very impressive. She licked her lips as she imagined herself on her knees before him, taking that magnificent shaft in her mouth…

He turned toward the closet. Now she could see his back and buttocks. They looked as delicious as the rest of his body.

She wanted to run her tongue over every bit of that tan skin.

You're here, you're real, and you'll be in my suite in less than two hours.

That thought made Kaci gasp. "Less than *two hours*? *Shit*!"

She released the charm and tugged off her sweater as she hurried toward the bathroom.

*****

Kaci lit the tall cream-colored tapers and spiced vanilla-scented votives ten minutes before Ryne was due to arrive. She checked the arrangement of fresh flowers and tapers on the dining table, and straightened the placemats and silverware. A bottle of Merlot sat on the table. Dinner would be served at seven-thirty. The drapes were open in the living and dining rooms, exposing the nighttime lights of Seattle.

The suite looked perfect. Kaci hoped she looked the same.

She rubbed her damp palms down her thighs and straightened her blouse. Kaci had stood in front of her closet for almost fifteen minutes, choosing and then rejecting what to wear. She'd finally decided on dark green, flare-legged slacks and an ivory, long-sleeved silk blouse with a Mandarin collar. She pinned up her hair in a simple twist, with loose tendrils touching her neck. Diamond studs, a gift from Nana on Kaci's twenty-first birthday, adorned her ears.

Outwardly, she'd wanted to appear sophisticated and feminine in case she'd misunderstood the heated looks Ryne had given her today. Underneath her clothes, she wore a new lacy white bra and tiny thong she'd picked up at the lingerie shop on the second floor. They screamed for him to push her against the wall and fuck her.

The doorbell rang. Kaci's stomach jumped. She folded her hands across her waist, took a deep, steadying breath, and let it out slowly before walking to the door.

Dressed in black pants and a crew-necked sweater in multiple shades of gray, he looked more handsome than any man she'd ever seen. Kaci completely forgot how to talk as she stared at him.

Ryne brought his hand from behind his back and held up a single red rose. "Good evening."

His thoughtfulness helped her find her voice. Smiling, she took the rose from him and sniffed it. "Thank you." She moved aside and opened the door wider. "Come in."

He stepped inside and Kaci closed the door. She sniffed the rose again as she watched him gaze around the open living and dining areas.

"Very nice."

"I like it." She motioned toward the L-shaped couch. "Please sit down. Would you like a glass of Merlot, or something a bit stronger?"

"Merlot sounds good."

"I'll be right back after I put this in a vase."

Finding a bud vase for the rose gave Kaci a few moments to get her heart out of her throat. She took her time getting the vase from a kitchen cabinet and filling it with water. When she turned, she saw Ryne leaning on the bar that separated the kitchen from the dining room.

Her heart jumped right back up into her throat.

"I saw the wine on the table," Ryne said, "but no corkscrew."

Kaci set the vase on the bar and reached into a drawer. "Sorry about that." She withdrew the corkscrew and handed it to Ryne. Their fingertips touched. The warmth, the tingling, she experienced in her hand and arm whenever she held the charm happened again.

His eyes widened slightly, as if he had experienced the same thing.

"No problem," he said softly. "Shall I open the wine?"

"Yes, please."

Kaci followed him to the dining room table and watched him expertly open the bottle of Merlot. He poured the ruby liquid into two glasses then held one out to her.

"To a long business relationship," Ryne said, clinking his glass against hers, "and wherever that relationship may lead."

She sipped her wine, gazing into his eyes the entire time. They were intense in the mirror, drawing her close to him, making her want to follow anywhere he wanted to lead her. In real life, they were…

Spellbinding.

"Very good," Ryne said. He lifted the bottle and looked at the label. "From a Washington winery?"

"Yes. I use local suppliers whenever possible. You won't find an apple grown in California anywhere in this hotel. All our meat comes from ranches in Eastern Washington." She twirled her wine in her glass. "And speaking of meat, dinner will be served soon. My chef makes an incredible chateaubriand with béarnaise sauce."

Kaci knew she was rambling. She always rambled when she was nervous. Right now, her nervousness climbed right off the scale.

Ryne smiled. "It sounds delicious. But first…" He took her glass and set it and his on the table. Stepping closer to her, he tilted up her chin with one finger. "I suspect there's something that would taste even *more* delicious."

He covered her lips with his. He didn't deepen the kiss or use his tongue. He kissed her softly, gently, touching her only with his lips and that lone finger.

Everything inside Kaci's body turned to liquid heat.

Ryne ended the kiss and ran his thumb over her lower lip. "Yes, definitely delicious." He raised his gaze from her mouth to her eyes. "I've wanted to do that ever since I saw you in your office." His thumb skated over her lip again. "And a lot more. I want to touch you, feel your skin against mine."

He was being completely honest with her, so Kaci had to be the same. "So do I."

"Do you feel it too, this…? I don't know what to call it."

"Fire? Electricity? Desire?"

"All of the above."

"Yes," Kaci whispered, "I feel it too."

He cradled her face in his hands. "I have things to tell you, things you probably won't believe."

Things I won't believe? What will you think when I tell you about the mirror? She touched his hands, running her fingers over the warm skin. "What do you have to tell me?"

The doorbell rang before he said anything else. Kaci silently sighed. She'd lost all interest in food. All she wanted now was Ryne. "That's probably dinner. Excuse me."

Kaci walked to the door, although she didn't know how when her legs were shaky. She wasn't a virgin. Other men had touched her, made love to her. Their caresses, their kisses, had never affected her as quickly or as strongly as one kiss from Ryne.

Jorge stood outside her door with a rolling cart. He smiled, flashing all those straight white teeth that earned him a lot of tips from the ladies. "Good evening, Ms. Montgomery."

Kaci returned his smile. "Good evening, Jorge. Come in."

"Shall I set up for you?" he asked as he rolled the cart past her.

"Yes, please. In the dining room."

Jorge tipped his head at Ryne and wished him a good evening also as he moved the items from his cart to the table. He chatted easily with Kaci about people in the hotel and upcoming events that he would be working. She listened and made the appropriate responses, but her attention was glued to Ryne…his handsome face, his intense eyes, his dark mane of hair, his broad shoulders. She didn't dare look any farther down his body for fear of attacking him. That wouldn't be a good idea with one of her employees in the room.

Hurry up, Jorge. I want to get dinner over with so I can have Ryne for dessert!

"Anything else, Ms. Montgomery?" Jorge asked.

"No, thank you. This is fine."

"Enjoy your meal, ma'am, sir."

Kaci saw Jorge out and made sure the door was securely locked before she returned to the dining room. Ryne watched her approach. His gaze traveled over her body, lingering on her breasts and hips. Her body grew warm when she thought about his hands touching her instead of only his gaze.

"Everything smells delicious," he said when she stood next to him again.

"I have wonderful chefs. Here, you have to taste the bread first."

Kaci uncovered the basket of small loaves. Tearing off a piece of the warm, soft bread, she slathered butter over it and held it up for Ryne to taste. He took a bite and chewed slowly.

"Very good." Taking her wrist, he held the bread up to her mouth. She took a bite from the same spot that he had tasted. Somehow, despite the lump of desire in her throat, she managed to swallow the bite.

Ryne took the bread from her and returned it to the basket. "I'm not hungry for food, Kaci."

"Neither am I." Tunneling her fingers into his hair, she pulled his head lower and kissed him.

He'd kissed her softly and gently. Kaci didn't. She kissed him with all the hunger she was feeling, moving her lips over his, sliding her tongue along the seam. It took him only a second to respond. He wrapped his arms around her and returned her hungry kiss, his tongue pushing past her lips. Moaning deep in her throat, Kaci opened her mouth and accepted the thrust of his tongue.

Oh, yes, definitely a good kisser.

Ryne's hands cupped her buttocks and pulled her pelvis into his. "Where?" he whispered against her throat.

Kaci didn't ask what he meant, she knew exactly what he wanted to know. "My bedroom."

Ryne scooped Kaci up in his arms. She buried her face against his neck, licking and nipping on his skin as he walked toward her bedroom. Her tongue slid up to his ear and dipped inside. Chills raced down his spine.

"We won't make it to the bedroom if you keep that up, Kaci."

"I don't care." Her tongue dipped into his ear again, then she bit his lobe. "You smell so good. And taste even better."

Ryne groaned and quickened his pace. He wanted her naked and beneath him as soon as possible.

The sight that greeted him when he stepped past her bedroom doorway made him stop in his tracks. Dozens of candles were lit around the room, releasing a spicy vanilla scent. They filled the room with pale yellow light. He could see reflections of the flames in the large glass window and mirrors.

She'd obviously planned for them to make love tonight. That realization made him want her even more.

Continuing to the bed, Ryne laid Kaci on top of the quilted bedspread and reclined beside her. He stared down into her face. The candlelight made her skin golden, her eyes glow. "You're beautiful, Kaci."

"Thank you," she whispered. Her breath hitched when he licked her bottom lip. "And you're even more handsome in real life."

Confused by what she'd said, Ryne stopped exploring her jaw with his tongue and looked at her. "In real life?"

"Nothing. Ryne, please, take off your sweater. I want to touch your chest."

He had to taste her mouth once more before he moved away from her. Rising to his knees, he jerked his sweater over his head and tossed it to the floor.

Kaci propped herself on one elbow and ran her hand over his chest and stomach. Her fingertips brushed over his nipple, and Ryne hissed. He wanted to take this slow, make their first time together special. If she kept touching him with that soft hand, taking it slow wouldn't be a remote possibility.

Her fingers drifted across his stomach again before venturing below his belt. Ryne spread his knees wider and let her touch him however she wanted. She outlined his cock, tickled his balls, explored between his legs. When she repeated the journey a second time, Ryne grabbed her wrist.

"Time for you to take off some clothes, too."

Kaci gave his balls one more gentle squeeze before she rose to her knees. Looking him straight in the eyes, she unbuttoned the cuffs of her blouse. Ryne clenched his fists on his thighs to keep from reaching out to help her. He wanted to watch her undress, wanted to see her ivory skin revealed to him a bit at a time.

The top button on her blouse slipped through the buttonhole. The next one followed, giving him a glimpse of her chest. The next one exposed the tops of her breasts.

Why did women's blouses have to have so many damn buttons?

By the time Kaci reached the last one, Ryne was struggling to breathe. He wanted her so much, his body trembled. He'd never experienced desire so fierce, so overpowering. The need to claim her, make her *his*, overruled all his intentions to take this slowly. He had to have her *now*.

She removed her blouse and let it fall to the bed behind her. A lacy white bra pushed her breasts up, making them look even larger, more tempting.

More delicious.

He motioned toward the piece of lingerie covering her breasts. "Off."

She obeyed him with no hesitation. Her bra joined her blouse on the bed.

Large, round, with big nipples made for him to suck. Ryne's mouth watered with the need to taste her. Unable to resist, he cradled both heavy breasts in his hands, lifted them, and took one nipple in his mouth. Kaci arched her back and moaned softly. That sound of pleasure urged him to suckle harder. He moved from one nipple to the other, treating each to his tongue, his teeth, his lips.

"That feels so good, Ryne. Oh, more, *please*!"

Only too happy to do as she requested, Ryne alternated between sucking on her nipples and licking the areolas while he kneaded the firm flesh. The sounds he made, along with Kaci's increased breathing, filled the room. She gripped his hair, holding him even closer to her. Her breathing became erratic, choppy, until she gasped and her body shook.

Ryne looked at her face. Her head was tilted back, her eyes closed. Surely she hadn't… "Did you come?"

"Mmm, yes." She slowly brought her head forward and opened her eyes. "My breasts are very sensitive."

Ryne grinned. "Oh, yeah? I like that." He squeezed her breasts and skated his thumbs over the nipples. "So how many different ways can you come?"

"Why don't we find out?"

"Oh, lady, I like the way you think." He unbuttoned her slacks and slowly lowered the zipper. "Let's get you out of the rest of your clothes, all right? Lie down."

She reclined on the bed, resting her head on a pillow. Ryne tugged her slacks past her waist. Kaci lifted her hips and he pulled them farther down her legs. He had to stop a moment and admire the tiny scrap of white covering her pussy before sliding them off her legs. She toed off her flats, leaving her wearing nothing but the thong.

He'd dreamed of seeing her ass for months. Finally, he had the chance to make his dream come true. "Roll over," he said, his voice thick.

She did, and he got his first look at those rounded, perfect cheeks. The thought of being buried inside her ass made his cock throb.

Ryne rose long enough to remove the rest of his clothes. When he returned to the bed, he lay on top of her, settling his cock against her ass. Slipping his hands beneath her, he palmed her breasts and squeezed them.

"You have an incredible ass," he whispered in her ear. Moving down her body, Ryne dropped kisses on her spine until he reached those beautiful globes. He palmed her cheeks and spread them while gently nipping her with his teeth. Soft moans from her throat and the shifting of her hips proved to Ryne that Kaci liked what he was doing.

He pulled aside the thong's string and ran his tongue from her anus to her clit and back again. Kaci lifted her hips when he wiggled his tongue across her puckered hole.

"Do you like this?" he asked before dipping his tongue inside her.

"Yes."

"Do you want more?"

"Oh, yes."

Spreading her cheeks wider, he began to fuck her ass with his tongue. Kaci writhed on the bed, moving her hips up and down in rhythm with his movements. Ryne released one cheek so he could slip his hand inside her thong. Warm cream coated his fingers.

"My God, you're wet."

Ryne easily pushed two fingers inside her pussy. He pumped them in and out, in and out, while he continued to tongue-fuck her ass. No more than a few moments passed when he felt her walls clamp around his fingers. He continued to pump them and lick her as she shuddered from her climax.

Finally, she stilled. Desperate to be inside her, Ryne rolled Kaci to her back and jerked off her thong. He straddled her body on his hands and knees.

"I bought condoms this afternoon. I don't want to use one, but I will if you want me to. Do you?"

Kaci touched his face, his shoulders, his chest. Her gaze followed the movement of her hands as she explored his stomach and groin. When she palmed his cock, she looked back into his eyes.

"No."

Ryne moved his legs between hers. He kissed her deeply as he entered her with one thrust.

Kaci wrapped her arms tightly around Ryne's neck and returned his ravenous kiss. Two orgasms hadn't diminished her desire for him, and she didn't understand that. Orgasms usually occurred for her, but she rarely experienced more than two during sex.

The heat taking over her body again told her she would definitely experience more than two tonight.

She moved with him, meeting every deep thrust. He slid his hands beneath her buttocks and lifted them, letting him drive even farther inside her. Sweat covered his skin. She could feel his heart pounding, could hear his ragged breathing. So close. They were both so close…

Ryne stopped moving. Kaci crashed back to earth without reaching the peak. "Oh, don't stop!"

"I'm sorry," he rasped in her ear. "I don't want to come yet."

"*I* do!"

His chuckle tickled her ear. Raising his head, he smiled at her. "You're a horny little thing, aren't you?"

"It's been a long time between lovers."

"For me too." He kissed her once, twice. "I want you to come again."

She swatted one of his buttocks. "Then *move*."

"I want *you* to come, not me." He kissed her again. "How about if I lick on your clit for awhile?"

Kaci's pussy clenched in response to his question. "Oh, yes."

She propped her feet on the bed and spread her thighs as wide as she could. Ryne lay on his stomach between them. One long lick up her entire slit made Kaci groan.

"Mmm, you're delicious." His tongue wiggled over her clit. "I could do this all night."

Kaci would've popped off a joke, but the intense sensations kept her from speaking. She'd been with men who were too rough with their tongue, or too fast, or too slow. Ryne's movements were perfect, as if they'd been lovers for years instead of this being their first time together. He licked her as if he really did want to do it all night. Kaci quickly climbed up toward the heavens again. This time, she reached the peak and fell over it.

When she could think again, she realized that Ryne still gently licked her pussy. Kaci touched his cheek. He raised his head and grinned at her.

"That's three. My tongue isn't tired. Want to try for four?"

She laughed. What a delightful, funny, sexy man. She couldn't remember any time when she'd laughed during sex. Falling hard for him wouldn't be at all difficult. "I think before we worry about four for me, we should concentrate on one for you."

"Deal."

He quickly scrambled up over her body and thrust inside her. Kaci laughed again at his silly action. Her laughter turned to moans when he began to move.

The feeling of fullness. The sound of heavy breathing, and hard flesh sliding into wet. The scent of sex. The salty taste of sweat when she licked his neck. Everything combined to raise Kaci's desire once more. Holding tightly to Ryne, she accepted his powerful thrusts, his passionate kisses. The heat slowly built in her body, the prelude to orgasm.

Ryne gripped her buttocks, thrust hard, and released a loud moan. Kaci's heat dissipated. Instead of feeling disappointed that she didn't reach orgasm again, she reveled in Ryne's climax.

Long moments passed before he raised his head. "Wow. That was… Wow."

Kaci ran her hands through his thick hair. "I like a man of few words."

"I'll talk more when my tongue will work again."

"Your tongue was working just fine a few minutes ago."

He grinned. "You liked that, huh?"

"Very much."

She tugged on his hair until he lowered his head for her kiss. He returned it as he began to slowly thrust again. "I'm not through," he said against her lips. "Do you mind?"

A brush of his thumb across her clit made her breath catch. "No, I don't mind at all."

Chapter Seven

Kaci sipped her coffee while gazing at downtown Seattle as it greeted the new day. She had no idea of the time, but it had to be early since the sun hadn't risen. It would be a glorious day with sunshine and blue skies...a very untypical March day in the Pacific Northwest.

Despite the promise of a cloud-free day, the temperature hovered in the mid 40s here on her balcony. She hunched her shoulders, trying to burrow her body farther into her thick terry-cloth robe without releasing her coffee mug. The warm mug felt too good in her hands to release it.

The start of another day was always a blessing to Kaci. Today was especially joyful to her because of the sexy man still sleeping in her bed.

Kaci smiled and looked up at the lightening sky. *Ryne is wonderful, Nana. Thank you for sending him to me.*

Warm lips caressed her neck, making Kaci's smile widen. She looked over her shoulder into Ryne's sleepy eyes.

"Good morning."

"Good morning. Why didn't you wake me?"

"You were sleeping so soundly, I didn't want to bother you."

His arms encircled her waist and he entwined his fingers over her stomach. "You're a very considerate lady." He kissed the tip of her nose. "Thanks for the robe."

"You're welcome." She ran one hand up the sleeve of his blue terry-cloth robe that matched the one she wore. "I'm not the only one who's considerate."

He raised his eyebrows. "Oh?"

"Someone put away our dinner. I forgot all about it."

Ryne grinned devilishly. "You were too busy having orgasms to think about putting away the food."

"True. But since we didn't have dinner last night, I'm absolutely ravenous this morning. How about you?"

A smoky, seductive look filled his eyes. "Oh, yeah. I'm absolutely ravenous, too."

Kaci didn't realize he'd untied her robe until she felt him touch her bare stomach. She almost dropped her coffee mug when his hand began a slow descent down her abdomen. "Ryne!"

He kissed her cheek, her jaw, before traveling up her neck. He nipped her lobe then darted his tongue inside her ear. "Hmm?"

Goose bumps erupted on her skin. "We're outside. And it's cold!"

"You won't feel the cold in a minute."

"You can't do this here."

"No one can see us."

"There's an office building right across the street. Ryne!" Her voice came out as a squeak when he slid one hand between her legs. She couldn't believe he was touching her like this standing on her balcony.

"Relax, Kaci. Just enjoy me touching you." One finger circled her clit, ever so lightly. "Feel good?"

Kaci tilted her head back until it rested on his shoulder. Yes, it felt good, but she shouldn't allow him to…

Oh, my.

His finger dipped inside her, gathering up the moisture from her body. He returned to her clit, massaging it a bit harder this time. His other hand pushed her robe completely open and cradled her breast, his thumb brushing across the hard nipple.

"Does it excite you to think someone could be watching us?" His hot breath in her ear sent another scattering of goose bumps across her skin. "You're getting wetter and your clit is getting harder. You like this, don't you? You like knowing your body is exposed, that someone can see me touching you."

Two fingers plunged inside her pussy. Kaci had to lock her knees to keep from falling. The mug slipped from her hand and landed on a cushioned chair.

"Oh, yeah." Ryne's fingers pumped faster as he tugged harder on her nipple with his thumb and forefinger. "You are so hot." He bit her neck, her shoulder. "Think about it, Kaci. Think about a man standing at the window across the street, watching me fuck you with my fingers. Think of him stroking his hard cock while he looks at your tits. He won't let himself come until you do. Come now, Kaci. *Now*!"

He pinched her clit and Kaci shattered. Her knees stopped supporting her. Only Ryne's arms encircling her body kept her from falling.

Kaci didn't have time to catch her breath before Ryne turned her toward him. Pushing his robe open, he pulled her against his hot body. His hands gripped her buttocks as he kissed her deeply. His tongue lunged into her mouth, over and over, while he shifted his hips from side to side.

"I've got to get inside you." He bent his knees, as if he planned to penetrate her. Kaci stepped back so he couldn't.

"Not here. Come inside with me."

Ryne let her take his hand and lead him toward the bedroom. He would've been happy to take her on the couch. Hell, he would've been happy with the *floor*. If Kaci thought they always needed a bed to make love, he had a lot to teach her.

His cock throbbed when he thought of giving lessons to his willing student.

She stopped beside the bed. Releasing his hand, she pushed his robe off his shoulders and let it fall to the floor. After doing the same with hers, she lay on the bed, legs spread wide.

Ryne looked at pink, swollen lips glistening with her juices. He definitely wanted to fuck her, but he wanted to do something else first. He tugged on her ankles until her buttocks were halfway off the bed. Dropping to his knees, he thrust his tongue into her pussy.

She tasted like woman and sex. Ryne wiggled his tongue across her flesh as he breathed deeply of her scent. He'd always enjoyed performing oral sex on a woman. He especially enjoyed it with Kaci since she received so much pleasure from it. He licked her clit, her wet folds, her anus.

By the time he returned to her clit, she was writhing on the bed while she plucked at her nipples. Wetting his fingers with her own moisture, he pushed one inside her pussy and one inside her ass.

"Oh, yes," she groaned. "That feels soooo good. What you do with your tongue should be illegal."

Ryne chuckled. "Do you want me to stop?" he asked before giving her clit a gentle tug with his lips.

"Don't you dare! You..." Her breath hitched. "Oh, yes, right there. Faster. Yes, like that. Ryne!"

The contractions inside her body grabbed both his fingers. Wanting to prolong her pleasure as long as possible, he pushed them farther inside her body while he gently licked her clit. Kaci shuddered and the contractions grabbed his fingers again.

Ryne nipped the inside of each thigh. He loved the way Kaci responded to him, loved giving her pleasure.

But his cock was making demands...demands he couldn't deny any longer. He had to get inside her. He stood, slipped his arms under her thighs, and entered her with one hard thrust.

Kaci gasped. "Wait."

Ryne couldn't believe what he'd just heard. "*Wait*? I don't think so." He pulled almost completely out of her pussy then lunged back in.

"Ryne, please, I want to do something else."

Taking a deep breath, Ryne closed his eyes. He wanted to please her, but a man could only take so much before he had to *move*. He opened his eyes again. "Kaci, you're killing me here."

She scooted away from him until his shaft popped free of her. Ryne groaned at the loss of that warm, wet heat surrounding his aching flesh. Rising to her knees, Kaci cradled his face in her hands and kissed him. "I've never…" She stopped and bit her bottom lip. "I want to try something with you, something I've never done."

"What?"

"I really like it when you lick me. I want to try anal sex."

Ryne's cock jerked. He'd love to thrust inside that beautiful ass, but he had to be sure she truly wanted to. He didn't want Kaci to do anything only to please him. "Are you sure?"

She nodded. "I'm sure. I'm…curious. I mean, only if you want to."

Ryne chuckled. "Oh, yes, sweetheart, I definitely want to." Sliding his hands down her back, he cupped her buttocks. "We'll have to do something about satisfying your curiosity. Do you have any lubricant?"

"Second drawer of the nightstand."

"Lie down on your stomach."

Kaci lay diagonally across the bed, her head resting on her arms. Ryne took a moment to simply look at her, enjoying the sight of her back and shapely legs as well as her rounded buttocks. Nothing was more beautiful to him than a woman's body. Any size, any shape, they were all beautiful.

Especially the lovely woman lying before him.

Crawling up on the bed, he reached for one of the pillows. "Lift your hips." Kaci did, and he slid the pillow beneath her stomach. Not satisfied with the height, he grabbed the other pillow and added it to the first. Her legs fell open, exposing that luscious pink pussy and anus.

Ryne's cock throbbed as he stared at her tempting flesh. Desperate to be inside her, he fumbled for the nightstand drawer and pulled it open. Pushing aside a notepad, pen, and two books, he located the bottle of lubricating gel.

And three dildos of various sizes.

Ryne's eyebrows rose at that sight, then he grinned. He'd love to use those dildos on her, but not now. Right now, he didn't want anything touching her but him.

Kaci lay still, waiting for Ryne to touch her again. She'd loved when he'd licked her anus last night and thrust his tongue inside her ass. His penis would be another story. He wasn't exactly small. Although curious, she couldn't help but wonder if it would hurt.

The mattress dipped as he moved between her legs. She tensed, waiting. It surprised her to feel the head of his cock slip inside her pussy.

"I want to play a little," he said. "Okay?"

"Okay," she whispered.

Oh, yes, it was very okay to feel that hard shaft sliding in and out of her. His movements were slow, steady, building up her desire a bit at a time. With her stomach propped up on two pillows she couldn't lift her hips any higher, but she spread her legs another inch, trying to draw him even farther inside her.

Something cool and wet dribbled between her buttocks. Kaci tensed again, but quickly made herself relax as Ryne softly touched her anus. He rubbed the lube around the area while he continued to slowly pump inside her.

"Feel good?" he asked.

"Yes."

"I want you to tell me if I do something you don't like, all right?"

"I will."

His warm lips touched the middle of her back. Kaci sighed with pleasure. His kisses continued up her spine, so light they almost tickled. With each kiss, his finger caressed her anus a bit firmer.

By the time his lips reached her nape, he'd pushed his finger all the way inside her.

"Still okay?" he asked.

"Mmm-hmm."

More lube dribbled on her skin. A second finger joined the first. Kaci took a deep breath and released it slowly through her mouth.

"That's the way, sweetheart. Relax and let me touch you." His fingers began to slowly move. "You have no idea how good this feels to me, to have my cock and my fingers both inside you."

He had no idea how good it felt to Kaci. Other men had touched her anus with fingers and tongue, but she'd never had any desire for more with them. With Ryne, she wanted *everything*.

He withdrew both his shaft and fingers from her body. Kaci closed her eyes and waited for what he would do next. She felt a cool sensation inside her ass. Realizing he'd squirted some of the lube into her body, she tensed again.

"Take a breath, babe. I promise I'll stop any time you tell me to."

She believed that. Despite his own arousal, Kaci knew he'd stop the moment she told him to. "I know you will."

The head of his penis touched her anus while his fingers massaged her clit. A gentle pressure, a sensation of stretching, then his head was inside her.

"Okay, sweetheart?"

Kaci nodded. She was more than okay. The feeling of fullness was incredible.

It became even more incredible when Ryne began to slowly move. Each time he thrust he drove a bit deeper into her. He withdrew and advanced, repeating the action over and over until she could feel his balls snug against her feminine lips.

"I'm all the way inside you, Kaci. You still okay?"

"Yes."

Gripping her hips, he began to lazily pump. Kaci lay still, accepting what he gave her, until it wasn't enough. She reached back with one hand and grabbed his thigh. "Faster."

He obeyed her instantly, gaining speed until he was pounding into her ass. The fever built inside her, surprising her. She never would have believed she could reach orgasm this way. The heat climbed higher and higher until it erupted in a shattering climax.

"Oh, God, Ryne!"

She heard a loud guttural sound from Ryne before he collapsed on top of her. Sweat and heat poured off his skin. She could barely breathe from his weight, but she didn't care. She felt too good, too satisfied, to ask him to move.

Several moments passed before Ryne lifted his torso. Kaci immediately inhaled a much needed breath.

"I'm sorry. I didn't mean to smother you, but I couldn't move." He dropped a kiss between her shoulder blades. "And to be honest, I didn't *want* to move."

"Mmm, me either. But we're going to have to stop this fooling around and find some food. My stomach is really mad at me for ignoring it."

Ryne chuckled. "Mine too. Shower first?"

"Oh, absolutely."

He slowly withdrew from her and helped her roll to her back. He kissed her long and deeply while his fingers played with her clit. "You came, but do you need anything else?"

She shook her head. "I am completely satisfied."

Ryne smiled. "That's what I like to hear." He dropped one more kiss on her lips. "I'll get the shower started for us while you order breakfast. Deal?"

Chapter Eight

Ryne had three sisters. As the oldest of the siblings and the first one who could drive, there had been times when they'd conned him into taking them shopping "just for a few minutes". When Kaci had uttered those same words, he should've known better. A woman couldn't shop only a few minutes. They'd walked through a shopping mall for almost four hours. Each store they came to that caught Kaci's eye, she'd said those misleading words again about only needing a few minutes.

He had to admit he did enjoy the fashion show she'd put on for him at Victoria's Secret. He'd been thankful she'd already purchased some items. Holding the sacks in front of him hid his erection.

Kaci handed him a glass of iced tea. After slipping off her shoes, she sat beside him on the couch. "All better now that you're sitting down?"

The mischievous twinkle in her eyes made him scowl. "You're proud of yourself for putting me through that misery, aren't you?"

"*You're* the one who said you wanted to see some of the local sights."

"Kaci, 'the local sights' don't include the inside of a mall. I was thinking more along the lines of the Space Needle or Pike Place Market." He drained half his glass and set it on the coffee table. "You're a lousy tour guide."

She giggled. "Sorry. But I just needed a few things—"

"Yeah, yeah, I heard *that* line at least a dozen times."

She leaned forward and kissed him softly. "I'll make it up to you."

He thought of the red bra, thong, and thigh-high stockings she'd bought. "When?"

"When do you want me to make it up to you?"

"Now is good."

"We made love before we went shopping."

"Now is good," he repeated, trying hard not to grin.

She slid her hand beneath his sweater and caressed his stomach. "Do you have something particular in mind?"

"Yeah. I'd like to see you in that red lingerie."

Smiling wickedly, she pulled his sweater over his head and tossed it to the floor. She kissed the center of his chest then ran her tongue down his stomach to the waistband of his jeans. "I thought I'd save that for later. How about..." She unfastened his belt. "...I do something else..." The snap of his jeans popped open under her skillful fingers. "...instead?"

The rasp of his zipper made Ryne inhale sharply. "I really had my heart set on that red lingerie."

"Oh, I think you'll like this too." Dipping her hand inside his briefs, she drew out his hardening cock. She licked her lips before opening her mouth over the head.

Ryne groaned. "Oh, yeah, that works."

"I thought it might." He lifted his hips a few inches off the couch so she could tug his jeans and briefs down to his thighs. She took him deep in her throat then returned to the head. Her tongue circled, stroked, licked. Her mouth caressed his cock as if it were the most delicious thing she'd ever tasted.

Ryne tilted his head back to rest on the couch and watched her lips slide up and down his shaft. Her mouth was so warm and wet.

"That feels good, babe."

"Mmm."

Her mumble made him smile. "Can't talk with your mouth full, huh?"

Kaci slid her tongue up the underside of his cock from base to tip. "Do you want me to talk, or do you want me to do this?"

Ryne lifted his hips and drove the head past her lips. "I want you to do that."

She minded very well. Kaci added her hands to the play, caressing the base of his cock while she licked the tip, and vice versa. Her tongue lapped at his balls and the sensitive area between them and his ass.

It wouldn't take long to send him over the top. Cradling her jaws, he gently tugged her away from him. She looked at him, her expression confused.

"You need to climb up here and ride me."

The tip of her tongue tickled his slit. "I'm having fun here."

"So am I, but I really want to be inside you. Take off your clothes."

Kaci stood and reached for the hem of her sweater. "Slowly," Ryne said. "Give me a show."

"Give me one, too. Touch yourself."

Ryne wrapped his hand around his cock and lazily pumped it while Kaci drew her sweater over her head. It fell to the floor on top of her shoes. Watching his hand, she unfastened her jeans and pushed them past her hips. When they reached her thighs, she turned around, wiggling her hips as she continued to push them down her legs. Blood surged in Ryne's cock at the sight of that gorgeous ass as she bent over to remove her jeans.

He silently blessed whoever invented the thong.

She turned back to face him, now wearing only her cream-colored underwear. She reached behind her, unhooked her bra, and let it fall to the floor. The thong quickly followed. Kaci stood before him totally nude, watching his hand as he continued to stroke his cock.

"Come here," Ryne said, his voice husky.

Kaci straddled his thighs. Ryne held his shaft as she lowered her pussy over it. Once he was totally sheathed inside her, they both groaned.

Ryne knew he'd come much too soon if he began to thrust. To hold off his climax and give Kaci the chance to have one first, he had to let her be in charge. "Take whatever you need from me, babe."

She leaned forward, pressed her breasts against his chest, and kissed him hungrily. Lips slid together, tongues dueled, breaths mingled.

Her taste made his head swim.

"I love kissing you." Kaci nibbled on his neck as she began to ride him.

"I love it too." Ryne slid his hands up and down her back, enjoying the smoothness of her silky skin. "You feel incredible. Lean back so I can touch you."

Kaci sat up, bracing her hands on his stomach. Ryne splayed one hand low on her abdomen and slid his thumb over her clit. He caressed her breasts with his free hand, cupped them, tugged on the nipples. Kaci moved faster, picking up speed as he applied more pressure to her clit. She stared into his eyes while she rode him. Looking into her eyes, he felt the connection between them, the pull of their souls to be one.

He'd never in his life felt anything more powerful.

The walls of her pussy clamped onto his cock, milking it as she came. Her eyes slid closed, her back arched. Ryne kneaded her breasts, wanting to give her as much sensation as possible while she rode out her climax.

She opened her eyes. He saw the fire in them, the desire, and knew she was far from through with him. She proved him right when she dragged her fingernails down his chest…not enough to hurt him, but enough to make him catch his breath at the sensation. His cock surged inside her.

"Mmm," she purred, "that felt good." She scratched him again, her nails raking over his nipples this time. Ryne hissed in his breath through his teeth.

"*Damn,* Kaci."

"You don't like that?"

"Hell, yes, I like it!" He shifted his hips, driving his shaft inside her. "Can't you *feel* how much I like it?" He gripped her waist tightly. "Move for me, babe."

She held onto his shoulders as she rode him a second time. Ryne didn't hold back this time, the need to mate was too overpowering. He moved with her, establishing a rhythm in only moments that drove up his blood pressure and made sweat break out on his skin.

The contractions inside her body brought on his release. Ryne growled and shuddered beneath her.

The ability to think, much less form any coherent words, disappeared for several seconds. When he decided he could speak without slurring his words, he grinned.

"God, I love sex."

Kaci laughed as she caressed his chest. "I like it too."

Quickly becoming serious again, Ryne ran his hands up and down her thighs. "Kaci, I…" He stopped and took a breath. "That thing on the balcony this morning."

She tilted her head to the side. "Yes?"

"I shouldn't have done that…exposed you that way."

"I don't think anyone saw us."

"That doesn't matter. It wasn't the type of thing a gentleman would do with a lady." He squeezed her thighs. "And you're very much a lady, Kaci." He grinned. "Even if you're also a horny wench."

Laughing, she laid her forehead on his chest. Ryne hugged her then slipped his hand beneath her chin and lifted her face for his kiss. "It's never been like this, Kaci. I've never felt for a woman what I feel for you."

Her eyes filled with tears, even though she smiled. "I know what you mean," she whispered.

"It's kinda scary, huh?"

She nodded. "Kinda."

"So what do we do about it?"

"I don't know."

He slid his hands up and down her arms. "I'm supposed to go back to L.A. tomorrow."

A look of despair filled her eyes. "So soon?"

Ryne nodded. "This was a business trip. I didn't expect to meet the woman who..." He stopped, unsure if he should continue. He hesitated to say "the woman who I want to spend the rest of my life with," even though that's how he felt.

Kaci took his hands and held them between her breasts. "Ryne, I need...I need to tell you something, and I don't know how."

He knew the feeling. He still hadn't told her about Shae. Of course, they'd been so busy enjoying each other's bodies, he hadn't given the little fairy a thought.

It would really piss Shae off to know she'd been ignored.

He fingered the charm around her neck. He'd seen the necklace the first time she'd taken off her blouse. At the time, his hormones had been ruling his body, not his brain. He hadn't truly looked at the charm until later, when they'd lain in each other's arms after making love. It matched the one he carried in his pocket, except for the diamonds on Kaci's charm. "Does it have anything to do with this?"

She looked surprised. "How did you know?"

"Do you remember me saying last night that I had things to tell you you wouldn't believe?"

"Yes."

"It's time we talked, Kaci."

Chapter Nine

How do I tell him? Kaci wondered while she slipped into a pair of comfortable sweats and watched Ryne do the same with a pair he'd brought from his room. *How do I tell him about the mirror, the necklace, Nana's letter? He'll think I'm nuts.*

Once dressed, Kaci sat on the end of the bed and faced the mirror. She watched Ryne's reflection as he sat beside her.

"So, who goes first?" he asked, looking at her in the mirror.

"Me, as soon as I figure out how to start." She fingered the necklace, hoping the charm would give her courage. "My great-grandmother died one month ago today. She left me the mirror and this necklace in her will."

"Were you close?"

Kaci nodded. "Very. I miss her terribly."

He squeezed her hand. His support made it easier for her to continue. "She also left me a personal letter. In it, she explained about the mirror and necklace, and how they'd help me find my true love." Turning toward Ryne, she rested one knee on the bed. She waited to speak again until he'd turned toward her also. "When I touch the charm and look in the mirror, I see you."

She expected to see surprise, shock, or total disbelief in his eyes. She saw none of those. He continued to hold her hand, giving her his silent support.

"The visions came from something that happened hundreds of years ago. I know that from the clothing. It was you, or an ancestor of yours. I watched you ride horses, fight with swords, sleep...make love."

His eyebrows rose at that last part, but he remained silent.

"Yesterday, after I agreed to have dinner with you, I held the charm and looked in the mirror. I saw you in your room. You were talking on your cell phone. Your hair was damp and you had a towel wrapped around your waist."

"I'd just gotten out of the shower when my secretary called me."

Kaci released his hand and pushed her hair back from her face. "I know this sounds crazy—"

"No, not really."

Confused by his easy acceptance of what must sound like something from a writer's fertile imagination, Kaci watched Ryne reach behind him. He picked up his pair of jeans from the bed. Reaching into the front pocket, he brought out what looked like a coin. He held it up so Kaci could see it.

"Look familiar?"

Her eyes widened. He held a charm identical to the one she wore, except it was a bit larger.

Her gaze flew from the charm to his eyes and back to the charm. "How...?"

"I found it in a pawnshop in Miami three months ago. I never go into pawnshops, I never even look in the window of pawnshops, yet I did. I saw this lying on a piece of green fabric and knew I had to buy it. It's been with me ever since."

Ryne picked up Kaci's hand, laid the charm in it, and closed her fingers around it. "The first evening I had that charm, I saw a vision...a vision of you."

Kaci swallowed.

"I thought I'd gone crazy. I was alone in my house, having a glass of wine, and there you were, hovering in midair. Needless to say, I wore the rest of the wine instead of drinking it."

"I'm sure you did."

"After having several more visions, I learned to expect them, even look forward to them. The last one I had was in Denver, the night before I met you."

The piece of jewelry felt warm, vibrant, in her hand. Kaci tightened her fingers around it. "What does this mean? How can we both have the same charm?" Suddenly, Kaci remembered Kaylen's story about a charm being stolen from their ancestor. "Ryne, my great-great-grandfather had a charm just like yours. It was stolen from him shortly after he arrived in America from Ireland. Do you think this is it?"

"I don't know *what* to think, but I suppose anything's possible. We each saw visions of the other one without any idea that we'd actually meet."

"So do you think Nana told me the truth, that we're destined to be together?"

Ryne rubbed one hand over his face. "I don't know if I believe in 'destiny', Kaci."

"Then how do you explain what's happened to us?"

"I can't." He blew out a heavy breath. "We live hundreds of miles apart. How are we supposed to be together, to build a relationship?"

"You could move here."

"Kaci, I have dozens of employees. I can't just close my business and move to Seattle. I can't take jobs away from all those people." He laid his hand over hers. "Are you willing to move to Los Angeles to be with me?"

Her first instinct was to say no. She'd been to Los Angeles several times and didn't like it. To keep from saying anything yet, she bit her bottom lip.

"Well, there's my answer."

"Ryne, it isn't that I don't want to be with you—"

"This is your home, Kaci. I know that. And you employ even more people than I do."

"So what do we do?" she asked softly.

"I wish I knew." Ryne cradled her cheek with one palm. "I've loved being with you. You're a lovely, charming, passionate woman. But we can't let superstition dictate what we do."

Kaci knew Ryne was leaving without him having to say the words, but she had to hear him say them anyway. "You're still leaving tomorrow, aren't you?"

He nodded. "Everything that's happened between us has been incredibly fast. I think we need to step back, decide how we *really* feel about each other without some Irish legend messing with our minds."

I know how I feel! she wanted to scream. Instead, she tilted her head into his palm. "We still have tonight, right?"

Ryne smiled. "Absolutely." He skated his thumb over her lower lip. "I think we ought to go out to dinner, anywhere you want to go. Then maybe a movie, or a club...whatever you want."

I just want you to love me the way I love you. "That sounds wonderful."

*****

"You are making a huge mistake."

Ryne ignored Shae as she buzzed around his head. Or he tried to ignore her. She flew so close to his face, he could feel the breeze from her rapidly-fluttering wings.

"How can you leave her? She is your soul mate, your true love."

Realizing he wouldn't get his packing finished until he calmed down the fairy, Ryne sat on the bed. "It isn't that simple, Shae."

"I do not understand. She loves you. It is so obvious by the way she responds to your touch, your kiss."

Her comment made him raise his eyebrows. "Shae, did you watch us make love?"

If possible, her wings fluttered even faster as her cheeks turned red. "Of course not. I simply...checked on you."

Ryne chuckled. "Then why are you embarrassed?"

"I am *not*... Master Ryne, do not change the subject. You cannot leave her!"

"I don't have a choice, Shae. I have a life in Los Angeles."

"You have an empty life. Why do you want to go back to that?"

He couldn't explain his reason for returning to L.A. to the little fairy when he wasn't even sure himself why he was leaving Kaci. "It's complicated."

Shae crossed her arms beneath her small breasts and tapped one foot. He wondered how she could tap her foot while hovering in the air. "I have met a lot of stubborn Irishmen in my life, Master Ryne, but none as stubborn as you."

"Should I feel honored?"

"No, you should feel stupid! You have finally met the woman of your dreams, and you're leaving her. That is...is...*stupid*!"

He didn't want to be mad at Shae, but this whole conversation wouldn't change anything. "Kaci and I decided to take some time, to decide if we really want to be together. What happened between us... Everything was really fast."

"It was fast because it was fate, and fate works that way!"

Hanging his head, Ryne released a heavy breath. "Shae, you have to give up on this."

"I will *not* give up. I promise you that, Master Ryne!"

Ryne raised his head, ready to continue the argument. Shae had disappeared.

A knock on the door made him rise from the bed. He opened the door to see Kaci on the other side.

His heart lurched in his chest. "Hi."

"Hi," she said softly. "May I come in?"

"Of course." Stepping to the side, he let her enter the room and closed the door behind her. "I planned to come back to your suite once I was packed."

"I thought I'd save you the trip."

She wore a pair of brown slacks, a matching brown jacket, and tan scooped-neck T-shirt. The browns made her eyes look even more green.

God, she was lovely.

She slipped her hands into the pockets of her jacket and faced him. "When do you need to leave for the airport?"

"In about half an hour."

"I'll have the hotel's limo waiting for you."

The mention of the hotel's luxurious limousine brought up memories from last night. They'd gone to dinner at a fabulous seafood restaurant right on the Sound then to a late movie. On the drive back to the hotel, Kaci had instructed her driver to "take the scenic route". She'd then closed the privacy window and proceeded to seduce Ryne.

He'd carry the memory of her straddling his hips, taking his cock deep inside her while the limousine roamed the streets of Seattle, until his dying day.

Realizing he hadn't responded to her comment, he said, "Thank you. I appreciate that."

She looked away from him, her gaze falling on his open suitcase. "Do you need any help?"

"No. I've traveled so much, I'm good at this packing stuff."

"Okay."

He saw her throat work while she swallowed. She blinked several times, as if fighting back tears. Knowing she was in pain made his own throat tighten.

"I, uh, just need a few more minutes to finish packing then I'll go down and check out."

"You don't have to worry about that. I've already taken care of it."

"Thank you," he said softly. He took a step forward and reached out a hand toward her face. She quickly moved out of his reach.

"Please don't. I don't think I can handle you touching me."

"Kaci—"

"No, it's all right. We agreed to spend some time apart, and that's the right decision. This happened really fast between us. I've never fallen into bed with a man so quickly in my life. We have to know if what we feel is real or we only believe it's real because of the charms."

"I know I care about you."

Tears filled her eyes and overflowed. "I care about you, too," she whispered.

Despite her telling him not to touch her, he cradled her face in his hands and wiped away her tears with his thumbs. "Do you regret making love with me?"

"No. Never."

More tears fell and Ryne wiped them away. "I can't leave you without a goodbye kiss."

Silently, she nodded. Ryne covered her lips with his. He wanted to leave her with a special memory of their last kiss. He kissed her slowly, tenderly, using only the tip of his tongue along the seam of her lips. When he felt her hands on his waist, he tilted his head and deepened the kiss. Still keeping it slow and tender, he parted his lips and accepted her tongue inside his mouth. It rubbed against his own, and blood rushed to his cock.

Instead of pulling her against his growing erection, Ryne ended the kiss. He rested his forehead against hers and took even breaths to regain control of his hormones.

"I have to go," he whispered.

"I know you do." She slid her arms around his back and hugged him. "Call me?"

He returned her hug. "You bet."

She dropped a quick peck on his lips and left.

The quiet, the emptiness, seeped into him. Ryne had to fight the urge to go after her. Being with Kaci had made him feel alive, whole.

Now, he felt only the loneliness.

Chapter Ten

Kaci's heart jumped when her phone rang. Her first thought was of Ryne. He'd called her last night to tell her he'd arrived home. She figured it was too soon for him to call again, but she'd take any chance to hear his voice.

Hurrying into the living room, she grabbed up the receiver after the third ring. "Hello?"

"Hey, sis."

Trying not to feel disappointed to hear her brother's voice instead of Ryne's, Kaci forced herself to sound cheerful. "Hey, bro."

"I need a favor."

"Aren't you even going to ask me how I am before you hit on me?"

"How are you, sis? I need a favor."

Kaci laughed. "What's up?"

"Let me give you Nana's house. Please. I can't take any more of Mauri's phone calls."

"Why do you let her push you around?"

"I can't help it. I have a hard time saying no to a woman, even a witch like her."

"Kaylen—"

"She's afraid of you, Kaci. If I give you the house, she won't bug you about it."

"She isn't afraid of me. She simply knows I won't take any shit from her."

"Which is why you should take the house. Please. *Pleeeaaassseee*!"

Kaci laughed at her twin's ridiculous begging. "All right, I'll take the house."

"Thank you! I owe you big time."

"And I promise I won't let you forget it."

"I have no doubt of that. Now, seriously, how are you?"

"I'm fine."

"You have to sound more convincing than that, Kac. What's wrong?"

With a sigh, Kaci flopped down on the couch. She and her twin shared a connection that she sometimes wished didn't exist. "Nothing's wrong, Kaylen."

"Don't give me that shit, Kac. I know you're upset. What happened?"

If she talked about Ryne, she wouldn't be able to keep from crying. "Not now, okay?"

Kaylen remained silent for several moments. "Do you need me to fly up there?"

That did it. His tender voice and obvious concern made her eyes flood. "No," she whispered.

"Then talk to me, or I'll hang up and go to the airport right now." He paused. "Is it a guy?"

"Isn't it always when a woman is upset?"

"Do I need to beat up someone?"

Kaci couldn't help but laugh at the mental picture of Kaylen challenging Ryne. "No."

"Are you serious about him?"

Fresh tears filled her eyes. "Yes," she murmured.

She heard his heavy sigh. "You fall in love too easily, Kac."

"I can't help the way I feel."

"I know you can't. So what happened?"

"He doesn't feel what I feel. It's that simple."

"Love is never that simple."

"This coming from a man who's never been in love."

"Hey, this isn't about me, it's about you."

Kaci pulled a tissue from the box on the end table and wiped her nose. "It hurts a lot this time, Kaylen. I fell really hard, really fast."

"The man's pretty stupid not to fall just as hard for you."

"You're a good brother, Kaylen."

"I know." She heard ice cubes tinkle against a glass, as if he'd taken a drink. "When I was there three weeks ago, you talked about taking a trip in April. That sounds like a good idea to me. A change of scenery will help you forget ol' what's-his-name."

"It'll take more than a change of scenery for me to forget Ryne."

"Ryne, huh? Sounds Irish. Hey, that's where you need to go. You need to go to Ireland and look at the land Nana left you."

"Ireland? By myself?"

"Why not? You're a big girl. I'll bet you can book a trip with one of those tourist groups. Talk to your travel agent about it."

Actually, going to Ireland wasn't a bad idea. Kaci would love to see the land that Nana had left to her. It was located on the Dingle Peninsula in County Kerry, close to a town called Tralee. That's all she knew about it.

"I'd offer to tag along, but I don't think you want your big brother with you."

"No offense, but no."

"So, does that mean you're going?"

"I have to think about it—"

"Kaci, don't think, don't plan, just *do*."

Just do. Kaylen was right. For once, she should simply do something because she wanted to. "You talked me into a vacation, big brother."

*****

The rain had been falling off and on for two days. Ryne stared out his office window at the dark clouds. A Southern Californian was used to blue skies, not gray ones.

It reminded him of Seattle on the day he'd left Kaci. The dark sky had matched his mood perfectly.

"Why are you so troubled, Master Ryne?"

Surprised to hear Shae's voice, Ryne spun his chair back to face his desk. The little fairy sat perched on the edge of his telephone. "Well, where have you been? I haven't seen you in almost a week."

Shae shrugged. "I did not want to make you angry again."

His heart softened at the sad expression on her face. "I don't stay angry long, Shae. And I wasn't *angry* at you. I was…frustrated."

Shae cocked her head to the side. "Are you feelin' better?"

"Not really."

"You miss Mistress Kaci. Why have you not called her more than once?"

Ryne almost asked her how she knew he'd called Kaci only once. He stopped before he uttered the question. Shae seemed to know *everything*. "Kaci and I decided to spend some time apart."

"Did she not ask you to call her?"

The little fairy knew far more than she should. "I don't think it's a good idea yet."

"You prefer to be alone and miserable?"

"Shae," he said, a note of warning in his voice.

"I apologize, Master Ryne," she said, her head lowered. "I only wish to help you."

"I know that." He held out his hand, palm up. "C'mere."

She flew over and landed on the edge of his hand. "I'm surprised you're still here, Shae. I've stopped having visions of Kaci."

"My job is not complete, Master Ryne. I will be with you until you are with your true love."

"You still think I'm destined to be with Kaci."

"I do, but I will no longer mention her since it makes you sad." She shifted on his hand, folding her legs beneath her. "Perhaps you should take a trip."

"I just got back from a trip."

"I do not mean a business trip, Master Ryne. You should go somewhere for pleasure. I believe you call it a vacation."

Ryne couldn't remember the last time he'd had an actual vacation. With all the traveling he did for his business, he liked to simply relax at home whenever he had the chance.

Shae clapped her hands. "I know what you should do! You should go to Ireland."

Ryne laughed. "Why should I go to Ireland?"

"Because it is the home of your ancestors. Oh, that is a perfect idea!"

"Shae—"

"You should go to County Kerry. The coast, the green hills…you will love it there. The scenery is so beautiful."

"My ancestors lived in County Longford."

Shae frowned. "Oh, no, no, no. You do not want to go there. It is inland. You want to be able to breathe in the fresh air off the Atlantic."

That made sense. Ryne saw no reason to go to Ireland if he didn't see the incredible coastal views the country offered. "I like your idea, Shae."

She clapped her hands again and her wings fluttered. "Wonderful!"

"I wonder if June or July would be better?"

Shae frowned. "Why wait? Why not go now?"

"Well, the weather is a factor. I'd like the chance to walk on the coast without having rain pour over me."

"There is less average rainfall in April than in June."

"Really." He chuckled. "You're just full of important information, aren't you?"

She grinned. "I do my best."

"Can you recommend a particular place in County Kerry?"

Her grin widened. "Oh, aye."

* * * * *

"Are you sure this is where I'm supposed to go?" Ryne asked Shae.

The little fairy nodded vigorously. "Aye."

He glanced at Shae, sitting on the headrest of the passenger seat. She'd been with him almost every moment since he'd decided to come on this trip. She'd flown on the plane with him, making herself right at home on his seat tray, chatting practically non-stop. He'd had to catch himself several times when he'd almost talked back to her. The gentleman sitting next to him probably wouldn't have appreciated that.

"Well, I have to admit the scenery is breathtaking."

"Oh, aye. 'Tis a lovely drive. I am enjoying it very much."

Ryne looked back and forth from the narrow road to the ocean pounding against the shore. As soon as he found a place to park, he planned to walk along the beach and stretch his legs. He wasn't sure how long he'd been driving, but a rest stop would be a good idea. So would having a bite to eat. Surely he'd come to a restaurant or pub somewhere on this road—

Slamming on his brakes, his gaze whipped back to the beach. A woman stood facing the ocean, dressed in an ivory sweater, jeans, and boots. Her long blonde curls whipped around her head. He couldn't see her face, but the way she stood, the shape of her body…he would swear it was Kaci.

"Shae, do you think that…"

He stopped when he realized the little fairy had disappeared.

"Shae?" Ryne turned and looked over his shoulder into the back seat. No fairy. He thought that strange since she'd been practically under his nose for almost three weeks.

He turned his attention back to the woman. It couldn't be Kaci. The odds of them being in the same place at the same time were… He couldn't even fathom how high those odds were.

Even though he wished with all his heart that it was Kaci.

She'd occupied his thoughts almost every waking moment since he'd left her. It hadn't taken him long to realize he'd made a huge mistake in letting her go. He'd wanted to do the right thing, make sure they both felt the same way about each other, and not just because of some Irish legend.

Being noble was the stupidest thing he'd ever done.

Realizing he still had his car stopped in the middle of the narrow road, Ryne pulled over to the side and turned off the ignition. He watched the woman for another few moments before he couldn't stand it anymore. He had to know for sure whether or not that was Kaci.

Ryne opened the door and got out of the car.

*****

It reminded Kaci of home. The cloudy sky, the light mist in the air, the rolling green hills. It was no wonder Nana had loved Western Washington when she'd been born in this beautiful country.

She tucked her hands beneath her armpits to warm them. The ocean's breeze whipped through her hair, tossing it around her head. Although the breeze off the water was cool, she felt toasty in her thick fisherman's sweater—her first official purchase in Ireland.

Nana would be proud of her.

Coming to a foreign country all by herself took courage...courage Kaci hadn't realized she possessed. She'd always considered herself a strong person, but she was proud of herself for booking this trip. Even on short notice, her travel agent had been able to get her the flight and accommodations mere kilometers from the land that now belonged to her...the land where she stood right now and breathed in the air off the Atlantic Ocean.

She wished Ryne stood beside her.

She hadn't heard from him in the three weeks since he left Seattle, other than the one phone call to tell her he'd arrived back in Los Angeles safely. No other phone calls, no faxes, no e-mails. She was surprised...and hurt. After the intense lovemaking they'd shared, Kaci was sure they'd keep seeing each other, despite living so far apart.

Apparently, he hadn't fallen in love with her the way she had with him.

Reaching inside the thick turtleneck, Kaci withdrew the necklace and clutched the charm. *What did I do wrong, Nana? This necklace and the mirror brought Ryne and me together, just like you said it would. Why couldn't I keep him? Why couldn't he love me?*

No magical answer popped into her head. The only sound she heard was the waves rolling into the shore.

Determined not to let self-pity control her, Kaci straightened her shoulders. She didn't need Ryne. She didn't need *any* man. She had a loving father and incredible brother. She had a wonderful place to live, a great job, plenty of money in the bank. This trip had proven that she could do whatever she desired simply by picking up the telephone.

Her shoulders slumped. She didn't *need* Ryne, but she *wanted* him.

A sense of someone behind her made Kaci tense for a moment. She stood out in the open, but that didn't mean she couldn't be prey for some lunatic. Trying not to be too obvious, she slowly turned her body to the left.

The sight of Ryne walking toward her made Kaci gasp.

He didn't stop until he stood directly in front of her. "It *is* you," he said, a note of wonder in his voice. "I couldn't believe it when I thought I saw you. What are you doing here?"

"This is my land." She gestured around them with one hand. "My great-grandmother left it to me. I decided I wanted to see it, so here I am."

"You're here alone?"

Kaci nodded. "Are you?"

"Yes. I took a friend's advice and came here for a vacation." His gaze traveled over her hair and face. "I still can't believe you're here, in front of me. God, I've thought of you every moment."

If he'd thought of her, she didn't understand his silence. "Then why didn't you call me? You promised you would."

"I don't know." Ryne stuffed his hands in the front pockets of his jeans. "Partly because of stupidity. I handled everything wrong with you, Kaci. You have to admit, the way we met was pretty strange."

"Yes, I suppose it was. That didn't make the feelings any less powerful."

Withdrawing one hand from his pocket, he touched her face. "I've missed you."

His gentle voice made a lump form in her throat. "I've missed you too." She covered his hand with hers. "We're here at the same time. What does that mean? Is this fate too?"

"It means," he said, tilting her face up to his, "that we're supposed to be together. I'm a fool for not believing that from the first." He kissed her softly, sweetly. "I want a life with you, Kaci."

"How? The distance between our homes hasn't changed."

"Actually, I have a solution for that. I've toyed with the idea in the past of expanding my business. Being without you these last three weeks made me do more than toy with the idea. Seattle would be a good place for a branch office of Wilkinson Conference Services, don't you think?"

Tears of happiness filled Kaci's eyes. "I think it would be an excellent place."

Ryne slid his hands down her arms and clasped her hands. "I do have one problem with moving to Seattle."

"What?"

"Your suite is beautiful, but I want us to live in a house. I want a yard for our son to play in. Or a daughter. I'm not picky."

"Maybe one of each?"

He smiled. "Maybe."

"I assume there'll be a wedding somewhere in there before the children arrive?"

"That could be arranged," he said with a grin. Raising her hands to his mouth, he kissed each palm. "What do you think about us buying a house?"

Kaci thought of Nana's beautiful house on the water with the huge yard…the house that now belonged to her thanks to her brother. "That won't be a problem at all."

Ryne drew Kaci into his arms. "I love you," he whispered in her ear.

"I love you too."

A flash of green made Ryne lift his chin. Shae fluttered less than a foot away, smiling broadly. When she gave him a thumbs up, he knew he'd been had. The little minx had planned this whole thing. She'd been subtle with all her hints about Ireland being the perfect place for a vacation. He didn't realize she'd wrapped him around her little finger until this moment.

You tricked me, he mouthed.

I did, she mouthed back.

Thank you.

You're welcome.

He watched Shae do a series of somersaults that would make any Olympic gymnastic coach proud, then she disappeared with a soft *pop*.

The End

About the author:

Lynn LaFleur was born and raised in a small town in Texas close to the Dallas/Fort Worth area. Writing has been in her blood since she was eight years old and wrote her first "story" for an English assignment.

Besides writing at every possible moment, Lynn loves reading, sewing, gardening, and learning new things on the computer. (She is determined to master Paint Shop Pro and Photoshop!) After living in various places on the West Coast for 21 years, she is back in Texas, 17 miles from her hometown.

Lynn would love to hear from her readers about her writing, her books, the look of her website...whatever! Comments, praise, and criticism all equally welcome.

Lynn welcomes mail from readers. You can write to her c/o Ellora's Cave Publishing at 1056 Home Avenue, Akron OH 44310-3502.

Also by Lynn LaFleur:

Happy Birthday, Baby
Holiday Heat anthology
Two Men and a Lady anthology

You've Got Irish Male!

Titania Ladley

Trademarks Acknowledgement

The author acknowledges the trademarked status and trademark owners of the following wordmarks mentioned in this work of fiction:

Guinness: Arthur Guinness, Son & Co

Lucky Charms: General Mills, Inc. Corporation

Ouija: Hasbro, Inc.

Barbie: Mattel, Inc.

Ken: Mattel, Inc.

Waterford: Waterford Wedgwood Plc. Company Ireland

Chapter One

Goodluck, Tennessee
March 17
12:00 midnight

"You've got mail!"

Mischa Roxbury started and turned back to her computer. Though her adult Internet toy business certainly thrived, she didn't normally receive Celtic Sins orders at this time of night.

She plucked up her green-tinted beer from the deco kitchen table and crossed to her desk. Something—what was it?—*something* exciting slithered into her shorts and settled right between her legs. Her heart pitter-pattered in her chest, and she couldn't take her eyes from the dancing leprechaun screensaver she'd downloaded hours ago. Mischa hadn't really noticed it much before, but it now seemed to come to life. It beckoned to her, wiggling in time to a sudden cheery Irish tune blaring out over the speakers. Wide, eerie eyes twinkled at her as dew-covered shamrocks might under an Irish spring sun.

Without taking her gaze from the little redheaded pixie, she lowered herself into the desk chair.

"What…what's going on here?"

"*Ye've got mail!*" the voice said again. But this time, it wasn't the usual ISP's mailman she heard. No. This voice oozed a deep and utterly sensual brogue, as thick, sweet and warm as hot fudge.

"Okay, okay. I gotcha. I've got mail." She reached for the mouse and jiggled it until the leprechaun disappeared. Pointing the cursor to the *Read Mail* button, she clicked it and watched as her inbox popped up. The space was empty—with the exception of one E-mail.

Her brow furrowed. Strange, she thought. It hadn't been there two minutes ago when she'd finished processing today's ninety-seven toy orders. It was as if the person had known to wait until he or she could get Mischa's undivided attention.

And that possibility sent a brief shiver of creepiness through every muscle in her body.

The sender's E-mail address read GradyODonovan@IrishMale.com. "Well. If that doesn't sound like the sexiest name I've ever heard. Hmm, and you're apparently an Irish *man*."

She grinned and scanned the subject line. *Lucky you! Open me to change your dull life to exciting…*

Her grin faded. She glared at the screen as her pulse began to thud angrily in her throat. "Now how arrogant is that?" Aligning the cursor over the spam mail, she highlighted it and pointed to *Delete*.

"Please, do no' delete me," the voice echoed over the speaker system.

She gasped, dropped the mouse and shoved the chair away from the desk. "Who—? How did you know I was about to delete that mail?" And why was she even talking out loud to a computer?

"'Twould be more accurate to inquire…why would *ye delete such an opportunity from your…quiet life?"* The Irish, singsong lilt eased its way into her system. But she chose to ignore the strange ripples of desire that dominoed into her womb.

"Who are you?" The fear that squeaked from her voice sounded extremely pathetic. She sobered instantly, straightening her shoulders. Where was her usual bravery? Normally, as a single recluse, she voluntarily chose not to have a man around to coddle and protect her. How could one voice, one delusional moment—she'd been going nonstop since eight a.m.—make her long for the secure, safe haven of a man?

"Grady O'Donovan."

"No kidding." She swallowed a lump and inched closer, rolling the chair slowly toward the desk until the leprechaun screensaver popped back up. Hand trembling, she joggled the mouse again and zapped him off the screen. "I already saw that in your E-mail."

"Open it, me lass. Ye won't regret it." There was a long pause in which she just sat there staring at the monitor, while bagpipes and cheery Irish music played over the speakers. *"Please,"* he added softly, almost tenderly.

Though she resented it, that tone did strange things to her insides, instantly dashing away her fear. She could feel herself weakening, melting like ice cream below the blazing sun.

"Well, let's get one thing straight up front, here. I'm not your lass. But…" she trailed off, debating her options. "If I open it, do I win a prize or something?"

"Aye."

She waited a full ten seconds. Silence. "Um, care to elaborate?"

"Ye'll just have to open the mail to see now, won't ye?"

Mischa sighed and ground the heels of her hands into her eye sockets. "This is ridiculous, talking to my mail. I'm obviously exhausted, definitely in need of some Zs."

"Nay, 'tisn't blarney, milady. And exhaustion 'tis the very truth, I should say. But first, ye need some lovin', a taste of your own pleasures ye provide to your beloved customers."

She lifted a single eyebrow. "And how would you know that, Mister Irish?"

"Why, I've purchased every one of your clever sex devices, that I have. And don't ye be goin' and thinkin' I did no' sample them." He added a deep-timbre chuckle that made her think of mind-blowing orgasms and adoring affection all rolled up in one package. She tightened her groin muscles and inhaled sharply when a flood of wetness soaked her panties.

"See there? Your life is already excitin' and chock full o' arousal."

"Arousal?"

"Aye, arousal. As in, your wet panties."

"How—? Wait a minute!" She leaped to her feet. The chair tipped backward and cracked on the hardwood floor. Her eyes darted from corner to corner of her lofty warehouse apartment searching for a hidden intruder. Two shelf-lined walls housed every adult toy imaginable. Across the open area of the one-room living space, the larger, much more expensive toys were on display. Moonlight filtered in through the high windows, slicing across the cluttered room like enormous silver swords. But she saw no one among the inventory, no one invading her private living space.

Her eyes darted to the living room scattered with worn sofa and chairs, low end tables and a small entertainment center. No, it couldn't be coming from there. She didn't own a surround-sound speaker system, and the stereo and television were off.

She struggled to control her sudden shallow breathing. Fear roiled in her belly, whooshing her pulse into a painful thump in her throat. Her gaze zipped across to the old, cage-style elevator, her only exit. The metal, fencelike barrier was drawn down and locked in place, just as she always left it, and she could see that the cubicle of the elevator was empty. She flicked a look up. Being on the third and highest level of the building, the windows were way too high for someone to be peeking in, even with a ladder. And yet...she sensed she wasn't alone.

"Waiting..."

"Shut up! I-I'm no fool. Who's there? Where are you?" Without waiting for a reply, she plucked up the handset of the cordless and poised her finger over the 9-1-1 speed-dial button. "This is a trick, a setup of some kind. Who *are* you? And if you don't give me an honest answer and reveal yourself, I call the cops and you get hauled in."

He tsked—actually *tsked!*—at her.

"Now, now, Mischa. Calm yourself down, love. No need to have a canary. Ye want me to reveal meself? That would be fine and oh-so dandy with me. 'Tis gettin' a might bit stuffy here in your cable line."

Her laughter had all the qualities of a lunatic as it echoed through the warehouse. "Cable line? You say you're in my cable line?"

A low, long sigh eased out through the speakers. It somehow affected her like none of his words had before. Honesty. She detected honesty and true exasperation. She could swear the clock on her desk stopped ticking. Deafening silence blared in her ears.

Ohmigod! She was all-out losing her frickin' mind. He was in her cable line? But that was ridiculous. Unless…unless she were really in a dream. Anything was possible in dreams, wasn't it? She'd been burning her ass at both ends for months now. It was highly possible she was having stress-induced delusions.

Which meant, at least in her made-up mind, he was telling her the truth.

He *was* in her Internet line—wasn't he? Well, if her pulse would quit choking her, cutting off the blood supply to her brain, she might be able to reason this out.

Aha, a brain-deprived, alcohol-induced hallucination. All those long, lonely hours, day in, night out, staring at the monitor, processing sex-toy orders, surfing the Net. All she'd wanted was to treat herself to a stress-relieving beer or two. At least that's the way she remembered it, what she thought had been reality as opposed to a dream. True, she'd had more than she'd planned, and currently had a pleasant buzz going. Closing one eye, she mentally crossed beer off her future allowable-list. No more alcohol for Mischa Roxbury.

She let out a pent-up sigh. The knots in her belly unwound, her heart shrunk back to its normal size. This is ludicrous, she thought. She pressed her lips together. In her cable line. *Hmph!* Well, whatever. Next, horses would fly. With a roll of her eyes, she tossed the phone onto her desk and righted the chair.

Plopping down into its softness, she groaned and slouched down in the seat.

Staring up at the iron-beamed ceiling, she said blandly. "I need a vacation."

"Ah, 'tis the absolute truth! And ye should see the likes o' Ireland these days." He went on, his voice deep and breathy. *"Just grand, I tell ye. Spring just 'round the corner, the birth o' green, lush meadows all about the bog, shamrocks galore, breathtaking seascapes and—"*

"Um, Grady, was it?"

"Aye, Grady O'Donovan."

"Grady O'Donovan. Well, ya see, Mr. O, I don't have the time or the inclination to so much as go into town and buy groceries. I'm busy. I have a hectic life right here that requires my constant attention. I *need* a vacation, yes. But I can't *take* one. Not to Ireland or Alaska or the South Pole or anywhere else outside these four walls."

"Well, we shall see..."

"No, *we* shall not see." God, was she really arguing with voices in her head? "Now, would you please just go away and get out of my brain? I have nearly a hundred orders to pull from stock and prepare for pickup by tomorrow morning."

"That I will...but only if ye open the E-mail. Give me a chance to prove me good intentions. Open it, and I promise ye, I'll be on me way if ye do no' like what ye see."

Mischa's gaze riveted to the leprechaun screensaver. He now did a tap dance atop a soft, pastel rainbow that hadn't been there before. There at the end of the rainbow sat a gleaming pot of gold. As if he tempted her to partake of his riches, he slid down the curved ribbon of colors and giggled almost heinously as he fell into the pot with a splash. A merry melody piped softly in the background bringing to mind a mental image of his vivid Ireland descriptions. She could almost smell the scent of wildflowers in the meadow and the salt of the Celtic Sea. Peace and tranquility settled into her bones. It *would* be nice to visit

Ireland. Her mother had passed away months ago, but during her long hospitalization, Mischa could recall her deathbed wish.

"Your roots are in Ireland, Mischa." Her mother's voice echoed in her head. *"I should have taken you there a long time ago. But promise me…promise me that you'll go there one day and see what your heritage is all about."*

Mischa shook the mental image of death from her mind. There was a life here to live, her present, her future. A demanding life being lived just the way she wanted it. Or was—

"She was right, ye know, that sweet ma of yours."

"Oh…" A groan rumbled from deep within her chest. "Now you're reading minds? Well let me tell you, Irish, I refuse to open that mail if you insist on butting into my *private* thoughts."

"Bargain wholeheartedly accepted. I stay out o' your pretty little mind and ye let me out o' this bloody wire."

She propped her feet up on the desk and twined her fingers together over her belly. "And how am I supposed to know you're *not* reading my mind if you don't tell me?"

"Oh, 'tis a suspicious beaut ye be. Ye'll just have to take me word for it, now, won't ye, Mischa?"

Mischa hadn't a clue how he knew her name and, surprised, she realized she loved the sound of it laced with that Irish accent. But she wouldn't think about it anymore. No, she'd do all she could to keep her mind blank and free from his prying, telepathic powers.

With a sudden flutter in her belly, she reached for her beer and defiantly drained the last few ounces. She was going to do it. The excitement of clicking on that E-mail suddenly took her with stormy anticipation. Why not? Most likely, she was in a drunken stupor and imagining this whole thing, anyway. Go ahead, she silently coaxed herself—or was that him subtly brainwashing her? But the sudden impatience at matching a face to a sexy voice, won out. No doubt about it, she wanted to see what he looked like. And she supposed she felt a tad bit sorry for him being cooped up in that Internet line...*if* it was true...within her hallucination, that is.

But she would soon find out one way or the other.

"Well..." Her sneakered feet fell to the wood floor with a clunk. The mouse, it seemed, leaped into her hand in the blink of an eye. Once again, she got rid of the screensaver and stared at the single E-mail in her box. She felt foolish, but she said it anyway. "You promise, right? Promise not to read my mind anymore?"

"*Cross me heart and hope to die.*"

She snorted. "I never understood that *hoping* to die part, but here goes..." The cursor moved over the E-mail line and she thought of Ouija and how its little planchette always scooted itself across the mystical wooden board awakening excitement in its players. Shivers stirred at her roots making her hair stand on end. Her heart did a pleasant flutter behind her breastbone. Mouth now dry as sand, she longed for another swallow of beer. But instead, she licked her lips and inhaled slowly.

And she clicked on the mail.

The music changed tunes. No longer did the jolly melody play over and over. A sensual song of flutes and soft wind poured from the speakers. The mail opened, revealing a page full of shamrocks decorated over the top of...cocks? Each of two leaves of the four-leaf clovers strategically covered the scrotums, while the top two wrapped themselves around the many thick shafts. They weren't animated cocks, but so real, she reached up to the screen to touch one. Her clitoris immediately filled with blood, and throbbed almost painfully in response.

"Ah, I see ye like me shamcock gifts. Very fittin', I thought, for a woman who sells cocks for a livin'."

She shrieked and snatched her hand from the screen just before making contact with it. Her back went ramrod straight.

The voice had come from behind her!

Whirling in her chair, she ignored the wave of dizziness that assailed her. Either she'd had too much beer, or she needed another one, she wasn't sure which. But what she was sure of was that the most gorgeous man she'd ever seen stood tall and proud in the middle of her warehouse apartment. The only light in the entire room was that of her computer monitor and the lunar beams seeping in. Clouds moved across the moon just then, and through the high windows of the building, the filtered moonlight cast him in a bluish glow. He wore a black, felt top hat tipped rakishly over one brow and adorned with a gold buckle. Thick midnight hair was drawn back and fastened away from his arresting face, and she wondered just how long the ponytail was, how far it trailed down that long back. She itched to rise and circle him, to examine every inch of him, but a mixture of fear and astonishment kept her rooted to her seat.

"Holy son of a bitch."

"Nay. Me ma was no bitch. Holy, perhaps, but nay…no' a bitch."

The voice no longer came through the computer speakers but from his vocal cords—vocal cords in a thick, muscular neck atop a broad, *real* man's body. At his words, her eyes riveted to the wide mouth with its full lips. And she determined she no longer thirsted for a beer, but for a kiss. In unison, her pussy and mouth watered, both craving the steely-soft invasion of manly parts.

With the brim of the hat obscuring his upper face in a faint shade, she couldn't discern the color of the irises from where she sat. But the dark, eerie tint of them shimmered diamond-like by the scattered beams of light around him. Her gaze scanned his costume—the only word she could think to describe his garb. It was old-fashioned, almost elf-like in style, yet he wore it well, all man. The deep, hunter green suit coat over a red and gold plaid vest emphasized broad, massive shoulders cut to a narrow waist and hips. And beneath that vest, beneath the crisp white ruffled shirt, she couldn't mistake the wide expanse of chest. Mischa flexed her hands. Oh, how she itched to run her palms over that sculpted wall. Her eyelids grew heavy. She imagined his chest would be hard and unyielding against her breasts. The tender flesh of her nipples would be brought to an instant state of tautness; he'd no doubt be solid and powerful enough to snatch her breath from her lungs.

Mischa slid her gaze slowly downward. His pants were of the same color as the coat, but they ran snug along well-muscled thighs…and cradled an impressive thickness in his crotch. Her breath quickened, as did the snake of desire that coiled between her legs. It seemed to wrap about her clit like a boa constrictor, and flick up and across her breasts bringing her nipples to tight, tingly knots. She forced herself to study every inch of him, coaching her stare away from that delectable bulge. The ankles of the pants were stuffed into the tops of high, black boots with gold buckles along the length of his shins. By the style of his clothes, she thought of an elf again, and yet…he was *way* too large for that.

Unable to remain in her seat, she rose slowly and approached him with her arms crossed over her rib cage. "My, but you weren't kidding, were you? You are quite the prize."

"Kiddin'?" Up into the brim of the hat, he arched both eyebrows, two slashes of midnight lightning above ominous, cloudy eyes. "Ye mean about no' regrettin' it? No, ma'am. I would no' do that to ye, that I wouldn't."

Mischa pursed her lips and blew out a long breath as she circled him. Yes, the ponytail was long, almost to the small of his back, just as she'd hoped. And mental images filled her mind of it falling over his thick shoulder onto her naked breast as he took her with animalistic passion. She could just feel it swishing over one nipple, sending a flood of heat to her already soaked pussy.

"Hmm." She raised a hand and tapped a finger on her chin. *This was definitely a hallucination.* "You're…you're a…?"

"Leprechaun," he supplied. But the flush of red to his cheeks and the way his shaded eyes darted away, didn't go unnoticed.

"And that embarrasses you?"

She stopped directly in front of him. His scent smelled so real, so potent. It engulfed her, rugged forest mixed with an ocean breeze. The aroma was pleasing, unique and it sent her pulse into a new rhythm of need. Though she stood tall herself, she still had to tip her head back to look up into his face. And wow, what a face! Close up, it was even more striking than it had been from farther away. The strong bone structure and interesting planes and shadows beneath the rim of the hat made her think of a ruthless pirate. The clouds slid away from the moon at that very moment, pouring a flood of soft, blue-white light over him. And small, gold hoops glittered on each of his earlobes dazzling her with the roguish look it lent him.

Under scrutiny, he suddenly swiped the hat from his head, and she saw that those ears were slightly pointed at the top…almost like an elf.

The abrupt movement wiped the shadows from his face, submerging it in the mysterious glow of moonlight. Magnetically, her gaze shot to the eyes. Shamrock-green, they bore into her very soul. Mischa had never seen eyes quite that shade, quite so very stunning before now. It rendered her dizzy and giddy. Unable to remove her stare from his, she pressed her hands upon his chest to steady herself. Heat waves, slow and cozy, permeated her palms and entered her bloodstream. Just as she'd thought, the soft woolen fabric of his vest couldn't disguise the steely hardness of the man beneath it. And that knowledge sent a whiplash of fire to her womb.

He snaked out one arm and wrapped it around her waist to steady her. "Nay, no' embarrassed that I'm a leprechaun," he finally replied, though she'd already forgotten her question. "That I'm no' your typical elf, to be sure. A bloody mutant, as me people call it. Much, much taller, and me hair is no' as fiery as yours is, that's plain to see."

"To be sure." She swayed at the lilt to his voice, at the nearness of it as it filled her ears with its deep timbre. The hard length of him barely touched her from abdomen to knee, yet his warmth eased into her chilled bones. One of his hands came up to comb through her hair, and her eyelids grew heavy and lazy at the adoring touch. But he didn't pet her for long. His hand, large and hot, glided down over her torso and clasped with the other behind her waist.

"To be sure," she repeated, still unable to tear her eyes from his.

"Mischa..." He whispered it, but it came out more as a growl of restraint. "Ye feel so pliant in me arms, so very right. Just as I imagined, just as I knew 'twould be."

His gaze moved in a caress over her face and settled on her mouth, which she was sure had to be hanging open to her ribs. She licked her lips, again squelching the urge to kiss him.

"Well, I can't deny that."

She needed to breathe, to think. With great effort, she drew her hands from his chest and stepped out of the circle of his arms. Inhaling, she rolled her head around on her shoulders until she heard the satisfying crack of her neck. This was ridiculous. She had to get away, to reason out just what was happening to her. Crossing to her desk, she lowered herself very slowly into the seat. And her eyes returned to stake some sort of odd claim to this...this *leprechaun*?

He stood there, his arms out as if she'd stunned him with her retreat. "'Tis a mystery, then, ye know, that ye would walk away from me."

"I haven't decided yet how to handle you. It's called a woman's prerogative to make her own decisions."

"Even if..." he said cryptically as he sauntered toward her, "that decision has already been made for ye?"

*****

Grady leaned down and gripped the arms of the chair, caging her in. Her sweet, floral scent filled his nostrils, so like the wildflowers of his beloved Ireland. He filled his gaze with the mane of shoulder-length, burnished tresses. The eyes, framed by those thick, auburn lashes, were the epitome of twin spheres of dark, rich Guinness ale. They rose to soak him with a sharp and wary fire. The guardedness became apparent, as well, in the sudden stiffness of her body, the paleness that washed over her face at his ominous words. It made him long to hold her, to make her forget, to protect her from the tragedy that had forced this particular suspicious, untrusting trait into her personality.

But that would come with time.

Though she fought it, the virus worked powerfully and forcefully through her system. He could tell that now by the look of honesty and raw emotion emerging there in her eyes, in her lovely expression. Though it had no control over the apparent suspicion and possible fear she exhibited at the moment, its side effects were always the same. Inhibitions would crumble, true feelings would emerge, and the real inner person would shed any shells formed in crusty protection over the years. He'd been with her, watching her for months in the dormant period of the pre-virus. But its nature was such that its potency, its symptoms, could only be displayed during the twenty-four hour period of the holy day of St. Patrick—and only if the subject accepted the virus-spell.

Ah, and thank the faeries of Emerald Isle that she had!

His gaze moved to the plump, red mouth open now in adorable shock. He longed to cover her lips with his own, to taste of the ale on her tongue, to plunge his own tongue deep within her warm mouth. Even before she'd accepted his virus-spell through the computer system, he'd remained in an almost constant state of arousal. Just the sound of her husky, twangy voice had set him on edge and sent every ounce of his blood into his loins. And it had been crowded enough inside that computer cord *before* the erection affliction.

His thorough assessment fell to the large twin swell of breasts beneath the tiny blouse she wore. Nay, it could no' be classified as a blouse, he mused. 'Twas a whittled-down, tightened form of a man's undergarment. But it had been cut low by the tailor—bless his very soul!—and revealed the oh-so deep valley between the globes. His *bollocks* grew heavy and tight, the sac pulling down on his hard rod. He glanced further down to find her lean legs spread apart, the short, tight drawers she wore emphasizing every curve of her female lips. *Ah, to sink his very rod into that pussy! What heaven, to be sure.*

"Um, no one makes my decisions for me. I repeat, *no* one." Her voice, though strong in conviction, came up short in tone and believability. The virus was, indeed, starting to work.

Grady knelt between her legs. Their heat embraced him, and he conjured up visions of the long length of them locked around his hips. "I did no' make any decision for ye, me Mischa. Ye've made this one yourself. Ye had the power to say nay. Ye could have deleted me and sent me tumblin' back into cyberspace onto me arse. But ye did no' do it."

Her eyes flared and he thought of bittersweet pools of warm, melted chocolate. "You tempted me! You talked me into it. You—you— Oh, Lord..." She groaned and covered her face with her hands. "I'm trying to reason with a sly, underhanded leprechaun in an apparent hallucination brought on by too much friggin' beer and lack of sleep. I *do* need a vacation."

And ye're feeling the strong effects of the virus, love. "Me magic dust can fix that."

She peeped between splayed fingers. "Magic dust?"

"Magic dust."

The slender hands slid down to cover her mouth. Copper strands of hair fell across the high cheekbones, brushing the soft cup of her knuckles. Her muffled voice came out between feminine, well-manicured fingers. "Okay, your magic...whatever, can fix what?"

"The headache ye've got comin' on by imbibin' too much."

She slapped her hands on her thighs. "And *how* did you know I had a headache? You—oh! You promised not to read my mind anymore."

He chuckled. "No. I can see the pain of it in your lovely eyes. But...consider it an ailment long past."

Grady drew in a breath and straightened his shoulders. There was the usual tinkling tune his Irish magic always conjured up, accompanied by faint bagpipes as he circled his arms in the air and crossed his wrists. He clapped his hands sharply and tossed sparkles of rainbow dust above Mischa's head. As it settled around her in a cloud, he petted her silky hair and held her head in his hands.

"Be gone with ye, oh pain, with the soothing tune of the fife..." He massaged her temples and watched as her facial muscles went flaccid and serene. The scent of wildflowers and the sea swirled around them in the cocoon of glistening dust. She inhaled and closed her eyes, as if a peaceful drug had just been forced into her system.

"I call upon ye, Lord Leprechaun King, rid her of this excruciating slice of the knife. Lend her comfort and the power, so bright, to vanquish the pain on this, our mystical night!"

Mischa jerked and jolted as streaks of lightning materialized from above and struck her on top of the head. He held her face stable within his powerful grip, waiting patiently for the ritual to commence. Pure bliss filled her eyes, as if she'd just bitten into a delicious scone. The power ebbed, the static-filled noises quieted. Grady slowly drew his hands from her. It was over. The headache had been eradicated in no time. His spells never took long, just as the initiation of the virus-spell had taken but one click of the mouse.

She stared into his eyes for the longest time. There wasn't one whit of a doubt the pain had been banished. Every muscle in her lean body seemed to melt at his feet as if he'd performed a full-body massage and turned her to mush. His immortal heart rolled over dangerously in his chest at both the emotional confusion and passion he saw buried there. Dangerous because immortal hearts, though allowed to dally for sheer pleasure alone, were forbidden to mix with mortal hearts. And yet, with his sharp, see-through vision, he could see her heart beating in rapid, companionable rhythm with his own.

A careless, possibly deadly mistake had brought him here in the first place, but now it was his responsibility to aright the wrongs he'd amassed. With or without the help of the virus-spell, he would do what must be done. Yet he sensed that somehow, with each thump of his heart, with each mesmerizing blink of her dark lashes, *he* was infected rather than her!

"Wow. That was definitely a memorable moment." She shook her head and grinned. "And whoa, now that my headache's gone, I can see promise of great *sex* in your eyes." One hand came up to slap her mouth. "Did I just say that?"

"Oh, aye, that ye did. But never fear, the truth comes out when the spirits go in." *And always when the virus infection begins.*

"Spirits?"

"The potent ale ye've consumed."

She sighed with a nod of understanding, and he suddenly craved to gobble her up. Whether it was the virus, the ale, or a mixture of the two as the current dominator of her boldness, he didn't know just yet. It was too early to tell, but oh, how his mouth watered as she raised a trembling hand and cupped his cheek. As scattered as she was, she swayed a bit, despite the support of the chair and his tight grip on its arms to imprison her in safety.

"You're really quite handsome." Her voice held a slight slur, adding a flair of reckless daring to her words. "And you know something? I've never had sex with a leprechaun before."

He guffawed, his laughter echoing throughout her airy home. "Nay, that ye haven't, Mischa love, that ye haven't. But 'tis what ye agreed to—among other things—when ye clicked on me E-mail."

"No," she countered with an emphatic shake of her head. Her eyes raked up and down him greedily. "If I'd have known *you* were what I agreed to, I'd have clicked on it from the start. But the fact is, Mr. Lucky Charms, I had no idea what I was agreeing to."

"Nonetheless, ye agreed to accept me spell, whether knowing or no'. Now," he said hastily, holding up a single finger to halt her words, "ye do have the option of reversing it and engaging your antivirus software retroactively."

Her lips curved. A trace of mischief twinkled in her eyes. "Really? I've got all that power, huh?" She snapped her fingers. "To zap you outta my life, just like that?"

"Aye, that ye do, Mischa, dear, that ye do."

"Cool. Well," she said with a wink. "I'll save that trump card for later. When I'm done with *ye* and this bizarre hallucination."

Before he could inform her there would be no more chances, she hooked a hand about his neck. Yanking him to her, she slammed her mouth into his. The hunger she devoured him with rivaled that of all wild beasts of the many Irish forests he'd traveled. Her lips caressed his with velvety wetness, and it seemed her tongue flickered over his cock rather than into his mouth. Jolts of magical fire scorched his very soul and rendered his tool as hard as the boulders overlooking the Irish Sea. The flavor of her, a potent conglomeration of ale and sugary tarts, fueled his hunger. As his heart ceased beating, then leaped into a rapid beat, he drew in a breath of her unique aroma. She didn't reek of too much perfume as some women he'd encountered in his many centuries of life. The fresh scent of floral, feminine soap and female sex-cream filled his lungs. Tiny whimpers of desire escaped her mouth as she tilted her head in order to go at him from a different angle. With each guttural moan that escaped her throat, he returned one of equal measure.

Her arms, warm and bare, slid around his neck, twining and capturing him with bold fervor. She dragged him close and clamped her legs about his hips while still sitting in the chair. On his knees, the movement brought his erection up against the damp stretch of fabric between her legs. And he nearly lost himself then and there.

The knowledge that the nature of the virus did not induce sexual arousal unless the subject truly wished it filled him with glee. Its function was to guide one toward the goal—in this case, marriage. If carnal drive came naturally with the infection, the recipient would be as lucky as a bloke surrounded by a million four-leaf clovers.

And tonight would be Grady O'Donovan's luck-o'-the-Irish night. No malarkey here. Mischa wanted him, and he definitely wanted her.

There was no getting around it. He had to get inside her. With his lips locked to hers, he opened his eyes and scanned the room. Two life-sized pleasure dolls, one male and one female, stood mannequin-like in the corner. Directly to their right, Mischa's unmade brass bed was shoved against one towering, redbrick wall. High windows above it allowed in streams of silver-blue moonlight lending it a stage-like appeal. Further out into the large, one-room space, various pieces of sexual equipment were set and ready for use. His blood quickened. Yes, they were ready for *his* use.

But first he needed her in the bed.

He tore his lips from hers. "Em…Mischa, me sweet vixen."

"Huh—what?" Her husky voice seemed to blend with the glaze of passion in her dark eyes. The ridges of her fine cheeks were splashed with pink, as if she'd basked in the high-noon sun for days on end. And when he looked at her moist, swollen lips, trembling now with want, he groaned and combed his hand through the thickness of hair at her nape.

"'Tis a wee bit quick, that I'm aware, but I'm fierce mad for ye." He drew her to him with a firm tug and pressed his lips to her stunned ones. Against her mouth, he whispered, "I need—no, I *must*—get me flute into your softness."

She giggled and swayed so that she leaned away from him. Her eyes widened. "Flute?"

Jaysus, the difference in dialects! He hadn't the time or the inclination to fuss with it. "Me cock."

"Hmm…" The pupils in her eyes, edged by lighter shades of brown, dilated into large circles. "Flute. Well, I've played a *flute* before…with my hands and my tongue and my lips. I'm very…musical."

The implication of her words strummed him in precisely that manner, musically, entrancing. The smoldering notes entered his ears seductive and low, and played adeptly on the keys of his flute, hardening it like the taut cover of a drum. "Your tongue and lips, eh?"

She smiled sweetly. "And my hands." As if to prove her words, she pressed her palm, hot and small, to his chest. With her eyes boring into his, she trailed it down over one nipple, springing it to life. Rainbow flames of fire shot in colorful bursts toward his manhood. Already hard, it throbbed with an aching need so powerful, he nearly cried out with the blessed pain of it.

But the excruciating sensations only intensified when her hand moved ever lower over his ribs, down across his quivering belly, right to the protruding mass in his britches. He gasped when she closed her palm over him and stroked him through the thick fabric.

The heat of her body, of her hand and mouth so near his, seemed to engulf him with madness. He shot to his feet and jerked her up into his arms. She squealed, though with delight or fear, he didn't know. With a firm hold on her waist, he stabbed his hands down into her short little pants and dug his fingers into her ass cheeks. They were full and firm, yet soft and small against his large hands. Leaning down far enough to clutch those fleshy buns with adeptness, he yanked her upward so that her legs spread and automatically wrapped about his hips. The sensation of the weight of her body pushing that hot, clothed pussy against his hardness was nearly enough to bring him to his knees.

Instead, he gathered her close, turned on his booted heel, and strode across the room to the bed. He dove onto it with her body twined around him. Inhaling the scent of womanly soaps and sexual arousal, he covered her body with his and her mouth with his hungry one.

"I..." she panted against his mouth, kicking off her shoes. They thudded, one at a time, upon the hardwood floor. "I don't know why I'm doing this."

"I told ye it's the—" He gasped for air and swept the small cave of her mouth with his tongue. She greedily accepted it, dueling back with her own wet passion. Ah, honey and ale, he thought. She tasted of his favorite treats.

"The virus-spell," he continued. Grady had to sample her lovely breasts before he went any further. Through the cottony fabric of the tiny shirt, he cupped one full globe and flicked his thumb over the pebbled knot. She cried out, and her eyes first widened in shock, then narrowed with ecstasy.

"Ye've been infected and chose not to clean me out with your antivirus software. 'Tis now your fate to be with me, to love me, to devour me, to be devoured..."

Chapter Two

If this was what it meant to be devoured, Mischa thought as a beastlike urgency slammed into her, she was ready to surrender and be eaten. The length of his cock abraded erotically over her thin shorts, locating her clit as an arrow might find its bull's-eye. The musky, male aroma of him filled her lungs, making her think of lush, Irish forests and sunny, spring days. She lifted her head and sealed her mouth over his, drawing him down to her. The firm yet soft control of his tongue sent a slow roll of fireballs tumbling into her belly. His full lips melded perfectly to hers, damp and sweet and flavored with warm passion.

"Oh, God," she whimpered. Her hands found the gap of his jacket and yanked it down over his shoulders. "I've gotta have you. It's been too long for me."

"Aye," he said, his voice gravelly. He leaned up and away from her, and hastily ripped his jacket the rest of the way off. It went zinging across the bed and fell somewhere at the feet of the life-sized female doll standing nearby. "'Tis been months for me, as well, love. But I've watched ye..."

She hastily unfastened the plaid vest, peeled it away from his white shirt, and sent it reeling off across space.

In spite of the shocking confession he'd just made, she couldn't help but note the thick chest she now unearthed with each shirt button she released. "Watching me? You were spying on me?" She shoved frantically against the cottony shirt. She had to get him naked *now*!

He accommodated her, lifting first one arm, then the other, as she ripped his shirt from him. Her eyes went wide. Oh *my*. Luscious. No faerie or wimpy leprechaun, here. Pure, tasty, hot eye-candy, she thought. Wide, finely cut shoulders spread above a tanned, bare chest. His nipples were hard, dark knots, the manly swell of his breasts set in mounds of lean muscle. Though pleasant shock assailed her, she had to touch, to explore. He growled deep in his chest when she plucked each nipple, twisting and pulling.

That long, midnight-black ponytail fell over his shoulder when he stiffened. Her mouth curved into a small smile as she recalled not fifteen minutes earlier, fantasizing about how she longed for it to tease her breasts as he took her.

"Oh, aye, Mischa, I spied on ye," he finally replied, his voice deep and dewy-soft. She watched, mesmerized, when his eyes narrowed to slits of emerald lust as she continued to pluck and knead his chest. "I watched ye fuck yourself with your vibrating bullets and flesh-like cocks. I stood by," he rasped between wet kisses, "and watched in agony as ye pleasured yourself beyond bliss."

Her face flushed warm with embarrassment, yet the thought of him watching her play with herself, with all her wondrous toys, sent her spiraling into an altogether different level of desire. With a sure and swift rhythm, her heart pounded against her breastbone, her breath wheezed as she forced it in and out of her windpipe with each erotic mental picture she conjured up. And a puddle of wetness flooded her panties engulfing her in her own scent of arousal.

Grady shoved his hand between them and unfastened his fly. She looked down between their bodies, she fully clothed, him partially. Wiggling and readjusting, he freed the thickest, longest, most erect cock she'd ever seen from the open gap of his pants. A gasping moan escaped her lips, her mouth watered like Pavlov's dog, and her eyelids went limpid with hunger.

"Now I'm goin' to fuck ye with me own bullet." The threat filled her with a wild abandon, a sort of a thrilling panic that ignited her pussy with lava-like heat and engorged her nub so tight, she feared it would burst.

Suddenly, she grinned wickedly. Oh yeah, she was going to get lucky tonight—with a horny leprechaun!

His breath came in short bursts as he ground his hardness into her, nearly fucking her as if her clothing was a condom between them. The initial thick sensation of the fabric of both her underwear and her shorts pressing against her, made Mischa stiffen against the abrasiveness of it. Until he pushed further, deeper, rougher into her. The warm crotch of her panties was shoved almost a full inch inside her by the tip of his rod. The feel of it was one she'd never encountered before. Sticky, slick panty silk dragged against her lips, stretching the tender flesh.

Gliding a hand up her torso, he cupped one breast through the cloth of her shirt, and plucked the nipple between his thumb and forefinger. A gooey heat, like hot, melted caramel, flooded her panties again, soaking them through to his shaft. But apparently, it wasn't enough for him to explore her nipple through the fabric. He yanked up her baby-doll T-shirt and closed his large hand over her flesh.

A long, low growl escaped her throat. The rough texture of his palm abraded her breast sending ripples of desire straight to her vee. She spread her legs further and he pushed another fraction of an inch into her. "Ah…holy shit, Grady. You have hot hands." She swallowed audibly. "And a huge…flute."

"Oh, and ye have hot, delectable breasts, just as I imagined they would feel. And ye're tight…oh-so tight."

She looked up into glazed, sparkling eyes. Never had a man been so horny so fast for her. Joy and excitement burst in her chest. It was odd, very odd, but for some reason, she wanted him to fuck her this way, to shove her clothes up inside her with his rod. Somehow, it made her feel wild, animal-like, as if she were an untamed beast mating with haphazard abandon.

The notion briefly entered her mind that he must be reading her thoughts, because he suddenly drove himself inside her. The movement caused the waistband of her shorts to slide down across her lower pelvis. But there was no time to ponder, to ask or to accuse. Sweet pain and dry-wet pleasure shot through to her core. The covering of her clothing over his penis made him thicker, longer, if that were even possible. The fullness of it had her fighting to get away, yet clawing to get him closer, deeper. She could already feel—no, sense—the outer edges of the orgasm somewhere within reach, and there wasn't a thing she could do to stop it. It was as if one of her long, thick vibrators was being shoved up inside her, and no matter how hard she tried to draw out the pleasure, to fight it and make it last longer, it was inevitable, way too intense to delay.

"Grady..."

He ducked his head and closed his mouth over her nipple. Her vision blurred and sweat beaded on her brow. She'd barely moved and was already on her way to a mind-blowing release. Now that he flickered his slick tongue over her nipple, and took her other breast in his free hand, kneading and cupping it roughly, she was a goner. Icy bursts of lust shattered through her, from deep in her womb to the very tips of her toes and fingers, and back again. She shuddered as it went on and on. Tidal wave after tidal wave of bliss washed through her, leaving her breathless, stunned. It permeated into every single one of her cells, injecting her with a level of euphoria she'd never reached before.

"Yes, me faerie angel, what is it?" he asked between his teeth as he clamped them over the areola.

But it was too late to warn him.

"I..." She gulped in a breath, filling her lungs with warm air. "I just came."

*****

It wasn't over for Grady. No, it was only just beginning. He yanked himself from inside her, and with an impatience he'd never before experienced, he kicked off his boots and stripped himself naked.

Mischa lay there stunned, her chest rising and falling as she struggled to catch her breath. Her shirt was shoved up into her armpits. The small britches were taut across her upper thighs, the strip between her legs soaked, stained and all but disappearing up inside her. Grady closed his palm around his throbbing cock as he studied her with restrained hunger. His balls drew up in aching protest for release. He'd never, in all his centuries of existence, fucked a woman that way before with clothing still on—with it still between them! He'd been like a starving ogre forcing his way inside a woman, desperate for some unknown goal.

He stood beside the bed looking down at her, his hand stroking up and down the length of his rod. It felt hard and dry in his hand, but he needed it wet and sticky now. "Mischa…"

She blinked and tore her eyes from the ceiling. "Mm?" It came out husky, seductive.

"Are you all right, darlin'?"

The smile that spread across her face sent his heart into a tumbling roll. It reached her eyes, warm and fluid with an undefined emotion. "Well, I'm suddenly exhausted, but oh, yeah. You better believe it, O'Donovan. I've never been better."

It was all he needed to hear. He dove on top of her. Wild male aggression slammed into him and raged through his leprechaun's blood. He had to have her, now, fast, rough. With a growl, he hooked his fingers at the neckline of her shirt. The sound of the ripping fabric brought a gasp from her, and Grady blinked at the sharp sound of it. A slap of cold, it awakened him to awareness at what he'd just done.

"Mischa…I…I'm sorry—"

"No!" Her hands sought his out as he withdrew them. She dragged them back to the tattered edges of the fabric. "Don't stop. Please. It…it's a real turn-on, it's…it's making me *very* wet again."

There was no stopping him now, though he briefly wondered with self-disgust if he ever could have been stopped in the first place. Had the virus-spell infected him, too, for Paddy's sake? Throughout time, he'd had his share of women, every shape, age, temperament and color in the world. But never before had he been with a woman who brought out this beastly behavior, almost like an uncontrollable sexual rage in him.

Even now, as he wondered about the virus, it was as if his body took over and ignored the worry of it. He just had to have her slick passage cloaked around his cock. *Now.*

The shirt came off with a final rip. Next came the pants. He yanked them down her legs, watching as the soaked fabric popped from inside her. Ah, such a fine thing she was there in the heart of her soul, he thought, with the coppery shade of the *baz* trimmed short and neat, the lips shaved smooth as ice. The sweet scent of her womanly juices wafted up to tease him, to make him hunger for a taste of her. With unrestrained need, he buried his face in the damp fabric of her panties, inhaling, tasting of her creamy, salty juices on the cloth. But he had to have the source of it. His gaze riveted to the flowery petals of her pussy, and his dick throbbed in demanding protest at the delay. Obedient to his libido, he tossed the panties over his shoulder.

Grady draped the long, smooth length of her legs on either side of him as he knelt between her legs. The mounds of her breasts swelled with fullness, the nipples pebbly, dark silk sitting atop them like the mountain peaks of Macgillycuddy's Reeks. Her hair was fanned out behind her, glittery cinnamon against the stark-white pillow. He groaned when she lifted her arms in welcome to him, her body moving in a seductive, eager dance upon the cool sheet. And he could see right into her soul. Her eyes sparkled with passion and some undefined emotion. He'd never heard of a virus-spell affecting anyone quite this drastically before. Which told him this was the real her, that she was far more passion-filled than an average woman. It meant it had been buried inside her, longing to be freed. The virus only brought out what was real, what one truly desired inside, but did not normally have the bravery to display.

And just knowing he'd freed this beast within her made him harder, more desperate to get inside her.

"Mischa..." He planted his forearms beside her head, covered her body with his, and touched the tip of his penis to her heat. Sticky sap coated the head, preparing it for entry.

She sucked in a little pant of breath at the contact, but didn't reply. Instead, she cupped his face with her hands and brought his lips to hers. He sighed, content yet hungry for more.

"I'm going to fuck you like you've never been fucked before." He clamped a mental vise around his restraint when her tongue flickered out to trace his lips as he spoke to her. "Is that okay?"

The throaty laugh surprised yet pleased him. "Newsflash, my leprechaun. You don't have to ask my permission. Just shut up and fuck my brains out, would you?"

He chuckled, but it was cut off by his own howl as he rammed himself inside her with a force that shook his own control. She screamed out her shock at the sudden invasion, and it echoed in his head, sweet and sexy as it turned to a whimper of pleasure.

"Okay, me love, ye asked for it. I'll be fuckin' your brains out..." He gulped for air as the slick fire of her passage overwhelmed him with lust. Ah, but she was as wet and powerful as the River Liffey, he thought.

"Oh God, oh hell, you're so big." She squirmed away from him, but he held her tight like a helpless animal in a deadly trap. "I've never had such a huge—" she rocked forward, then away, as if she couldn't decide if it pleased or displeased her. "Oh shit, it feels *so* good!"

Relief flooded him; carnal hunger ate away at him. "Ye're such a horny lass. Such passion ye've had buried inside ye." He yanked her arms above her head, secured them with one large hand, and drew back and drove into her again.

She cried out, and her hips rose up to slam against his defiantly. He looked down to see her breasts jiggling high upon her chest, her smooth underarms faintly moist with sweat. Inhaling her musky scent, he yearned to explore every hidden treasure of her body. With her arms held high above her head, and his throbbing, granite-hard cock shoved to the tip of her womb, he reached around with his free hand and found her asshole. She flinched against his probing finger.

"Hold still, Mischa. Hold real still."

"No…don't…" She squeezed her eyes shut and thrashed her head from side to side. Her hot breath fanned across his neck at the very instant her buttocks tightened.

"Ye want it, ye know ye do, love. I've seen ye use the anal toys, almost like an addiction." Gently, he pushed through the tight cheeks and flickered his fingertip over the rigid hole. A moan, soft and hesitant, escaped from deep within her throat. He felt her cunt muscles spasm around his shaft, eager, hungry.

She relaxed a small measure and nodded, shook her head, nodded again. "Yes…"

All he could think was that he wanted to fill every hole in her entire voluptuous body with every finger and appendage he had.

And he did.

At the very second he sank his middle finger into her ass, he claimed her mouth voraciously, and plunged his tongue into her yielding, open cavern. She whimpered into his mouth, thrashing weakly against the weight of his body and the strength of his hold on her wrists. The hole tightened against his finger but gave way when he withdrew all invading parts and again, rammed his cock, his tongue and his finger deep inside her orifices at the same instant.

The sensation of being inside her in three different places at the same time engulfed him in wild abandon. He could smell her excitement, taste her eagerness, feel her tight, wet pussy and ass around him. The song of her labored breathing and guttural moans filled his ears, pleasing him far more than the Irish folk music he so loved.

He soared on the melody of Mischa, the flavors, the scents, the heat of her soft body. And with unbridled lust, he sank himself into her one last time, spilling his hot juice inside her. Mischa convulsed beneath him, her perspiring body twitching against his hold. Her quivers of ecstasy rippled against his invading flesh, from his finger to his cock, to his greedy tongue. As the waves of mutual pleasure ebbed, Grady slowly withdrew from her. He buried his face in her fragrant hair, throwing one leg across her thighs.

If I were to die tonight, I'd die the luckiest leprechaun in the entire fucking elfin world.

Mischa panted as he rolled over and dragged her on top of him, her back against his chest, her rear pressed to his still quivering cock. She gulped in a lungful of air.

"Wowza." Her breath wheezed in and out past her windpipe as she stared up at the iron beams across the ceiling. "I've now had sex with a leprechaun. And it was the best frickin' sex I've ever had in my entire life!"

Chapter Three

Moments later, she rolled off him, landing on the mattress with a thud. The headache seemed to be coming back with a dull, almost indiscernible ache. And, damn, but it was hot in here! Mischa raised a trembling hand and tested the temperature of her forehead. Yes, her skin felt warm, almost flushed. Was she getting sick? There was the vague feeling of muscle and joint aches, fatigue and a general ran-over-by-a-truck sense pumping faintly through her system.

She turned and studied Grady. He appeared exhausted, as well. His massive, cut-like-a-diamond chest rose and fell with his labored breathing. Sweat beaded on his tanned, naked flesh in tiny, silver droplets of perspiration. The aromas of sex and passion clung to him, reminding her of their wild lovemaking, promising her more to come. Behind the closed lids where his thick lashes fanned dark over chiseled cheeks, she could see his eyes moving as if restless thoughts filled his mind.

Mischa reached out a hand, slow and deliberate. She touched his cheek, noting the moistness of his skin. But he wasn't hot, not like her. "You feel okay?" she asked.

His eyes popped open, two rich, green fields of clover. He smiled and the corners of his lips curved upward until his eyes twinkled with mischief. "Ah, what a question ye ask!"

Her eyelids fluttered helplessly as he pressed a gentle kiss into her palm. Fire re-ignited and swirled in her belly. Son of a bitch, was she getting turned on *again*?

She drew in a breath and sighed. "No, really. Do you feel…sick, like you're getting the flu or something?"

"Aye, I feel lovesick, Mischa." He drew her up against him so that they lay on their sides facing one another. His hand, large and warm, trailed up and down her side sending ripples of goose bumps up her spine.

She shrugged and yawned. "I guess you've just worn me out. So," she said as she nipped his bottom lip between her teeth, "what now?"

"More of me magic," he replied matter-of-factly.

Mischa pressed a hand against his chest so that he rolled over onto his back. She crawled up on top of him and straddled his hips. His half-flaccid cock twitched against the remaining stickiness between her legs, and as if he'd pumped air into a tire, his manhood thickened in response.

"Oh, goody. Magic again. Will you spray me with your dust again, or just chant and fling your hands about?" With each word, she dragged her pussy over him, and with each drag, his eyes went limp and narrow with hooded passion. The control of it both thrilled and endeared her further to him.

He gripped her pelvic bone and ground her down on him. His cock pressed against her wetness, spreading her lips so that he probed her inner folds. A gush of honey dribbled out when he raised his hands and filled them with her breasts. The nipples sprang to life, hard, tight rocks of anxious need.

"Nay, Mischa, I'll be sprayin' them—" he jerked his gaze toward the male and female mannequins "—with me magic dust."

"Barbie and Ken, my sex dolls?"

He grinned mischievously. "Aye, your sex dolls."

"But...but why? What will you do with them?" She placed her hands on his chest and mimicked his massaging of her breasts. The nipples tightened instantly between her fingertips, and she noted his indrawn breath with great female satisfaction.

"Bring them to fake life."

She halted her hands. "To fake life?"

"Aye, to fake life, Mischa, yours to play with as ye see fit—though as real as they'll seem, they won't be. Ye can play guilt-free as ye do with your many amazing toys. I've watched ye," he said softly, pulling her down for a draw of his lips across hers. "I've watched in agony as ye've masturbated while clutching their lifeless bodies, while mating with them, while pretending them to be real, to be loving ye."

Mischa gasped. She rolled off him and turned her back to him. She *was* sick! She'd done those things, she'd gotten off on them, so real and lifelike—and he'd watched? The thought of it both humiliated and lit a torch of wantonness deep inside her. It was one thing for someone to watch you screw yourself with a vibrator, but entirely another to have them watch you get off on a lifeless, human-sized doll. What a pervert he must think her.

God, she wanted to dig a hole and die!

"Mischa, love." His hand was firm but gentle as he rolled her over to face him. "Oh, no, no. Please, do no' cry."

Cry? She was crying? Well, hell yes, she was crying. The dampness of her cheeks and the hitch in her chest confirmed it. She was crying from utter humiliation and…

She glanced sharply away from the tenderness in his gaze.

He pressed a kiss to her forehead. "No need to feel embarrassed or to explain. I'm glad of it, to be sure. And I know why ye did it."

"You do?"

"Oh, ye bet, me hot little lover. And I don't blame ye one wee bit." He combed a hand through her hair, and the gentle look in his eyes nearly sent her tumbling into love.

"Don't blame me for what?" Her curiosity was piqued beyond reason now, yet she dreaded hearing his explanation. He seemed to know things, but he couldn't know her pain, her past—or could he?

"For substituting. When death enters a mortal's life, sometimes it's difficult to go on, to bring new relationships back into their life."

"This has nothing to do with my mother," Mischa protested, and sat upright to prove it, turning her back on him.

The hand that trailed up and down her spine, from the base of her neck to the swell of her ass, spoke of understanding, tenderness…or was it love?

"Nay, Mischa, I do no' speak of your mother. Though her illness and expected death were devastating losses in your life, your fiancé's untimely death brought ye pain like no other. A man, a woman, a love and bonding that seemed, at the time, beyond comprehension. Lost. Lost," he repeated as he pulled her back against him, "in one blink of an eye, one wrong turn of the wheel."

"I don't want to talk about this." The tears were dry now, but her voice sounded hollow in the large space of the ceiling above her.

"And ye do no' have to talk about it, for ye've done that enough. Ye've accepted his death in some ways, as well as your mother's, but life must go on. Your obsession with your business here," he whispered, his hands exploring every curve and plane of her body, bringing her back to life. "Ye've turned to your dolls and your toys as substitutes for the real thing. I'm here to change that, Mischa, to show ye that your life is precious, that 'tis meant to go on, that 'tis meant to be lived in joy and spent with me."

With *him*? But another burning question took precedence. She whirled and pinned him with narrowed eyes. "How did you know? About Mother, about Trent? You—you didn't…kill…or…?"

His jaw clenched. He snatched his hand from her flesh, leaving her cold and lonely. "No, I did no' cause your lover's death back then. And, damn it, I'd thank ye to remember it!"

The sharpness of his voice, the insult that filled his tone, made her feel suddenly foolish. Of course he hadn't killed Trent. It was a cruel thing to even imply. "I'm…I'm sorry." She heaved a sigh. "It was a normal reaction. I've often blamed others, never been able to accept fate."

"'Tis all right." Forgiveness seemed to come so easy to him. He returned his hand to her back and continued the delicious dance. She trembled beneath his touch, as if her skin sighed in bliss. "I do understand. And it seems ye do, too."

"I do?"

"Oh, aye. Ye see, and are aware of, your own faults, of the fact that ye can no' seem to accept fate. This is a start to a new beginning for ye, love."

She supposed he was right. After all, she'd just allowed herself to have sex with a stranger—with anyone, for that matter—for the first time since Trent's accident. True, this could be that fantasy dream, meaning she still hadn't, in reality, done such a thing, but what if it were real? Mischa tilted her head and studied him. Real, she wasn't sure. But no, he was not a stranger. That she was certain of. For some odd reason, she felt she'd known him for a long time. She didn't recognize the darkly handsome face, the powerful body, but it had a vague familiarity to it that she could not discount.

"Were you spying on me and Trent?"

He shook his head rapidly. The dark stream of hair trailed across the pillow behind him. "Nay. I only entered your life during the few months of the pre-virus infection. Three months to the day of St. Patrick's Day. "

She did a mental calculation, ticking her fingers as she did so. "December seventeenth?"

"That would be the day. At midnight."

Visions swam through her head. She'd been swamped with holiday orders. The Celtic Sins work had been a godsend, for Trent's late-summer death had still been raw in her heart. She'd had another impending death to deal with, but her mother's illness had been long coming. Cancer was a cruel killer, warning those who'd be left behind, yet dragging on until the victim suffered needlessly.

The seventeenth of December had been the very day her mother had finally been hospitalized. She'd never returned to her tiny cottage. Mischa had been forced to go through every little knickknack, every dish and box. And then put the house up for sale.

"And my mother? How did you know about her?"

He lifted a bare, beefy shoulder. "I told ye, I've been watchin' ye, I've been with ye, for months. I was there with ye when she passed on in January."

"You were?"

"Every hour, every minute."

The thought of it sent a creepy sensation down her back, yet a warm glow of something gooey filled her heart. She hadn't been alone. He'd been with her. Her eyes filled with icy tears as she flashed back to that bitingly cold winter night at the hospital. There'd been many odd occurrences, but she'd attributed them to nerves, to grief, to loneliness. At times, she'd wondered if the warm arms she'd felt around her, the scents of sea and gusty wind, had been Trent's spirit reaching out to her. But even then, she'd known it wasn't him. She'd loved Trent, but he'd definitely had his faults. And offering her comfort and an affectionate embrace during the uncomfortable, painful moments of a person's slow death was not one of his best traits.

"Mischa." He dashed a tear from her cheek with a thumb. "Do no' cry, sweetheart. Me heart can no' take it, just as your tears back then had crushed me. I reached out to ye, but there's nothing like the real thing, like flesh and blood closeness."

To prove it, he pulled her down next to him and tucked her against his side. She placed a hand on his thick chest, smooth and tight against her palm. He tipped her chin up so that her eyes were but inches from his. In them, she saw passion, affection, and something altogether deeper. His next words confirmed that depth.

"I've loved ye, Mischa, since that first eve, December seventeenth, when I came to ye across the Internet and watched ye. Due to the virus-spell codes, I could no' be with ye in the flesh until this night, until the E-mail was set to be sent and ye willingly brought me to ye. But I was allowed to be with ye in spirit, loving ye, guiding ye, comforting ye in your sorrow. Do ye understand?"

She could swear her heart burst at that one potent word. Love. But no, she most certainly didn't understand. "Love? You don't even know me."

He bolted upright, naked and magnificent. "Haven't ye been listening to me?"

"Yes, but—"

"I've been *with* ye for months, I've gotten to know your every quirk, your every nuance. Your every…thought," he added as his eyes clouded with guilt. "In fact, I only know of Trent from your thoughts of him since."

She scrambled up onto her knees, her breasts jiggling with the sudden movement. Though she didn't miss the shift of his eyes to them, the instant glaze of masked desire in his gaze, she ignored it and shrieked, "There it is again. Invading privacy. You've been reading my mind. For *three* goddamn months?"

Mischa didn't like the panicked loss of self-control in her voice, but Jesus, wasn't anything sacred with this man? What things had she unknowingly been revealing to him all this time? Did he know her better than she knew herself? The thought of it creeped her out, big-time.

"Aye, Mischa, for three goddamn months."

"Oh, aye, this, and aye, that!" She didn't like the mocking tone to her voice, but something of solid ire and the principal of things won out. With slow deliberation, she leaned in toward him, close enough that her nipples barely brushed his chest. His wild, earthy scent filled her nostrils, strumming her senses against her will. "Cut with the Irish shit. This is such crap! You're pulling my leg, playing a cruel joke on me."

His lips thinned. He opened his mouth as if to speak, then his teeth clattered together as he swallowed his words.

God, it was hot in here, she suddenly thought. No, it wasn't. It was guilt. It must be her own fucking guilt and the anger boiling her blood that was making her feverish. She inhaled deep and long. Damn, but she was suddenly exhausted. With her eyes locked to his, she plopped back onto the pillow.

"What's the matter?" He hovered above her like a mother hen. The concern in his eyes tore at her heart and further heaped on the guilt.

"I…I'm sorry. I was being quite the bitch, wasn't I?"

Like a gentleman, he refrained from answering the question honestly. He pressed a hand to her forehead, and she watched as the inky black slashes of his eyebrows furrowed into inverted curves. "Ye're on fire."

She smiled, but ignored his assessment. "This virus of yours certainly does make me say and do things I'd normally only *think* about."

Was that a lame excuse for her rude behavior, she wondered, or was it the truth? The fact was, she'd been acting out of character since she'd heard the "You've got mail" announcement of his E-mail delivery. Before that, there'd never been such shedding of inhibitions in her entire life. Hmm, and come to think of it, she'd never before went off on someone like she just had Grady. What was wrong with her? It was as if her usual feelings, thoughts, irritations and mental actions were coming to life, emerging without her being able to stop them. She didn't think about the consequences as she normally did with her usual, outward personality. She just did it, and made vague, lame decisions to deal with the consequences later.

"Your headache's back." It wasn't a question because, of course, he knew answers without asking.

She pressed her fingertips to her temples. "Yes, it is. Wow, what a wicked virus you gave me," she mumbled just before blackness engulfed her.

* * * * *

"Mischa!" Grady shook her. Her head rolled loosely as if it weren't attached. She was on fire, her skin wet with perspiration. Her cheeks were splashed with pink splotches, obvious evidence that she had a fever. Why hadn't he noted it before? Had he been that selfishly caught up in her charms to overlook her health and safety? Looking back, he recalled her asking if he felt sick. If he'd been paying attention, he'd have realized she meant *she* was feeling odd.

Fear such as he'd never known before ate at his gut like acid. Was it the virus causing this? And if so, why? Leprechauns had used this very virus numerous times, and in many different forms of delivery over the centuries. Except for the shedding of inhibitions and the emergence of honest, true feelings, not one human had ever been struck with these same symptoms. Fever, headache, unconsciousness, and, he added with a bit of self-loathing, dizziness. It was a symptom which he now realized she'd been experiencing from the moment he stood before her, right after his emergence from the cable line. Like an arrogant ass, he'd mistaken it for a womanly swoon or too much Guinness.

He crossed to the kitchen sink and wetted a dishrag with cold tap water. Next, he flung open the refrigerator freezer and loaded dozens of plastic storage zip-bags full of ice. With hurried steps, he moved to the tiny bathroom set in the far corner behind a tall curtain. He drew a tepid bath in the clawfoot tub and tossed the bags of ice in, sending splashes of water over the rim.

Turning, he raced to Mischa and mopped her brow with the cool rag. Pressing the cloth to her forehead, he lifted her gently into his arms. She was limp and lifeless, and fear crushed him, tumbling in his chest like a heavy boulder. His heart thudded painfully against his lungs, preventing him from drawing in a deep breath.

Please, my love, do no' die on me!

As he carried her across the room, he looked down into her lovely, heart-shaped face. Her lips were as swollen as ripe cherries, and he could swear he could still feel their soft silkiness against his mouth. Her nose, a straight, feminine, almost regal line, drew him so that he lifted her and planted a kiss on the tip. Her scent, her unique, floral perfume, filled his nostrils, and he briefly clamped his eyes shut at the sudden euphoric dizziness that washed over him. Beneath the closed lids, he could picture the deep brown of her eyes, the dilated black pupils rimmed with lighter brown. The heat of her skin against his chest made his eyes wander to her perfect, curvy body, the flesh, though normally creamy-white, now a bright pink and coated with feverish perspiration. Her nipples were dark roses tipped at each breast, but they were no longer hardened knots as they had been only moments ago. He recalled the feel and taste of them, solid nuggets of candy against his tongue, a sweet burst of flavor in his mouth. The vague roundness of her belly curved against his own abdomen while the long length of legs streamed over his arm.

She was downright gorgeous, all woman, all soft and cuddly and sultry-sexy. He sidestepped the bathroom curtain that hung from a metal bar across the corner, and crossed carefully over the wet floor to the bath. Gently, so as not to startle her, he lowered her into the cool vat, streaming her coppery tresses over the edge of the tub. The deep water closed over her, swallowing her with icy wetness, and he could swear he heard a sizzle, as if her body had protested at the drastic difference in temperatures. The ice bags floated around her breasts, above her abdomen, her pussy.

But he could see it wasn't going to be enough. She moaned in delirium, her skin now flaming red.

He stood beside her at the edge of the tub and threw his head back in chant. Carefully, skillfully, he crossed his wrists and immediately clapped his hands together in three sharp beats of succession. In contrast to the dire matter at hand, cheerful bagpipes accompanied by tinkling harps, filled the room.

Rose petals, pink, yellow, white and scarlet red, materialized in his hands. He closed his eyes and inhaled the fragrance of them, each color its own distinct, subtle hint of nature, each filled with their own healing quality.

"Oh, King of the Leprechauns, I call upon thee," he sang, and tossed the blooms above Mischa. They levitated and spun over her body. "Protect and heal her, mortal of my heart is she. Guide me, lead me, show me the spell, of love and of protection, a true Irish tell."

As the aromatic dusting whirled around her unconscious body, Grady stepped over the rim of the tub and stood above her in the water, naked, determined. He threw his arms up toward the high ceiling, chanting an ancient Gaelic spell as its exact rules and order poured into him from that place afar, of emerald fields and seas of power. Flutes and harps tinkled out a tune, while violent winds blew in, lifting his long ponytail, stirring the air and cooling the room.

"Aye, I hear ye, oh King of the Isle," he replied to the silent voice transmitting into his mind. "'Tis my very heart's wish to see her smile."

"Grady?"

His eyes popped open and riveted downward. "Mischa. Mischa. Ye're awake!"

He'd gotten his wish, for her mouth curved, revealing a pretty row of teeth. They gleamed as white as an Irish snow. "Well, of course I'm awake. All that racket and singing and howling wind—it's enough to wake the dead."

The wind stilled, and with it, his fear. He lowered his arms. The flowers fell to the surface of the bathwater, floating around her delectable breasts. But he wasn't concerned with the beauty of her at the moment. All that mattered was the fact that she'd awakened, that she appeared well and happy.

Grady collapsed in the water, a deep, rolling laughter erupting from his chest. Giddy, he cupped her chin and pressed a hand to her forehead. "Ye're cold."

She shivered to emphasize her agreement. "Freezing. Why the hell did you put me in a pool of ice water?"

"Eh, never mind. Just tell me…do ye feel okay now?"

Her eyebrows drew together into dark ribbons of auburn. "What a ridiculous question." She rose and he stared up at her, mesmerized. Water sluiced down, dribbling over her nipples, into her navel, down to those pink little love-lips. "Of course I feel fine. I did feel a bit...odd earlier, as if I'd maybe started with the flu or something, but now I feel wonderful. I'm cured, apparently."

"Oh, aye, ye're cured, me lass." *At least I pray ye are for good!* "So, what does me sexy faerie lady wish to do now?" He stood and pulled her into his arms, the frosty water lapping around knees and lower thighs, sloshing up and over the rim of the tub.

"I wanna get out of this ice water, for starters." She disentangled herself from his arms and climbed from the tub. Choosing a thick, white terry towel, she wrapped it around her luscious body. Her hair hung over her shoulders in long ropes of damp, burnished copper. Above the towel, he could see the shadowed valley of cleavage between her breasts, beaded with droplets of water. Her skin no longer glowed with that frightening feverish red tone. Oh, aye, he thought. The lass had been cured. But he'd be going and getting the first four-leaf clover he could find, the first chance he got.

He pulled the plug, and suction, along with the faint rush of water, filled the room. Snatching a towel from a nearby rack, he stepped from the tub and rubbed himself briskly down. "And what else would me lovely Irish beauty like to do?"

Eyes wide and doe-like, she twirled a lock of her hair around her finger while she stared openly at his naked body. He could swear her eyes touched his flesh, warming him to a feverish state of his own. They flicked upward and snared him with a steamy look.

"The mannequins."

"The mannequins?"

"You..." she began, but instead spun to pluck a brush from the vanity. She stared at herself in the mirror, avoiding his gaze, and absently dragged the brush through her mane. "You said something earlier about bringing them to life."

"Ah, yes, your imaginary lovers."

Her eyes flicked to his in the reflection of the mirror, a mixture of discomfort, curiosity and wicked desire. "You said they wouldn't be real, right?"

"Aye."

"So if you bring them to life, it'll be just like…making love to them as dummies. Only they'll *appear* real."

"By Killarney, I do believe she's got it!"

She set the brush down and turned. "Are you making fun of me?"

"No, no, 'course not, me love. 'Tis a grand thing ye've done, gettin' over your inhibitions and the like. Your wish is me every command, that 'tis." Naked, he bowed to her respectfully and threw out a handful of dust toward the half-open bathroom curtain. "After ye, me ladylove. 'Tis time to finally bring some Celtic Sin into your life."

Chapter Four

"Wee green one of the faeries, I say, turn them to flesh, only this day!" Grady's voice was all there was—he had no discernable form. His body, now zipping around both dolls in high speed, was much like the fluttering wings of a hummingbird. Nothing but a tan blur, and circling so swiftly, she could see through him. He stirred the room, sending his earthy scent across the space, and the air crackled with energy as flashes and zaps of red light clung here and there.

"'Tis wit and charm and a grand flair for sex, the couple—these two—I do grant them my hex!"

The forces died. Grady levitated above the cloudy space that had once held her vibrating, very real, life-sized dolls. He floated across the room and made one circle around Mischa before he settled on the floor beside her.

She flicked her gaze from his solid, nude body to the silver mist left behind. It swirled in long fingers of mystique, and she could swear she heard faint flutes trilling in the distance as the fog began to dissipate. Gradually, it thinned to nothingness, and the sight that met her eyes was more arousing, more exciting, than using the Triplezinger. One of her best-selling specialty toys, it consisted of a vibrating vaginal faux-cock, an outer finger for clitoral stimulation, and a ribbed, vibrating anal device all in one toy.

"Wow. Talk about knocking your socks off." She blew out a breath and glided halfway to the naked couple, stopped when the female's moan echoed in the room. It was much like, she mused as she studied them, looking upon one of those expensive sculptures in an art gallery, of a man and woman standing there locked in a sensual embrace. Where did her limbs end and his begin?

Taking one step closer, Mischa inhaled and caught the fragrance of female dew and warm male flesh. Instantly aware of a throbbing between her legs, it began a slow and welcome thaw, warming her skin, dampening her pussy lips.

Her eyes did a caressing appraisal, first memorizing every inch of woman. By the orange-silver beams of moonlight spearing down through the high windows, the female's voluptuous, bronzed body gleamed with perspiration. Everything was accentuated, every curve of hip and breast, every nook of waist, every line of fluid arms and graceful neck. A flaxen, short swing of hair covered her face as she looked down watching him suckle at her breast. But soon, her head fell back, a guttural cry escaping her red, pursed lips. The blonde curtain swung back revealing a porcelain face, perfect and femininely delicate, drawn in sweet ecstasy.

Mischa's gaze slid fluidly into the man. He wasn't quite as tall as Grady, but he carried with him a body built stone tough and statuesque strong. Cut and lean, from the thick shoulders to the legs lined with corded muscles, he emitted power and raw masculinity. His short-cropped mop of golden hair was tousled by the woman's zesty, voracious slide of hands. When he attacked the woman's mouth with his own, and angled his head to deepen the kiss, his eyes opened and flitted to Mischa. Her breath caught. As blue, deep and mysterious as the sea, they locked on hers with toxic accuracy. She shuddered, suppressing the swift wave of lust that swept her.

With his mouth still devouring the woman's, he crooked a finger at Mischa.

"What—? Oh, God."

"They want ye to go to them, Mischa, love. Enjoy."

Go to them? Be *with* them?

"Yes, go to them, be *with* them."

In a state of stunned giddiness, she noted he'd read her mind, but hadn't the heart to shatter the magic of this moment by pointing it out. Her body hummed with anticipation, her nipples hardened, tingling without so much as a brief touch upon them. A slow flow of hot, creamy syrup dribbled from her passage, down along her inner thighs.

Slowly, she picked up one bare foot and moved nearer. She halted, her back to Grady, and suddenly stiffened. "They're not real, right? I mean, I'm not normally promiscuous—unless I'm having sex with a toy."

He chuckled softly, a deep rumble of amusement. "Nay, lass, they're no more real than when ye mated with them before as toys. 'Tis merely magic."

"'Tis merely magic," she echoed with a nod. "Merely magic."

The couple broke their kiss and, still in a twist of slithering limbs, said together in a tranquil song, "Come. We are here only for your pleasure."

Ah, only for my pleasure. The sound of it thrilled her to distraction. When had anyone ever focused only on *her* pleasure? Her brow creased. Certainly not Trent, come to think of it, she decided. Oh, he'd been an okay lover, and she'd reached orgasm more often than not, but it had all been for him. His rabid, wild, short bouts of lovemaking had been more to get himself off, that she'd always known. If it weren't for her ability to take herself out of his arms and fantasize about a gentler, more attentive lover, she wouldn't have even one orgasm under her belt.

Only for your pleasure. The words resounded in her head…in Grady's voice. She turned to see him sprawled across the bed, his hands folded behind his head, biceps flexed and as large as tree trunks. She recalled the feel of them tightening against her palm as ecstasy reached for her. Her pussy went up in flames when her perusal skimmed across the tight abdomen to find his erection full and granite-hard. His long legs, with the sparse sprinkle of black curls over corded muscles, were crossed at the ankles. Finally, her eyes rose to his face. The smile that curved his mouth reached his eyes, a twinkle of deep, indefinable affection.

And her heart did a long, fluid thump-thump.

No one had ever focused on her pleasure…until Grady.

"Go. I want to watch ye being pleasured." His voice was a husky pitch of restrained passion. It had an aphrodisiac effect on her, branding her veins with a blast of hot blood.

Her breath quickened, as did her sex. "Will you end it when I ask?"

"Aye, ye can count on that, to be certain."

"Will you come to me when I ask?"

His smile faded. "I will always come to ye when ye ask. Always."

Suddenly, with all her soul, she knew he meant it. There wasn't the indecision and doubts that had forever plagued her relationship with Trent. Just complete confidence, understanding and true trust.

"No, Mischa, do no' cry, love. Go. Pleasure yourself, have fun. 'Tis all for ye, for once in your life—though I'll admit, I'll derive just as much, if not more pleasure from watching your gratification."

"Thank you." She choked it out, grateful the tears had not doused her desire, for all of a sudden she longed to give him his pleasure with hers. It was, she thought as she swiped the one lone tear from her cheek, much like putting on a show, acting for the purpose of arousing the watcher.

His eyes flickered beyond her to the man and woman who continued their act. "They call to ye. Hurry, before the magic fades."

She turned back. Indeed, they called to her…with a mating call. Her blood rushed thick and potent through her veins, engorging her clit. As she stepped nearer, they reached out and, together, plucked the towel from her. Their arms drew her in so that she was sandwiched between hard, solid male, and soft, curvy female. There was the pleasant, mixed aroma of perspiration, musky feminine juices…and faint, almost indiscernible rubber.

She almost laughed. Rubber. It was as if Grady had magically inserted it into the equation so that all of her doubts of mating with *real* people would be finally doused.

Mischa's gaze riveted to Grady's where he lay on her bed stroking his cock, pure male prowess and selfless devotion. He grinned ever so slightly, and she knew he reassured her, confirmed with her in a telepathic sort of way, that he had put the rubber smell there for her.

This was all for her. All of it.

So now, there was nothing else to do but be completely ravished by her mannequins.

*****

Limbs and bodies tangled, hands raced and plunged. Grady had never seen such a show of passion before now. The dummies weren't real, but he'd added to the spell an ingredient that, as Mischa pleased and became pleased, so did the mannequins…as best a rubber doll could. It would enhance Mischa's pleasure, make her feel as if they were real, yet she would always have that faint scent of rubber as a reminder that she did not mate with real people. There would be no shame for her, only complete and utter fulfillment.

And for him, as well.

He groaned, the hardness of his cock nearly bursting through its skin. Mischa was locked in a voracious kiss with the man while the woman stood behind her, one hand on Mischa's full breast strumming the nipple, the other stroking her clit. The man spread his legs to lower himself, and slipped inside her, his strong arms holding her, his hands clutching her delectable ass as he bounced her on his tool. Mischa's husky, muffled cry filled the room, tantalizing Grady's ears and bringing him to the bare edge of control.

Massaging his cock, he watched as the woman eased them down to the floor, Mischa straddling the man. The blonde reached for an anal plug and twisted its end, firing it up for power. As Mischa rode the male, the female slithered up between the man's legs and clutched Mischa's back to her ample breasts.

Grady could smell Mischa's dewy milk all the way from across the room. He lifted his nose, sniffing it in like a wolf in heat. His blood simmered, moving through his system in a slow boil. Soon, very soon, she'd come. He'd try his best to hold off, to slake his own desire inside her when she called to him, but he wasn't making any promises to himself. This show was starting to become the most absolute erotic one he'd ever had the pleasure of watching.

He sat up when the woman shoved her hand down between Mischa's back and her own abdomen, the vibrating plug whirring away. Mischa stiffened. The plug made contact, rubber tip to tight hole. Her head came up as she broke the kiss with the male doll. The woman shoved the plug up into Mischa's ass and mercilessly turned it to high speed.

"Oh, holy night!" The mewling noises that erupted from her throat sent Grady into a tailspin. He rushed across the room, his cock near to bursting with the need to come.

Mischa fell on the male mannequin and growled, taking his mouth with a hungry swoop. The woman climbed onto Mischa's back, holding the outer end of the plug against her own nub, as if it were her cock. Her eyes, a pale, almost white-blue, snared Grady's, and he sucked in a breath when she thrust her crotch against Mischa's ass where the plug barely hung out. Her mouth found the crook of Mischa's neck and suckled hungrily as she humped herself into Mischa's ass with the vibrating toy. The female doll reached around and wiggled her hand in between the two so that she could play with Mischa's breasts.

Mischa sucked in a sharp breath against the man's mouth. Her wild dance of pleasure ceased. She tore her lips from his and threw her head back onto the woman's shoulder. "*Grady!*" she screamed as the multiple orgasms slammed into her, wave after wave after wave. Her body convulsed and jerked, stopped, then convulsed again.

Dazed, Grady looked down at her as she slowly went limp. Despite his hardened state, he longed to take her in his arms and simply coddle her, pet her, love her.

Her head was now down on the man's chest, her breathing labored. Her voice muffled, she whispered, "Make them go away, Grady. Please. I want you now."

He clamped his eyes shut, drew in a long, tight breath. *She wanted him.* The words unlocked something in his heart, something that had been trapped inside it for centuries. Sure, women had always *wanted* him, for he was a very skilled lover. But not one had ever sincerely said she wanted him like *that*. Joy, coupled with bursting desire, filled his immortal soul.

Without a word, he moved his hands in a dance over the three lifeless bodies. Humming faintly to himself, he reversed the spell with a tinkle and a flash. The mannequins now stood ramrod still where they'd been from the start, and Mischa lay on the floor alone and in an exhausted, naked heap, the plug now forgotten at her side.

He knelt and lifted her into his arms. Sated fatigue riddled every cell of her body. He could sense it, not just with his powers but by her limp, quiet manner. She slid one arm around his neck and rested her head on his shoulder. And he thought he'd never felt a more tender, loving sensation in all his years.

"Thank you, Grady," she rasped. "That was wonderful, but I've determined I want you. *Only* you. Is that okay?"

"Ah, never fear, me love, never fear. 'Course 'tis okay." He carried her to the bed and laid her upon the rumpled sheets. Her hair, a fiery blaze of silk, streamed over the pillow behind her. Milky limbs and subtle curves called to him, hidden treasures beckoned.

She raised her arms, one leg drawn up in sensual modesty. "Make love to me, my leprechaun. Make love to me like you've never made love to anyone else before."

A lump clogged in his chest. It was a challenge, but one that would be easily conquered.

"Mischa..." he breathed, and climbed onto the bed, poised over her as a beast might do to his fallen prey. "Do ye know how I feel for ye?"

She touched his cheek. Her eyes sparkled. They brought to mind the gold coins in the cauldron at the end of his rainbow after a dewy rain. In them, he saw the glint of the sun slicing through a trailing cloud, pouring over his fortune.

"No, no words. Just show me. Already, my body yearns for you, even after that amazing gift you just gave me."

How could a leprechaun with a painful erection argue with that? He bent and took her mouth with his, a leisurely kiss that told her all he didn't speak. She still tasted of ale, but now there was an added flavor, one of pure, eager heat. Tongue slid across silky tongue, hands glided and skimmed. He filled his palm with her breast, even as he slipped inside her. She arched her back on a groan, and broke her mouth from his. He tasted of her faint, salty skin, there where her neck bowed slim and elegant, and rejoiced at the damp tightness that enveloped his shaft. So slick, so compact, so very incredible. There was no pussy in the world, never had been, never would be, like hers, he thought.

He moved with all the patience he didn't feel. Unhurriedly, he thrust and withdrew, thrust and withdrew. With each plunge, she whimpered his name. His hands skimmed up and over her hard-peaked globes, and pushed her arms above her head. There, by the waning light of the moon, he linked hands with her, and he linked his heart to hers. Though the virus-spell would guide them to the same end, he knew there was nothing more sure than true love.

She looked into his eyes, her hips rising to meet his. "Please, please, just make me come. No more thoughts, please."

Ah, the virus was in its later stages. She would now be able to read his mind intermittently, like random flashes of light. So, with careful, controlled powers, he mentally switched off that ability for now. Her eyelids blinked, as if she'd been slapped. But it wasn't long before her arms were twining around his neck, her legs locking at his waist. She shuddered against him, crying out her pleasure, but it wasn't the end for him.

Amazed at his restraint, he allowed her the last wave of orgasm before he withdrew from her. He kissed her mouth, her chin, her neck. Making a trail, he took first one nipple, then the other, into his mouth. He laved them, slapping his tongue against them until she gasped out her renewed pleasure. With a sudden urgency, he dragged his tongue over cushy breast, quivering ribs, down across sweet-salty flesh. When he reached her core, he inhaled her fragrance, a potent mixture of her creamy arousal and clean, floral soap.

He rained flutter-soft kisses over her hip, her inner thighs, that intriguing spot where leg met groin. She sucked in a breath and stabbed her hands into his hair. As he neared her swollen jewel, she bucked up and shoved his head down so that he had no choice but to cover his mouth over her sex. His first taste of her fed a thirst, yet he couldn't get enough. Sweet and potent as wine, he drank of her, intoxicating his senses with her flavor. The satiny feel of her clit against his tongue, and the moans each flicker elicited from her, were nearly enough to bring him to orgasm. Her female lips were soft and damp, parting like the petals of a tulip reaching for the sun. The heat of his tongue branded her as his woman, and to further seal that thought, he rammed two fingers into her sticky canal.

"Oh, shit! Ah…Grady…" her voice trailed off. The muscles of her passage convulsed around his fingers. With each jerk of her body, he finger-fucked her harder, drawing out her release.

When she collapsed against the bed, he crawled up her body, stealthy and sure. And he entered her flooded cunt with a guttural sigh. It didn't take long. After that show with the mannequins, then slipping inside her, only to draw it out longer and give her the ol' Aussie kiss, it didn't take long. He stiffened above her, his hands planted beside her head, his arms straight and taut. In seconds, he spilled his elfin seed into her, groaning when it gushed out around his penis, mixed with the overabundance of her own juices.

"That was," she panted, "*the* most fabulous sex I've ever had."

He grinned down at her. "Really? Even more than the mannequins?"

"Even more than the mannequins."

He withdrew and collapsed next to her.

"Is it hot in here to you?" she asked, fanning her face.

"No," he said sarcastically, throwing an arm over his eyes and snorting. "'Tis as cold as the ice I put in your bath, love. Of course 'tis hot. We just had an all-out marathon!" And would he ever get his breath back again? he wondered with a silent chuckle.

A sharp pain stabbed his side as she rammed her elbow into his ribs. "I'm serious."

"Well, don't get your knickers in a twist." He rubbed his side and glanced over at her. Just then, the cloud that had been hovering over the moon, floated away. Mischa was bathed in its soft, silvery glow.

He shot up at the sight that met his stare, his heart bursting in his chest. "Mischa, are you feeling ill again?"

She sighed and rubbed her temples. "Yeah. My head is suddenly pounding again, I feel like I've been tossed in a furnace—" she began scratching her body frantically, her eyes flaring with panic "—and I'm itching all over, all of a sudden."

He leapt to the bedside and towered over her. "That does it. I'm taking you to Ireland."

"To Ireland? Why Ireland?" But before he could answer, she cut in. "Grady?"

"Yes, Mischa, love, what is it?" He could hear his pulse pounding through the alarm in his voice. The splotchy, bright blue rash that covered her body made him choke on his bitter fear. *Oh, Leprechaun King, please help me!*

She set a hand on her forehead. "I…I feel like I'm going to—to pass out again."

"Mischa!"

Her hand flopped to the bed, the fingers curled in weakness. Beads of sweat formed on her blotchy skin, sparkles of impending death in the moonlight. And he watched, horrified, as her eyelids fluttered shut and her chest no longer rose and fell with her sweet breath.

Chapter Five

Grady paced back and forth through the meadow. At the base of his rainbow, he wore a long, deep rut into the fertile ground. He didn't notice the way the dew glistened diamond-like upon the shamrocks and spears of tall grass. Nor did he care that the sun finally bathed the ancient trees edging the pasture. The colorful ribbon rejoiced in the end of a long rain, arching breathtakingly through the cloudless, blue sky. But he cared not. Even the fragrance of wildflowers, and the sharp aroma of sea beyond the cliffs wafting in upon the cool breeze, did not jar his senses. All he could feel was the heaviness of his heart, the fear choking him in thick, sharp spurts around his neck.

He stopped again and stared across the field at his little thatched cottage that overlooked the Celtic Sea. She was there inside, abed and breathing again—thank the King—but remained unconscious, that frightening blue rash still splotching her milky skin. The virus, no matter how many spells he'd cast, would not leave her comatose body. He'd sent for Fahy, his one trusted little leprechaun friend, to watch over her so he could get this matter arighted.

Still, anxious blood pounded through his veins. He could not keep his eyes from the home, praying Fahy did not call to him, did not come racing across the countryside with tragic news of her death.

He clenched his jaw and his fists simultaneously. "If I ever get me hands on that sorry son of a bitch," he growled, thinking of the mortal who'd set Mischa's whole future onto a different path.

It was, he thought, all that greedy bastard's fault. But he halted his pacing and stared up at the rainbow. A little voice nagged at him. No. He couldn't completely blame the mortal, really. If Grady had been more careful while guarding his gold…if he hadn't been so miserly and underhanded himself over his own gold and riches, Mischa might be safe this very moment. He couldn't help but feel at least partially responsible, even though it had always been the leprechaun way to deceive mortals. For centuries following a blundering spell of one of Grady's forefathers, mortals had been allowed to gain fortune from a leprechaun's bountiful treasure in one way alone. If a leprechaun elf is caught by a mortal, his only choice is to offer great wealth if set free, else he be turned into a mortal himself and lose all that he owns.

In December, Grady had been here at this very spot rejoicing at his riches he guarded. His rainbow had appeared following a most lengthy, unseasonable period of rains. Giddy and careless, he'd not noticed the tall, redheaded man who'd crept upon him from behind and jammed a gunnysack over his head.

"Ah-ha! Caught ye, leprechaun!" he'd bellowed with wicked glee, his strong arms holding Grady immobile inside the musty bag.

Just the thought of it sent Grady's blood pressure to the top of the rainbow. He'd fought, he'd kicked, he'd done all he could, but the fact was, there was no fighting the spell. He'd been caught, and there was no way about it but to bargain with the mortal.

He still remembered the sound of the man's voice, thick with a slangy lilt, deep and gravelly. His hair the shade of burnt oranges, his body round and massive, he'd stared back at him with eyes as gold as the coins in Grady's black pot. They'd twinkled with delighted mischief and triumphant merriment. It riled him even now, even knowing he'd never have met Mischa if it hadn't been for the bloke's fierce malarkey. For if Grady hadn't been so careless, she would be well and pulling those toy orders from stock right now to be shipped to her beloved customers.

And she'd never have known a mutant leprechaun's love, one Grady O'Donovan.

He hadn't wanted to give up a single coin of his riches to a mortal, had never been in this predicament in all his centuries of life. The thought had riled him and had him bargaining in a way no other leprechaun in history had done before.

He remembered it oh-so well, as if it had been only yesterday. "Aye, ye want a piece of me riches, Toad—em, I mean Tad—MacPhain. I can give ye that, that I can, but how would ye like to double your riches?"

At the greedy craze that entered the man's eyes, Grady drew out a brown leather pouch from his green suit jacket. From it, he slid out a sparkling gold coin, balancing it and rolling it across the backs of each finger, enticing the mortal.

"Ah, that there coin is no silver shilling, that 'tis not," the man said, drool dribbling from the corners of his mouth. He wore a torn blue, plaid shirt with suspenders, worn trousers and a patched-up, thin jacket. His brown boots revealed one jiggling big toe through a ragged hole. Faint, white clouds of his breath puffed out as he panted in greediness. And Grady could smell the stench of him from several feet away. *Aye, the man would take all he could get, and I will get me riches back.*

"That 'tis, me poor, big bloke." He tossed the coin up in the air, watching with delight as the brown eyes followed its ascent, then its descent into Grady's palm. He slipped it into his pocket. The man wiggled his fingers, as if he itched to dive for it. "Now, ye care to make that bargain, sir?"

"Oh, that I do." Tad grinned, revealing surprisingly clean, straight, white teeth.

Grady clasped his hands behind the small of his back and paced. "This is how it goes. Ye let me go, I give ye tirty-tree gold coins, enough, ye see, to get ye some new clothes, a roof over your head, and a delicious pint o' the Dark Stuff."

At mention of a pint of Guinness, the mortal's eyes twinkled.

"I've a fierce throat on me—and a mouth, come ta think of it, boyo, ta be sure." He licked his pink lips and rubbed his round belly, indicating hunger and thirst.

Grady had held up a single finger and smiled slyly. "But…I can grant ye one wish in lieu of the coins. When 'tis complete, ye'll have your pint, shelter and clean clothes—but not the tirty-tree coins ye'd otherwise have gotten." *But if I'm unable to grant the wish for* any *reason at all, ye'll forfeit your wish and be left empty-handed.*

He chuckled to himself, knowing it was the nature of these types of relationships for the leprechaun to do all he could to fool the mortal, even by using omission. But Grady also knew that he must be clever, careful, and win this battle at all costs. If Tad decided to pass on the coins and the wish, Grady would forfeit his immortality and die in time as a mortal man. What mortals did not know is that by refusing the riches, they could use their captured leprechaun prey as one might a chimp in a circus, and gain even more riches in the future.

The man gasped. He blundered and mumbled his surprise. "Ye mean it, lad? Any wish?"

"With every ounce of me Irish, leprechaun's blood, ye can count on it."

"Well…" The man stumbled back and leaned against a smooth, gray boulder. "Well, there is one thing in this world I'd like ta see done."

Grady rocked back onto his heels, up onto his toes, back again. "And what, may I ask, would that be, Tad MacPhain?"

The man's eyes lowered to stare at the dead, brown grass at his feet. "Me daughter. I'd like ta see her wed *happily* and in love." He glanced up sharply and snared Grady with a steady stare. "Ta ye."

"Pardon? Did ye say to me?"

Tad nodded. "That I did, boyo."

Grady had studied the man, not caring where the idea had come from or who this daughter was. It was plain to see a leprechaun was forbidden to marry a mortal, to love her and make her happy, above all else! The only way one would be allowed such a farfetched thing was to give up immortality and become a mortal.

Grady shivered at the thought.

No. That wouldn't be happening. And the sorry bloke hadn't a clue that it would not work. Therefore, the spell of him being caught by a mortal man would be broken due to Grady's natural inability to completely grant the wish. By the laws of the Leprechaun King, he had to make a try of it, that he was aware of, but it wouldn't go anywhere near marriage—or love, to be certain.

He grinned. But he wasn't required to reveal any of those truths.

"Ah, 'tis a bleedin' deadly idea, that 'tis!" he laughed, the sound of it carrying through the snarled oaks, across to the sea. "Marry your daughter, ye say?"

Tad chuckled along with him. "Aye."

"Your wish, Mr. MacPhain," he could now clearly remember saying, "is hereby granted—if 'tis in me power."

Grady continued to pace now, drawing himself back to this day of reckoning. He scanned the line of woods, eager for the sight of Tad to emerge.

No, he hadn't counted on falling in love with Tad's long-lost daughter, Mischa Roxbury. Apparently, he'd learned from Fahy's recent inquiry of the old man, Tad had had a torrid affair with Mischa's mother over a score of years ago. She'd begun to breed, and Tad had promptly abandoned mother and child. Her mother had returned to the States with babe in arms, raised her daughter alone, and had never seen Tad again. And apparently, Grady thought with a snarl, Tad had felt guilty and had been willing to give up thirty-three golden coins just to see his daughter happy and married.

Gallant, to be sure, but downright stupid.

A movement caught his eye, a streak of burnt-red hair, a round figure. Tad materialized from behind a towering maple. And something about the way he strode arrogantly toward Grady, the richness of the fine clothes he wore, and the bevy of an elite assemblage of tiny, blue-clad elves at his back, sent Grady's pulse into a guarded rhythm.

Tad marched up to him and planted his feet so that his toes nearly touched Grady's. His eyes blazed with fury, like the flames of the very candles that sat at Mischa's bedside this very moment. He caught a whiff of regal cologne, and wondered how this man had come upon his riches before the wish was even complete.

Grady stepped back. "Do no' stand so close to a leprechaun, I warn ye."

"What spell did ye use on her?" Tad demanded, his voice booming, echoing across the meadow.

Something was not quite right here. Grady knew Tad had been informed of his daughter's dire situation by Aichlin, another of Grady's trusted leprechaun friends. But how did he know there'd been a spell used on Mischa? A mortal wouldn't know such workings of a leprechaun.

A mortal wouldn't, but…

Grady stiffened. He stepped closer to Tad so that their eyes were level. He looked deep inside them, conjuring up his powers to read the man's mind. But he ran into a painful wall. If he hadn't been prepared, he thought, alarmed, it would have knocked him straightaways onto his arse.

"Who are ye?"

Tad kept his eyes on Grady's, but he lifted his velvet-clad arms from his sides. The royal blue suit he wore strained across his massive body as he did so, nearly popping the solid-gold buttons from his belly.

At the enormous power that choked him, Grady stumbled back, indeed falling upon his arse. Green spikes of light shot from Tad's fingertips like javelins.

"I am the Leprechaun King, Grady O'Donovan." His voice boomed, rumbling like thunder, making the buds on the trees tremble, the limbs dip. And it sounded much more educated than the original Tad who'd "captured" him. "And ye have angered me to no end!"

The Leprechaun King? And if he was really Mischa's father, did that mean…?

Grady could only stare up at the man who'd months ago come to him as a greedy bum. His own anger began to simmer and rise to a boil. He'd been tricked!

"Aye, and chock full o' lies, that ye are." Grady hauled himself up and brushed off his smarting rear. "Ye may be the king, I'll give ye that, but ye deceived me, a tiny thing, I might add, that is against your own leprechaun-to-leprechaun laws. Scamming a fellow elf is punishable by immortal-strippin', that bein' your own law…*Your Royal Sir*."

The king flinched and crossed his arms over his barrel chest. His eyes suddenly danced with merriment. "Ye've got a lot o' nerve, that ye do, boyo. Hmm, but a good representative ye'd be for the ol' Fighting Irish."

Grady jammed his hands on his hips. "Nerve or no', your daughter lies on her deathbed. And I, for one, can no' bear to see her slip from me life. I do no' know what this is all about, your Royal Highness, but I'd like to know…what are ye goin' to do about savin' your daughter's life?"

Tad crossed to the base of Grady's rainbow. He glanced up, and Grady could swear he saw the prism of colors dull in Tad's eyes.

There was a long, heavy sigh. "Grady O'Donovan, I've tested ye, that I have. But only for a good cause, for all the leprechauns that roam the Emerald Isle."

"Tested me? For what, may I ask?"

Tad turned and wiggled his rear up onto Grady's black pot of gold. The coins were so in abundance, Tad—or rather, the king—could sit atop them and dangle his legs over the edge.

Finally, when he'd settled in comfortably, he planted an elbow on one knee and his chin on a fist. "I'm tired, son. So weary. 'Tis time for me to pass on the crown to ye." With those words, a shimmering gold crown appeared on his fiery head, and rubies, diamonds, sapphires and emeralds winked by the rays of the sun.

"What?"

"Ye've inherited the throne, Grady. For a time now, I've been searchin' for a worthy leprechaun, someone to love and care for me Mischa. Only the one who can prove his worth to me, to me beloved daughter, would be allowed to carry on me royalship."

"Bah! Away with ye." Grady whirled, crossed to the edge of the meadow, turned back. This couldn't be happening, he thought, stunned. There was only one Leprechaun King, and never a successor.

And especially not Grady O'Donovan, giant mutant leprechaun.

"Nay, ye can believe it. Ye *will* believe it. I command it of ye."

"So ye tricked me—"

The king interrupted with a cluck. "Tested ye," he corrected.

"Tested me," Grady went on, "so that ye could see if I'd fall for your daughter. A daughter, I might add, that ye abandoned all those years ago."

He threw up a hand and sent balls of fire zinging across the meadow at Grady. Grady ducked and dodged each and every one. And his anger came back full force.

"What, ye do no' have any words to add to that accusation? Just toss your arrogant powers about?"

"Nay! Except to say I loved her enough to let her go. I fell in love with her mortal mother, but had a duty as the king to no' give up me immortality. Mischa's mother wanted me all, or nothing. Nothing was the only way...at the time. C'mere, lad, do ye hear me? If I could change it, if I could turn back the clock, I would. Not even me own magical powers can rightly do such a deed. But once me young, Irish, selfish, pigheaded mind had been made up, the spell of sending her away could no' be reversed per the laws. I've lived me life watchin' over Mischa and her mother with me magical powers, searchin' for a leprechaun in me kingdom competent and carin' enough to love me own flesh and blood, me own daughter I cast out."

Tears glittered in the king's eyes. Grady's heart stopped. Never had he heard of the king crying or having any emotion at all. This was a time to mark in history, and yet Grady knew how it had come to be. Mischa. Special, loving, quirky and beautiful. Her magnetic personality stirred things in man, and even immortals, that were next to impossible.

"And ye chose me?" His own voice sounded weak, disbelieving.

"Aye." The king leapt from the treasure pot and glided to Grady, his buckled boots barely skimming the ground. He was a huge man, apparently a rare mutant leprechaun as was Grady, yet he still emitted compassion, a softness rare in a leprechaun.

"I was no' sure until your definite love for her was transmitted to me. I let a love go once, Grady O'Donovan of the Emerald Isle, that I did. But believe an old, tired king. Do no' do the same, lad, or ye'll find yourself regrettin' it to the ends of eternity."

He stopped, snared Grady with a fiery stare. "Now, I need to know one thing." He set his hands on Grady's shoulders and the warmth and power moved into him.

"Ask away."

"What spell did ye choose to use on her?"

He paused for a bit, but then replied, "The virus-spell number seven-seven-seven…via the Internet."

The king gasped. His eyes widened to round nuggets of terror before he turned his back on Grady. "Just as I feared," he choked out.

"What? What does it mean?" Grady gripped the huge, hard biceps and spun the king around to face him.

"Virus-spell number seven-seven-seven," he cried, tears streaming down his round face, "is the only one in the entire holy Leprechaun Book that will cause deadly illness upon a being—if accidentally cast upon one with even a single drop of elf blood. And Mischa is half-elf."

* * * * *

The stucco cottage with the thatched roof overlooked the Celtic Sea. At one side of the bungalow, there was the thick spread of forest. Through the trees, deep into the darkening space where elfin creatures prowled and spirits ruled, distant voices could be heard. Chants and cries echoed and mingled with the far-off hoot of an owl. Further still inland, at the center of a clearing in the forest, there was a small black cauldron swung over a blazing fire. It simmered and steamed, leaving an odd, pungent odor in the air. And every now and then, a chilly, coastal breeze would blast through the trees into the tiny clearing and send the flames into a frenzied dance.

Within the forest clearing, Mischa hovered above her body. Confused, she saw that it lay upon a long, high, flat stone near the fire. Her eyes were closed, Sleeping Beauty-like, as if she slumbered on into eternity. She reached down and caressed her own cheek, surprised but not alarmed to find it cool and smooth as ice. Her face, she thought as she continued to float in her current out-of-body state, seemed rather pasty. If not for the splotches, marbly and blue, she'd have compared it to a ghost. In contrast to her skin tone, her hair appeared rich and auburn by the light of the fire. It glittered and gleamed, the thick tresses spread out under her head in the shape of a fan. She noted with mild interest, the white, gauzy gown she wore. It clung to her body revealing every curve and plane. The elongated sleeves, draping over the edge of the altar, were wide and bell-like, as an angel might wear. Her hands, pale and rash-ridden like her face, were clasped together over her abdomen, while her feet peeped bare from the ankle-length hem of the gown.

Her eyes moved to her chest. A heavy silver chain lay around her neck, and an amulet as large as the pit of a peach nestled in the valley of her cleavage. Silver too, it glimmered by the firelight, and a huge, shamrock-shaped emerald adorned its surface.

Removing her gaze from the tantalizing jewel, she observed one final thing. Her chest did not rise and fall. Frosty-white breath did not stir beneath her nostrils. She was dead.

Suddenly distracted, she rotated so that she could see where the sudden escalation of chants had come from. Across the forest floor, a circle of stones had been laid. The sun had just dropped behind the horizon, and in its place, moonlight speared into the circle, flooding the misty, see-through occupants in glowing, silver light. There were four of them in attendance, two female, two male. They danced and hummed near a great white willow tree, throwing their arms up, reaching for the moon. Energy crackled around them, and jagged streaks of gold struck the rocks, as if to hold them in place.

Her eyes moved panoramically, and she noted the hundreds of green-garbed elves perched in the limbs of oak, ash and hawthorn trees, leaning against tree trunks, sitting cross-legged on the damp earth. All were tiny, maybe two to three feet in height, and most sported mops of carrot-top hair. Twinkling eyes of blue and green were the norm, though occasionally, an amber-eyed imp stared in awe at the rituals. Their features were sharp and pixie-like, their clothes of green velvet. But there, off to the right, was a band of blue-clad leprechauns surrounding a large, rotund man with deep, fiery hair. He commanded respect, love and power merely by the way he held his head high under the jeweled crown, and by the way he wore his clothing, rich and elegant.

And next to him stood Grady.

The sight of him, tall and proud in the forest, his midnight hair loose and billowing about his shoulders and back, his eyes ablaze with something fierce and determined, was like jarring her from a deep, dead sleep. Though varying only slightly in colors and style, he wore a costume similar to the one she'd first seen him in. Her eyes scanned him hungrily, noting the rippled muscles beneath the fabric, the command and strength he emitted, yet his handsome face was drawn in worry. She longed to press her lips to his, to wrap her arms and legs around that hard body and never let go.

Something…what was it? Something joyous and warm filled her blood. Fire hotter than that blazing below the cauldron, scorched her loins and brought her to a delicious awareness. Then it hit her.

I'm in love with him.

She felt the sudden sensation of her heart leaping into action. Mischa glanced sharply to her body, watching in awe as her chest began to rise, her head to shift and roll when she moaned.

And there was an excruciating *pop*. She slammed into herself, crying out when her soul crashed into bone and flesh before settling into place.

Inhaling sharply, she caught the mixed odors of garlic, lavender and some others that were indefinable, almost putrid. God, would her headache ever go away? She lifted a trembling hand and rubbed one temple. A pillow, she thought, annoyed. It would have helped to have had a pillow instead of the frickin' rock against her head. She smacked her dry lips together. Cottonmouth. Shit, was she in the midst of a full-blown hangover?

"She stirs!" Grady gasped. Mischa's gaze darted to him. Spears of white-hot pain shot behind her eyes, stilling her movement.

"No!" The large man gripped Grady's elbow and held him in place. "Ye can no' go to her while the ritual is in full force. Ye'll risk losing her. Let Fahy see to her."

Grady stopped in mid-stride and his eyes found hers. He mouthed her name, and she thought all of the world could just go away forever. She started to rise slowly, carefully, but relaxed in exhaustion against the cold stone at the sound of the voice.

"Do no' get up, me queen." The munchkin voice was male, but it held a little-girl quality. She rolled her head slowly to her left. A tiny leprechaun stood on a stone at her side. He wore the miniature green suit, a black felt hat with a gold buckle, and his eyes were as cool blue as the sea.

"Queen?" She chuckled huskily and raised her head again, her throat dry as sandpaper. "Hmm, well. And who are you?"

"Fahy, that I am. I've been watchin' over ye for days now. And I do no' wish ta anger our Celtic cousins, here, the gods and goddesses who've come along ta save ye."

"Save me?"

"Aye, ye died—and they've been kind enough ta travel here ta use their herbs and magic and whatnot, ta save ye."

Died. Mischa relaxed against the slab, despite the pain it caused to set her aching head back on the rock. "What…what's going on here, little guy. I…I'm kinda confused, scared."

"Grady O'Donovan cast the virus-spell number seven-seven-seven upon ye. Normally, 'twouldn't harm a flea, but ye…well, ye've got a tad more than just a wee bit of leprechaun blood in ye, and—"

"*What?*"

"Do no' fear. 'Tis all good. Ye're the long-coveted blood daughter o' our blessed Leprechaun King, Tad MacPhain, that ye are, lass." His eyes flitted to the tall, round man, and utter respect reflected there in his expression.

She followed his gaze, studying the man closer. His eyes…they were so like hers. And though his hair was a brighter shade of red, it was the same texture, the same thickness as hers. He'd obviously imbibed too much on food and spirits over the years, but beneath all the cushy flesh, she could see a familiar man.

"He's—my father? My *real* father?"

"Aye."

"It can't be." She stared in awe at the great man with the crown. Her father?

"Oh, 'tis, lass, 'tis verily the truth."

The truth. Well, she'd make that determination herself, in her own time. "But he's too big to be a leprechaun."

"He's a mutant, just as yer Grady is. Very rare, but 'tis a mutation that arises every century or so in our kind."

"Oh." A mutant. Well, thank the powers of genetic mishaps, she thought as the beautiful image of Grady floated through her mind. "And the large man there, the one you call my father…he's the Leprechaun *King*?"

"Well, ye see, 'tis accurate for the moment, but soon, our loyal Grady will be inheritin' the crown and the leprechaun throne."

Mischa sat bolt upright and winced. Nausea plowed through her stomach, while an excruciating, sharp pain sliced up her spine to her skull. Fahy pressed her back down with a small, warm, gentle hand. She caught the brief scent of clover but it slowly dissipated.

"Grady? He'll be the…?" Her voice sounded weak, almost deathly as it echoed in the forest.

The little man grinned impishly. "Leprechaun King."

"Oh, Lord." She stared up at the silhouette of gnarled limbs ripe with fresh spring buds against the moon-bathed sky. How could she love a king, and a leprechaun king, at that? "Am I still having that hallucination?"

"Nay, Mischa. Nay. Ye've no' been hallucinatin', darlin'. 'Tis all real. Now, ye've got ta lie back, miss, and allow the gods ta do their thing afore ye can rise again. Do ye understand?"

"Got it," she said tiredly. Exhaustion ached in her bones, every cell and muscle. "But, may I ask…? No, I don't think you need to tell me. I'm in Ireland, aren't I?"

Fahy nodded, but did not elaborate. He climbed down from the stone step and stood almost soldier-like at her side watching the performance.

Ireland. She was in Ireland with her real father and Grady, the man—the leprechaun—she loved. Somehow, the truth of it settled into her soul. In wonder, she slowly rolled her head to the side and studied the rituals.

The chants suddenly increased in volume and voracity. The mantra carried to her across the clearing. She watched, entranced almost magically, as the four spirits linked hands and punched them into the sky.

The small, flaxen-haired woman spoke then, her voice far more powerful than her tiny body reflected. She was adorned in lavender silk, and Mischa thought she'd never seen a more beautiful woman. The winds tore at her gown and at her long, thigh-length hair. But the woman ignored it, intent on her powers and purpose here.

"I am Aine, Goddess of healing and protection! Hear my plea, oh powerful beings, save the queen, the illness be done! I call upon you water, fire, air, earth. Align thy elements with Venus and Saturn; we summon our Mars, Mercury, and moon of the Earth, and pray to the sun of the Universe."

The foursome, shifted, hummed, threw their heads back in unison, and stared at the moon through the jagged limbs.

Aine went on, her blue eyes sending prisms of light to the center of the circle. "I offer up, on this dark and mystical night, bark of the black elder tree to purge the ailment bite."

"I, Diancecht, call up the same remedy," sang the tall man at Aine's right. His golden, long hair whipped in the wind, his green eyes boring beams of light to meet with Aine's. "Bring forth the bark of the black elder tree!"

Brown, jagged bark appeared in the circle, hovering several feet above the ground. Aine and Diancecht jerked their heads and the bark arced above them and landed in the boiling pot. It sizzled and bubbled. Steam and crackles of blue light shot upward from the green liquid surface.

"The herb of mugwort, nettle, and bulb of garlic, for protection and healing, to rid of the sick." Again, the items materialized within the circle. Aine sent them zipping into the pot. As each ingredient was added, clouds moved in, thunder rumbled in the far-off distance. Mischa could smell the fragrance of rain, could feel the crackle of energy as it filled the atmosphere. Pain and discomfort raged in her system, warring with her need to be with Grady, to feel his arms around her.

"A pot of freshly cut nettles beneath the sickbed, to aid in a speedy recovery, to prevent of the dead." Her voice rose, reverberating against tree and sky. She jerked her head, and that very item appeared and traveled toward Mischa. The cluster of small greenish flowers, set within a copper urn, settled below the slab she lay on.

"I am Bel, hear my plea," said the stocky man with midnight hair. His eyes of amber bore into the ring, its mighty beams of energy meeting with Aine's and Diancecht's. "Purify the coming queen with the tea. We've blue balm and goat's rue and lavender, too, white willow bark and cowslip, all yet to do." Flowers and herbs and bark appeared. And just as Mischa thought they would, they traveled from the gods' circle of stones, across the forest, to the pot. One by one, they plopped into the brew, and the liquid hissed in greedy acceptance. Thunder boomed and seemed to part the black sky with its anger.

"'Tis Scatha, I doth speak, oh wise ones, our fathers, our sons." The woman who had yet to speak, moaned, her wavy, copper hair billowing about her. Her almond-shaped eyes were soft and blue-green like the waters of a tropical sea. "Dizziness, fainting, migraines and fever—rid her all, rash and nausea, please leave her!"

Mischa's muscles twitched, first her fingers, her toes, then her arms and legs. She was cold, so cold. And her body began to shiver violently.

"In the cauldron we offer all of these," the four recited. Their combined voices became an intonation of authority, supremacy and strength. "Protection and healing and immortal keys!" Lightning crackled above, and with it, a smattering of large raindrops fell. The scent of sharp ozone and raw, natural herbs carried upon the gusty winds. A pleasant pitter-patter of rain against leaves, limb and ground, sounded. Elves took cover, snapping their fingers and bringing into existence small tents over their heads.

The cold droplets soaked Mischa's gown, and she looked down in horror to see the fabric slowly disappearing, as if it were made of wetted tissue paper. Now naked upon the stone, she trembled, and couldn't help but shriek when a straight bolt of lightning, like a majestic silver sword, struck her in the chest. Pain and bliss at once assailed her. She arced up on the table, smelling the acrid scent of burning flesh and hair.

"Fahy…" she called out, but he did not answer. Her body had crashed back to the slab and been immobilized. All she could do was look straight up into the flickering sky, black to white, white to black.

Was she dead?

The silent question sent her into a panic, but all too soon, blackness engulfed her. One of the last things she remembered was the sound of her own scream carrying out across the forest to the cliffs and the wild surf below.

The other was the agonizing cry of her name as it was wrenched painfully from Grady's throat.

Chapter Six

Grady took flight. White puffs of dragon-like mist shot from his mouth and nostrils. But a tight hand on his arm halted his steps. He turned to see the pain in Tad's eyes, yet determination won out.

"Ye must let them finish, Grady. Ye must, for 'tis imperative to riddin' her of the spell and also of the portion of her that is mortal. Else ye will no' be able to live on with her into eternity, as your queen."

"She cries in agony. Her body burns, damn it!" He could feel his pulse choking him, mocking him. The odor of burning hair and flesh churned in his gut.

"She will heal. What do you think all the healin' and protection chants of our cousin gods and goddesses were all about, son?"

Grady clenched his jaw and tears stung his eyes. Many herbs and substances had been used in their ceremony, but still he could not see how Mischa could heal. He'd stood by long enough watching, waiting, hoping. It was time to end this madness.

But even as Tad continued to hold him in place, he watched as Aine, Bel, Diancecht and Scatha stepped from the circle. Diancecht picked up the boiling cauldron, heedless of its scorching temperature, and, with the other three in attendance, he moved to Mischa's side. She lay unconscious, her body a brown, smoking, charred heap. Grady's stomach quivered, his heart ceased beating. There was a metallic taste in his mouth that ate away at the confidence he normally had in his spirit-cousins' powers.

And when the four lifted the pot in unison and dumped it over Mischa, Grady moaned, "*No*!" and he wrenched his arm from Tad's hold.

Within a split second, he was across the clearing shoving aside the gods, tearing his way to Mischa. There was the sickening sound of sizzling flesh. And somewhere in the lunacy of it, he could swear he heard her calling to him.

"She must bathe in it." Aine put out an arm, halting Grady's movement. It was as if he'd hit an iron wall.

"Bathe?" he shrieked. "You burn her alive! And you do no' understand. I love her. I want her to be with me, always. You can no' do this to her!"

Diancecht's olive-green eyes soaked Grady with kindness. "Yes. That is *why* we do this to her. Your kingdom of leprechauns will not be complete without her."

"Patience," Scatha said, and she placed a cool hand upon his cheek. Immediately, he relaxed, every muscle in his body going lax. And when he glanced back at the bubbling, steaming mess that had once been Mischa, he sucked in a sharp breath.

The rain stopped, the winds died. Clouds slithered away and the sky filled with diamonds of stars against inky black. There was the pleasing, faint scent of lavender mixed with the dewy aftermath of rain. The chill in the air warmed a measure, and collective sighs sounded from the many leprechauns in attendance. And the gods had disappeared, leaving behind only the circle of stones and a blackened ground in its center.

Grady swayed, wondering if he needed a bit of herbs for his own dizziness.

"Mischa!"

"Grady O'Donovan," she said with a note of scolding. Her body had returned intact—and naked—the gods' mixture gone. "If you *ever* cast another spell on me again, I swear, I'll use my antivirus software this time."

The relieved, bubbly laughter that escaped his lips, traveled across the woods, and a sudden uproar of chatter and cheering of leprechauns filled the air.

"Mischa, oh, love…" He dragged her into his arms. She turned upon the stone bed and wrapped her arms around his neck. The heat of her warmed him like a long drought of hot tea on a chilly winter's night. "Ye're back. Ye're back." And he couldn't keep his hands from her soft body. He raced them up her spine, over her shoulders to her full, nipple-hardened breasts, around and down to the cool cheeks of her rear.

Cool. She no longer raged with fever. Her skin was back to its smooth, creamy color, void of the ugly blue rash.

"Ye're no' dizzy, or plagued with migraines or nausea or itching?" He skimmed his hands over her hair and cupped her jaw. Forcing her eyes to his, he examined every cell of her body.

"Nay," she mocked him with his own brogue. "I've never felt better, me dashing leprechaun."

He sighed. "Ah, thank the gods."

She glanced across the clearing, her gaze settling on Tad. "I'd like to meet him, you know? Weird, huh? To say you want to meet your own dad."

"No, 'tisn't strange. But…"

"But…?" Her eyes flitted back to Grady.

"Your formal introduction to your father will have to come later."

"Later? Why?"

"You'll see…"

She pressed a hand to her abdomen. "Oh, yes, but…"

Oh, blarney and hell, she *was* still ill! Alarm raked through his belly, sure and deep. "But what, Mischa? *What*?"

She curved her hand against his ear and whispered, "I'm naked in front of my own father and hundreds of elves. Can we go to the cottage? I've a sudden yen for your flute inside me, and I'd prefer to do it in private."

He inhaled and held it, his eyelids fluttering shut in relief. But soon, the thrill of her words and the huskiness in her voice sent a ripple of lust through his blood. He shuddered and dragged his lips over hers. She tasted of Ireland and the salty, Celtic Sea. And he knew that meant she was all his, completely immortal, safe, forever his love.

Against her mouth, he rasped, "Aye, and I've a sudden yen for me flute to blow in ye."

*****

Mischa clung to Grady as he threw out a sprinkle of twinkling dust. It winked by the light of the moon while the cloud carried them up and above the forest, across the lunar-bathed meadow, to the cottage by the sea. Where the side of her breast pressed into him, she could feel his heart beating strong, and the tempo of it blended with the increasing volume of the surf pounding against scattered rock below. There were the distant sounds of cowbells in the grazing fields afar, night birds singing, and the quiet left behind by a soft, misty rain.

Her eyes scanned the horizon in all directions around them. There, up ahead, she saw the shimmering, silver-streaked surface of the ocean. Behind and below were the roughened treetops of the forest, where little leprechauns prowled and stirred up mischief. Inland, over the rolling, emerald fields, a ribbon of water sliced through the land. The River Liffey? she wondered, and eagerness welled up in her to find out for sure, to learn and explore every inch of this glorious land of her heritage. And way off afar, purple mountains jutted up and stabbed the star-filled sky. She sighed. Majestic diversity. Ireland. Home.

And joy filled her soul.

They angled down and approached the cottage door. Grady set her on the cold stone step and reached for the knob.

"Are ye ready?"

"Oh, yes." She spread her arms and indicated her nudity. "Very, wouldn't you say?"

He chuckled and pushed through the door. Mischa followed, and a groan of pleasure escaped her lips as she entered the room. Immediately, heat, slow and cozy, embraced her from the crackling fire in the huge hearth. Scents of sugary berry tarts filled the kitchen, and mingling on the edges were the aromas of frying bacon and warm, buttery potatoes.

Her stomach growled. "Mm, I just remembered, I have a hunger for food, as well."

"Come." He offered her his hand and drew her to the wooden slab table. Long and low, it dominated the room. "Wait here," he ordered, and urged her to sit upon the cool surface. Gradually, the chill thawed against her bottom, and a slow gush of desire oozed onto the table when he disrobed before the fire.

"Ah, you're a hunky leprechaun." Her gaze devoured the smooth ripple of muscle, the dark power of him.

He smiled, his eyes twinkling with merriment. Crossing his wrists and rapping his palms together, music low and romantic filled the room. There was a harp, a fiddle, a tin whistle, and now and then, a bagpipe and flute, all composing Irish folk music. Its song filled her heart with the urge to go to him.

He sauntered to her, naked and proud. And wrapped his arms around her.

She leaned away from him just enough to snare him with a scolding stare. "Are you reading my mind again?"

"Aye, Mischa. I sometimes prefer it to talking aloud. I'm pleased," he said, stroking her back, "that ye feel as if Ireland is your home. That ye were cozy and welcome when ye stepped over me threshold."

Now, how could she deny that? It warmed her heart that she'd pleased him. Her legs opened and she dragged him against the edge of the table so that his cock pressed against her swollen pussy lips. Her clit throbbed and tingled deliciously. She moaned and pressed her lips to his, tasting remnants of his earlier fear and concern for her life.

"I love you, Grady."

He blinked. "Really? Ye do?"

She snorted and tapped a finger against his moist mouth. "As if you didn't already know. You had to have read my mind."

"Nay," he replied, shaking his head emphatically. "I purposely pre-blocked any feelings or thoughts of love that may have come about. I prefer to hear such sentiments when they're professed."

"Really?" His confession surprised her. At times, he could be a sly leprechaun, but it delighted her that he'd waited to hear the words from her mouth.

"Absolutely. Now, will ye dance with me?" He held out a hand and she took it without pause. "We must seal our engagement of Leprechaun King to his Queen."

It still floored her at the sound of it. Mischa Roxbury, a queen? She chuckled to herself. And a *leprechaun* queen, at that!

He drew her to the edge of the room and, together, they levitated upward near the wooden beams, floating as one in a merry dance of love. The music guided and moved. Her limbs were fluid, relaxed, all knowing, as if the rhythm, the tune, the choreography of the dance, flowed into her with great Irish knowledge.

She inhaled his musky, male scent, and pressed her cheek to his bare chest. Could her heart swell anymore?

"Mischa," he whispered, and he brushed a kiss at her temple.

"Mm-hm." Shivers of bliss danced up her backside as he caressed her from shoulders to buttocks.

"I love ye, too."

She stilled her movements.

"'Tis a scary, often rare thing for a leprechaun to say to anyone or anything. But I swear to ye, I love ye with all me immortal heart."

Their eyes met, gold to emerald. She pressed a hand to her chest, calming the flutter of her heart. Though he'd admitted it before, at a time when it'd seemed out of place and like a silly dream, it now filled her with joy, with a completeness she couldn't quite define. "Oh, Grady..."

The kiss, wet and urgent, spoke of love almost lost. Mischa sighed into it, draping her arms around his neck. God, how she just wanted him to take her, to overpower her, to completely ravish her!

He groaned and broke the kiss, but ground his erection into her abdomen. "I'll be makin' love to ye, that ye can be sure of. But let's no' be in such a blazing hurry, eh? First, we dine and toast our upcoming union."

Disappointment assailed her, but due to a rabid hunger for food, she allowed him to lower her to the floor. Her bare feet touched wood already heated by the hearth. She eyed the food, now miraculously spread out on the table and arranged upon an antique, white lace tablecloth. Knowledge of all things Irish continued to pour into her. There was steeped beef and cabbage with a side of mash, or creamy mashed potatoes. Next to that, bangers—sausages fried in a batter and more curvy and thick than a hot dog—filled a basket lined with a red-checkered napkin. She imagined her mouth around one of those juicy hunks of meat, and instantly, in the picture frames of her mind, it turned to Grady's cock, all salty, firm and tasty. She sighed, battling with two hungers, two needs.

But more food called to her. Her mouth watered at the sight of a steaming spread of fry. The collection of fried breakfast foods included eggs, rashers of bacon, mushrooms and tomatoes. Her belly rumbled in protest. Scones and biscuits—here in Ireland, more like a cookie to be eaten with tea—and many afters, or desserts, were arranged on a lovely china plate edged in soft, yellow roses.

"Care for a spot of red wine, love?" Grady asked, and poured her a serving in a glass of Waterford crystal.

She smiled warmly and took the cup, sipping of the sweet, tart wine. "Oh, yes, and a *huge* spot of all this food. Mm, it looks *so* good. If you only knew how hungry I am."

"Oh, I'm very aware of your hunger. And if ye'd hurry and finish eatin', we'll get on to satisfyin' another kind of hunger..."

Mischa giggled, loving the sound of that threat. She plucked up a fried mushroom and popped it into her mouth. Her eyes rolled back into her head, and a moan slid from her throat at the salty, sharp succulence of it. She snatched up a tomato and sucked it in, the hot crispiness crunching against her teeth before the juicy, sweet tomato burst in her mouth.

But she didn't stop there. Before she knew it, her hands were coated with crumbs, her chin covered in potatoes and flakes of tart crust. She couldn't shove it in fast enough. Her stomach continued to growl in protest, as if it did not detect the mouthfuls and ounces of food filling it.

Is this what death did to you? she wondered, amazed. Make you rabid with hunger?

Grady forced his hanging mouth shut. His eyes were as wide as the round, crispy cracker she shoved into her mouth. "Eh, sweetheart...I do have silverware, if ye'd care to keep your hands clean."

She laughed and picked up the glass from the table. Tipping her head back, she drained every drop of the wine. With a swipe of the back of her hand across her smeared mouth, she sighed and collapsed back into her chair.

And she'd be damned if she wasn't getting dizzy again.

"Grady..."

But she couldn't fight the exhaustion long enough to wait for his response. Blessed sleep claimed her.

*****

"Ye've got Irish mail!"

Mischa's head popped up. Jarred awake, she blinked at the sudden flood of light that assaulted her eyes. Squinting, she held up her hands.

"What? Who…? Who's there?"

There was no response. But now that her eyes had adjusted, she could see that the light was *sun*light streaming in from the high windows of her warehouse apartment. She glanced down at her arm lying across her deco kitchen table where her head had rested. It was asleep, damn it, and all red and wrinkly. She wiggled her fingers. Pinpricks of tickly coldness shot through her palm, up into her forearm and elbow. With a sudden sweep of her eyes, she took in her nudity. Looking down at herself, she saw that she sat buck-naked on one of her vinyl, flowered kitchen chairs. Her labia felt soft and moist, like a sponge squishing against plastic.

Her eyebrows dipped as she struggled to remember how she'd gotten here in her kitchen, stark nude and passed out. Damn, she must have really whooped it up solo-style last night.

Alone. The word tore at her defenses, ate away at her ego like acid. She didn't want to be alone anymore. Why, she didn't know, but it hit her train-wreck-style, bowling her over with its urgency.

Suddenly distracted—something vague yet powerful nagged at her—she gripped her stomach. "Shit, I feel like I ate a whole cow."

Her gaze flicked up, she blinked then widened her eyes with a gasp.

At the mention of eating, it all came flooding back to her. An E-mail, a virus-spell, a magic leprechaun, Grady, illness, death, love and Ireland.

"No." It tore from her throat, painful and raw. "No. Please tell me it wasn't a dream."

"Ye've got Irish mail!"

Mischa pushed from the table with a squall of metal scraping wood. She spun in her chair. And there it was, the screensaver with the mischievous little red-haired leprechaun and the beautiful rainbow.

Carefully, she rose and crossed to her desk, one slow step at a time. Her heart pounded with dread. *Please. Please let it be Grady.*

Lowering herself into the chair, she reached for the mouse and joggled it. The screensaver disappeared. She clicked on the mail icon and the inbox popped up on the screen. Swallowing a lump of fear, she scanned the mail. Her box was full of new orders. But there at the top was one piece of mail that read *Open me* in the subject line. Her gaze jerked to the sender column.

GradyODonovan@IrishMale.com! Her shriek of sheer joy echoed in the room.

"Grady," she sighed. Her heart raced as she clicked on the mail. The box flicked up. His written words were there, but his voice—ah, there was no lilt more lyrical!—filled the space in her apartment, caressing her ears, her thoughts, her heart.

"Me dearest Queen… The top o' the morning to ye, me lovely lass! I'd wager to say ye're a bit confused, eh? Well, 'tis sorry I am to play such a cruel joke on ye, but the mischievous leprechaun in me just could no' help it." He chuckled deep and long. *"Your dream was a wee bit bizarre, aye, ye may say 'twas. Oh, but Mischa, me love, 'twasn't a dream! And right at this very second, ye're lookin' about your precious home and business and sayin' to yourself, 'Impossible'. Ah, but never fear. Go now, to the window set high above your bed. Do no' ask questions or furrow that lovely brow of yours. Just go. Much love, Grady, the Leprechaun King."*

Stunned, she stood and turned. Her eyes rose to the window. She crossed to the bed and stepped up onto the mattress. But her body kept going, up, up, up. Up until she could look straight out the window—at Ireland!

"Mischa…" Grady's arms slid around her from behind. A slow fire ignited in her chest and traveled to her womb. She could smell him, the scent of wind and campfire. His heat warmed her backside.

"Grady?" Her voice sounded husky to her own ears, and there was a trace of uncertainty there that saddened her.

He kissed her neck sending currents of desire to her nipples. They hardened and tingled with delicious obedience. "Ye're still in Ireland, Mischa, still in the cottage. But I brought your business, your familiar surroundings here to ye. We're in the attic—I made it over for ye in duplication. Is that okay by ye, to work your Celtic Sins from here?"

She whirled and let out a long, low breath of approval. He was here! It was really him! And he was naked.

"Aye, I'm here," he replied to her thoughts. "And so are ye." By the light of the sun, his teeth glittered like smooth, white diamonds in the curve of his mouth.

"But…but I fell asleep… I—"

He tapped a finger to her nose. "Aye, ye were knackered. A normal response to all the herbs your body had to metabolize. Ah, and your illness drained ye, too."

But now she felt oh-so revived. Starved.

"I ate and I ate," she recalled, tracing a finger down his bare chest. He shivered, but she went on. "I was so hungry—in two different ways."

He grinned and she felt her heart flop over and sigh.

"And we danced and you promised me you'd feed my hungers. But you only fed one, as I recall…" She pressed her lips to his, wet and salty, and delighted in the growl that escaped his throat.

"And by Dublin, ye've got me livin' the life o' Reilly, that ye do!"

"Yep," she agreed, and closed her hand over his cock, already spongy-hard, almost where she needed it. He hissed, his eyes narrowed. "We're living so carefree, so hedonistic. Isn't it grand?"

"Oh, 'tis!" And he gathered her close, so close, she thought his shaft would spear her. "Now that we've that determined, what would me fiancée queen like to do next?"

She scanned the rows and shelves of sex toys below, the many contraptions set up in the center of the room, the mannequins, now stiff, inanimate objects.

"Hmm." She pursed her lips in mock indecision. "How about…the Shrink-Fuck?"

His eyes twinkled. "The Shrink-Fuck, eh? 'Tis a wee bit of bravery ye've got there, me love."

She lifted her chin. "I've never tried it before, but I think I'd enjoy it."

"Then come." He offered his hand and floated her down to the showroom area.

The machine was one of her best sellers in the outrageous, expensive category. It wasn't as if she sold dozens a day as she did the standard vibrator, but when she sold even one Shrink-Fuck a month, it was cause for monetary celebration. He led her to the contraption set up in the center of the room. It was long and capsule-like and had always reminded Mischa of a tanning bed. Grady lifted the top half by the outer handle, revealing the inner surfaces. Indented and shaped like a person's body inside, the shell was made of see-through, cushioned materials that would conform to the body, allowing no movement whatsoever. And there was an elongated hole on the upper section where breasts might align when closed, as well as one for the crotch area. Once the capsule was sealed, an outer layer could be lifted away for the dominant partner to explore the submissive mate as she or he is held captive by the soft plastic of the machine.

Mischa had examined it many times, wondering what it might be like to be closed inside it. She wasn't the least bit claustrophobic, but she supposed the fact that one's head was left out to rest on a cushion might soothe those who were.

Just looking at it made her wet. Being held hostage by Grady, unable to stop him from doing naughty things to her as she lay bound inside the contraption, it was a fantasy come true.

"Ready?" His brows arched, his eyes danced with devilment.

"Yes." It came out on a pant. Already, juices dribbled down her inner thighs. Her heart raced with anticipation, her mouth watered with carnal hunger.

She turned and sat on the edge, the soft plastic caressing her thighs. The scent of vinyl drifted up to her nostrils mixed with her female scent. Lying back, she settled herself within the indentation, her head resting upon the pillow outside the capsule.

Grady took one of her hands and placed it on the emergency lever within the space. "In case you panic, love. I do no' want to scare ye."

She looked up at him, naked and sleek, his manhood standing erect and hard. Her breath caught in her chest, not only at the breathtaking body or the look of endearing love in his eyes, but at the thoughtfulness and care the gesture had spoken of.

Her hand closed around the lever. "Thank you, but I don't think I'll be needing it."

He chuckled. "Spread your legs."

When she obeyed, he lowered the top down. Cool vinyl covered her front side. Grady stepped out of view and she heard a button click. Immediately, the machine whirred and a suction noise followed. The plastic closed around her, holding her immobile. Excitement snapped through her system.

Grady lifted the outer layer, exposing her shrink-wrapped body to his hungry gaze. "Mm, ye look delicious enough to devour, love, like a zippered sandwich."

She grinned, even as her pussy gushed with sticky cream. "Then shut up and devour me."

"Oh, I will, ye wanton nympho. Ye're gettin' it every which way I can think of, and ye're not goin' to be able to do a thing about it."

With that, he threw up a cloud of pink dust. Babbling something in the Gaelic tongue, he waved his hand toward her stock shelves. The cloud zipped to the section where the Lovebugs were shelved. G-strings with tiny clit stimulators attached, Lovebugs were the cheapest yet most explosive, unpredictable devices in her inventory. Unpredictable due to the fact that the remote was wireless—anyone could control it, not just the wearer of the vibrator.

Several boxes leaped from the shelf and tumbled toward them. "Three?"

"Aye, three. One for each delectable nipple and one for your sweet little knot." His voice sounded strained, almost evil, as if he'd turned into some mad scientist with a wacky theory he was about to test.

He waved his arms and whacked his wrists together. The boxes popped open. Three beetle-shaped little vibrators slid out, the g-strings dangling in midair.

"Now what?" she asked, her breathing ragged.

"Ye'll see." He snatched the remotes as they emerged from the boxes. And with a snap of his fingers and a smattering of new dust, the devices were in place, one in the standard position over her nub, the satin, elasticized band abrading between her lips and cheeks of her ass. The remaining two, she was delighted to see, were magically sealed over each of her nipples, the straps hanging down unused at the sides of her breasts. It wasn't long before the cool plastic surfaces all warmed against the heat of her skin.

"Good, huh?" Grady asked, climbing up on the surface of the contraption. He laid over her, dragging his body up and down over plastic, careful not to dislodge the Lovebugs set inside the access holes. His scent swirled into her soul, a cologne of manly restraint and animalistic need.

"Very. Now, would you please just—" she gasped when he reached up to flip a switch "—get on with it before I implode." He'd initiated only one of the devices, the one over her left breast. Tingles of cold-hot lust rippled from her rock-hard nipple to her pussy.

"Your every wish, me queen, is me every command." And he inserted his cock through the plastic hole and pushed aside the straps so that the tip met with her outer wetness.

God, how she longed to wrap her arms around him, to lift her legs and clamp them behind his hips! "Another one, please." The tone in her voice begged for relief, for more torture. She struggled to move her fingers, her toes, but there was no give, no mercy in the clever Shrink-Fuck.

He pushed into her an inch, the head of his cock dragging over moist lips and inner folds. She trembled, unable to do anything but groan. Her clit throbbed as milky cream gushed from her hole. And he flipped the second switch. The right nipple exploded with quivers of delicious fire. She moaned out her satisfaction.

Apparently, Grady began to feel just as needy as she. With a whoosh of his breath, he shoved his cock into her so that he completely penetrated her. Before she could groan her pleasure, he threw up a hand and the Lovebugs buzzed into full speed, jolting her with pure, raw voltage. Her areolas twitched and hardened against the violent vibrations.

"Ah!"

"That won't be all, so don't be goin' and comin' just yet, babe."

As he panted his own restraint, ramming himself inside her, he lifted his head and shouted, "Now!"

"Oh, my God!" she screamed. The clit Lovebug sprung into action. With her arms held at her sides and her legs pinioned apart, Grady stroked in and out of her madly. And three Lovebugs stung her, injecting their wicked venom through her system from every angle, every sensitive nerve.

"Ah, Mischa," he groaned through gritted teeth. His cock spasmed with the oncoming orgasm. "I want to spend an eternity pleasuring you like this."

"No complaints—oh, oh..." And rainbows of blissful color exploded around her.

Enmeshed in the cry of Grady's release, soft flutes began to play in the distance, and she opened her eyes as the rapture engulfed her. Even as the last ripples of the orgasm eased from her body, she saw the beauty around her. They were together on top of a glorious rainbow. Fields of shamrocks and woods surrounded the base of the prism, and leprechauns dotted the ground below, their little heads tipped back looking up at the arch. The aroma of wild flowers and sea filled her head, and just then, she looked afar to see powerful waves rolling in toward the craggy cliffs below. They crashed and ebbed, and birds cawed in anxious protest.

Looking down, she saw that, once again, she wore the white, bell-sleeved gown she'd worn during the ceremony with the Celtic gods and goddesses in the woods. And the amulet, its emerald shamrock center glistening in the sunlight, lay nestled between her breasts once again.

"'Tis okay, love. No need to be shocked. Though 'tis been many centuries since a king of the leprechauns has taken a queen, this is the normal way of it. 'Tis our wedding, sealed by our union following the dinner and dance of our engagement."

Stunned, overjoyed, she didn't know what to say. Dropping her gaze, she noted Grady was now dressed in regal blue velvet, the jeweled crown upon his dark head. Her hand closed over the queen's amulet, cool and tingly with energy that seemed to soak into her like a sponge.

"Your mortal genes have been eradicated," came a deep, familiar voice.

She turned, the misty colors surrounding her ankles, to see Tad approach. He was dressed down in the clothes of a pauper.

No longer did he wear the styles of a king, no longer did he carry the crown arrogantly upon his head.

"Eradicated?" she asked, alarmed.

"Aye," Grady offered. He drew her up against his side so that the two of them faced Tad. "In addition to saving your life, 'twas part of the gods' ceremony. Ye're still your mother's daughter, Mischa, do no' fret over that, but ye've been made wholly immortal, in order to carry on your duty as the Leprechaun Queen."

"Oh—whew!" She pressed a hand to her forehead. "This is all happening so fast."

"Daughter."

At the word, her eyes snapped up to capture Tad's saddened gaze. So like her own, his eyes glittered as gold might in a leprechaun's treasure chest. He pressed a hand to her cheek, warm and fatherly.

"I've come to give ye to this man in marriage, to tell ye how very proud I am of ye, and to..."

She waited, her heart palpitating, but he didn't continue.

"To...?"

"I...well." He blew out a breath and tucked a lock of her hair behind her ear. "I need to tell ye that I've always loved ye, always. I was a fool to let your mother go, but even more than a fool, I was a selfish bastard. I treasured me immortality more than me love for her...and for ye, me own flesh and blood. Ah, Mischa—" He cut himself off with a choked cry.

"Hey," she soothed, touching a palm to his wet cheek. "It's okay. I understand you had responsibilities. In spite of it all, Mother loved you to her dying day."

"Yes, that I know," he replied, his eyes going all melancholy-soft. "I've watched ye both, loved ye from afar. Do ye no' remember when I'd visit ye?"

She could only smile and nod. Yes, she recalled her "imaginary" friend. She could never see him, but he was there.

And her mother would smile knowingly when Mischa would chatter about him. But Mischa now knew her mother had been aware of more than an imagination. She'd known her daughter was part leprechaun, and that it was Tad who spoke to her.

"Mischa, I've something more to tell ye..."

There was a long pause, and she could swear she could hear the tick-tock of a clock. His eyes were pained, almost guilty.

"What? What is it?"

"In order for a half-elf to become full-blooded leprechaun, another elf must give up their immortality during the ceremony."

She looked to Grady, but he simply tucked his arm tighter about her waist. For long seconds, she stared at her father, large and forbearing yet seeming so humbled and meek at the moment. And slowly, his words gained meaning to her.

"You...you gave up your immortality for me?"

He nodded, but she didn't see pain or regret there. She saw relief in the wrinkles about his eyes, in the faint curve of his mouth.

"But why?"

"Oh, 'tis an odd mixture of that dreaded selfishness and unconditional love for ye."

She blew out a breath. "Um, wanna elaborate?"

He threw his head back, and a rumble of deep laughter carried inland. "Ah, precious daughter, ye are so like your sweet mother, blunt yet soft around the edges."

She couldn't help but grin. "Okay, now that we've got that pointed out, how about telling me why you did such a thing for me?" She held up a hand to halt his words. "I know you love me. But still, that doesn't explain it."

Tad's gaze wandered to Grady and his smile faded. "Because I know ye love this man. In order for ye to have him into eternity, ye must be made immortal."

"That covers the 'unconditional love' half of the odd mixture—and tells me something I already knew."

He crossed his arms, clearly enjoying this banter with her. "Aye, that it does, daughter, that it does. But the 'selfishness' half… When I die, whatever me fate may be, I finally get to be with your mother, lass. Our souls will rejoin in what your previous kind call heaven."

Mischa stared at him and the arteries in her heart suddenly clogged. Her eyes stung with sentimental tears. She saw that Tad's eyes glittered with tears, as well, but they were tears of joy, tears of hope and a future he'd never been able to have before.

She swallowed a painful lump in her throat. Her parents would be together one day! Her mother would be happy again! The concept of it made her chest ache with elation, knowing neither one would be alone.

Mischa flew into her father's arms. She rejoiced in the feel of his big, protective arms around her. He smelled of raw earth and Irish winds. Warmth permeated her flesh and the breeze blew, fluttering her gown and tickling her nose with a long lock of his red hair.

"Father," she whispered. "Thank you so much."

He lifted her, squeezing her tight against his chest before setting her down and urging her back into Grady's embrace. "No, thank ye. By loving this man, by being who ye are, I'm now free. Free to love again."

Grady's arms came around her from behind. He kissed her temple. "I must release him now, Mischa."

"What? Release him from what?"

"He will go now and live in the village as any mortal does, and live out his days until death comes to him."

She whirled in his arms. "But—"

"No, no. Hush. Do no' worry. Ye'll be free to go to him, to visit him all ye wish. But our marriage is complete now. He's given ye to me. He must go now from the magical field."

Over her shoulder, she caught a glimpse of Tad's image fading. He waved to her, a glowing grin on his round face.

"Bye, me lovely daughter! Visit me often?"

She jammed her fists on her hips. "Well, you're damn right. I'm not letting you get away from me again, Father."

His booming laughter reverberated in the sky above them, and he faded into the mist.

"Well," she said, swiping the half-dried tears from her cheeks. "That was quite a revelation."

Grady drew her into his arms. Instantly, she became aware of the erection pressing into her abdomen. She leaned back in the circle of his embrace and snared him with a mock look of reproach. "Are you horny again?"

"Always."

She wrapped her arms around his neck and dragged her mouth over his. Already, her core throbbed with need for him. "So what do you want to do, my Leprechaun King?"

"How about...hmm. Cybersex?"

Mischa blinked. "Oh, yeah. You got cable Internet in that cottage of yours."

"Oh, aye, love. And just wait until ye see cyberspace. 'Tis grand, I tell ye, just grand!"

About the author:

Titania Ladley began her journey into reading romance at the tender age of 13. Soon, sweet romance just didn't cut it. She craved more detail, more sex, *way* more "creativity" between lovers. By her 20's, she discovered that people actually wrote what she needed to read—what she fantasized about. She then devoured the erotica genre. But, alas, restless as usual, she could no longer tolerate just *reading* about it. In her 30's, Titania couldn't suppress the need, the overwhelming drive to create her own fantasies. She had to write. So she did. Published in erotic romance novels and best-selling novellas, she just can't seem to tame her active imagination. So she writes some more…

Titania is a registered nurse, magazine freelance writer, book reviewer and has penned witty slogans. She resides in the Midwest with her very own hunky hero and three children. She enjoys reading erotic romances, walking, weightlifting, crocheting and baking fattening desserts.

Titania welcomes mail from readers. You can write to her c/o Ellora's Cave Publishing at 1056 Home Avenue, Akron OH 44310-3502.

Also by Titania Ladley:

Jennie In a Bottle
Me Tarzan, You Jewel
Moonlite Mirage
Spell of the Chameleon

Must Be Magic

Lani Aames

Chapter One

The rush of high winds displaced the roar of furiously beating Faerie wings as Prince Myghal darted through the doorway at the top of the tallest turret of Castle Faer. His trusted men, Malthe right behind him, and Sirrin bringing up the rear, slammed the heavy wooden door shut and leaned against it just in time.

Myghal relaxed. Two Pixies, especially if one of them was his massive friend and personal guard Sirrin, could easily hold back a horde of infernal Faeries.

As soon as Myghal stepped out from the shelter of stone around the doorway, the gusting wind made it difficult to stand, but he bent into the wind and made his way to the edge of the parapet. Leaning over in the narrow space between the protective blocks of stone, he looked down.

Winks of light, indicating cozy homes, dotted the storm-shrouded landscape as far as he could see to the right. In the other direction, there was nothing but the darkness that marked the edge of Wildwood, the dense and treacherous forest separating the Faerie Kingdom from his home, Pixieland.

Looking down, he saw that most of the Faerie Guard had made their way outside and were fighting the gusting wind to the top of the turret. The storm delayed them, but Myghal and his friends had to think of something. Fast.

"My liege," Malthe shouted from his side. "It appears we're trapped."

Myghal agreed with his Chancellor who had the most annoying habit of stating the obvious. Still, Malthe's habit allowed them both to look at a situation clearly.

Faeries at the door, Faeries swarming the turret by air, and even Faeries who probably thought they might reach them faster than braving the wind were climbing the side of the tower. Myghal had been held captive for nearly two moons, and he was sick to death of Faeries.

Sirrin joined them, his bulk blocking most of the wind. Beside him, Malthe was dwarfed, even though the Chancellor was as tall as Myghal himself. Sirrin made anyone in his vicinity look small and insignificant.

Myghal glanced back at the door. Sirrin had moved a huge block of stone from somewhere to hold the door closed. Myghal wouldn't be surprised to find out that he had ripped it from the sheltering wall. Unusually large and muscular for a Pixie, Sirrin's strength often came in handy.

"I'll fight to the death, Myghal." Sirrin's brown eyes sparked, and he punctuated his impassioned declaration by drawing his broadsword.

"No." Myghal laid his hand on his friend's shoulder. Sirrin had been with him since childhood and, since the death of Myghal's father had made Myghal ruler of Pixieland, the only person to call him by his given name. "We've not spilled Faerie blood so far and we won't. They won't be able to hold us responsible for this in any way."

Sirrin slid his weapon back into its sheath, but his wide forehead creased and his eyes narrowed. "We're not responsible at all. Who would blame us for defending ourselves and our prince?"

Myghal exchanged meaningful glances with his Chancellor. Sirrin was his best friend, but the politics of the princedom and their sometimes precarious position within the Faerie Realm escaped him.

"They'll find a way. They always do." Myghal looked out over the edge of the parapet again. The Faerie Guard drew closer, but battling the stiff winds would keep them at bay a while longer. Maybe long enough for them to think of something.

Sirrin snorted. "If I can't kill'em, can I clip their wings?"

"No!" Myghal shouted.

Sirrin's growl of disappointment was his only response.

"Do you have any dust?" Myghal asked when he turned back to his men. His supply of pixie dust had been confiscated at the time of his kidnapping.

"My liege," Malthe began in a tone of voice that signified what he was about to say was not good news at all. "Sir Sirrin and I brought as much as we could carry, but the Faeries were taking no chances. They had half the Guard on watch and it took all the dust we had to get past them and reach you. I used the last of it on the six guarding your cell."

Suddenly, Sirrin drew back and swung his meaty fist toward Myghal's head. Luckily, Myghal's reflexes were quick. He ducked and Sirrin's fist smashed into a Faerie face. The guardsman shrieked as he fell back.

Sirrin looked at Myghal and shrugged. "I didn't kill him and I didn't touch his wings."

Malthe frowned, his brows furrowing over his eyes. "We have to do something and soon. It won't be long before more than we can dispatch will be upon us."

Myghal agreed. But what could they do? Pixies didn't have wings. They could fly, but only for short distances. None of them would make it to the ground from this height or through these high winds alive. They needed dust.

Sirrin laughed and clapped Malthe's thin back, nearly sending the older man to his knees. "You have Myghal's Heart Match dust."

Malthe's pale blue eyes widened. "Of course. As required by law, I have the charmed dust on me at all times."

Myghal held out his hand. "Give it to me."

"But, my liege—" Malthe began with a splutter.

"We don't have time to argue and we don't have any other choice," Myghal snapped.

Malthe reached beneath his cloak and tunic, to a pouch fastened around his waist. "The dust has already been charmed and can't be used for anything else. You know this."

By the laws set upon them when Pixieland broke away from the Faerie Realm and declared their independence, a newly coronated prince must be wed by the next Equinox or the princedom would revert to Faerie rule. Myghal had had his share of women, but he'd never found one he favored over another. Having no preference, Myghal had decided to invoke the ancient custom of using Pixie magic to find the perfect mate to be his Princess.

The night before the ceremony was scheduled to take place, he had been kidnapped by the Faeries. Norfe, the Faerie King, had been trying to regain control of Pixieland for as long as he'd been on the throne. The Pixies supplied the Faeries with dust, and rulers before Norfe had recognized the importance of keeping the Pixies happy. Norfe's pride wouldn't have him or his realm beholden to anything or anyone.

Malthe and Sirrin had managed to infiltrate the castle and rescue Myghal, but now they all were trapped without Pixie dust. Using the Heart Match dust was the only way.

"The incantation brings your mate to you," Malthe reminded him, still clutching the pouch. "Transporting an unsuspecting maiden into the middle of this situation will only give King Norfe a greater advantage in preventing your marriage."

Myghal nodded, but the idea had already formed. "Can't I change the incantation?"

Malthe's eyes grew wide again. "My liege, that incantation was composed eons ago and has been tested by time. To change the spell without careful thought is to invite disaster."

"What could be more disastrous that the mess we're in now?" Myghal asked and took the bag from Malthe.

The three men huddled around the small bag of dust as Myghal untied the knot. "How does it go?"

Malthe recited the rhyme:

"In the realm of Fae and Kin,

"We have dwelled, alone, apart.

"Bring to me, in good will and good faith,

"The other half of my heart."

Myghal thought a moment, then put his hand into the bag and brought out a fistful of dust. "I'll change one line, to take us to my Heart Match instead of bringing her here. That should be all right, shouldn't it? Are you ready?"

"I think changing that one part won't be harmful. But my liege," Malthe added quietly, "the dust will only work on you."

Myghal looked at his friends. He'd forgotten about that. If he used the dust, he'd have to leave his two most valuable advisors—and friends—behind.

"Hurry!" Sirrin suddenly shouted. "Here they come!"

Myghal looked up. Two Faeries, with swords unsheathed, hovered over the parapet trying to land safely in the wind. He was glad it had always been standard procedure to charm the dust before it was shipped to the faeries so that they had limited use. They couldn't use it to transport and couldn't use it against Pixies. Otherwise, he and his friends would have been surrounded by faeries before they'd gone far from his cell. Now, at least, they had a chance, however slim.

"He's right, Prince Myghal," Malthe said. "Do it."

"As soon as I'm gone, give yourselves up," Myghal shouted his orders. "They don't have any reason to harm you, and they know if they do, they'll lose their shipments of dust."

Sirrin growled.

"You heard your Prince," Malthe said sternly.

But before Sirrin could agree, the Faeries landed. One leaned into the wind and, with a feral growl, charged.

Myghal watched as Sirrin blocked the Faerie. He grabbed the guardsman's slender wrist in his huge hand, and Myghal heard a bone snap. Myghal started toward them, but Malthe held him back.

"Hurry!" his Chancellor shouted into his ear. "You have to go. I'll keep Sirrin under control."

Myghal knew he had no choice. He tossed the dust straight up and as it fell the wind whisked it around him, the fine glittering crystals swirling around him in ever widening spirals. More Faeries landed and raced toward him. He didn't have time to recite the entire incantation.

"Take me to the other half of my heart!" he shouted.

Through the sparkling haze of the dust as it enveloped him and his body began to disintegrate, he saw Malthe's eyes widen in horror at his abbreviated spell. By Malthe's reaction, one would have thought he'd bring about an end to civilization as they knew it by shortening the incantation. Malthe was overreacting, as usual. What could go wrong? Myghal would be taken to the one woman who would make the best life-companion for him, and he for her.

Malthe and Sirrin had backed away from him.

Myghal didn't often use the dust to transport himself and the sensation was unsettling. His stomach lurched, and he felt as if every joint was being pulled apart. He knew he'd arrive in one piece, wherever he landed, but the journey there was never something he looked forward to.

Through the thickening haze, he saw several Faeries capture Malthe and Sirrin. A couple of the guardsmen braved the dust and reached in for him, but their hands went completely through his now transparent body.

Then everything went black.

Chapter Two

Kerry O'Neill bumped into the Leprechaun when she turned around from hanging the latest sale price sign. He caught her before she fell, his strong hands on her shoulders, and she clutched his arms to regain her balance. Her eyes swept over him. She'd seen any number of Leprechaun costumes since the first of March, but this one was the worst yet. Aside from his eyes, which were the color of tender spring shoots flecked with gold, he wasn't wearing a speck of green.

He wore brown leather half-boots, tan leggings, and a maroon tunic laced over a billowy sleeved shirt cinched in with a brown belt. His long ash-blond hair fell in thick waves below his shoulders, random strands in tiny braids decorated with beads and feathers. He reminded Kerry of the elf in the *Lord of the Rings* movies…except that his rugged face, height, and breadth was more than any elf could ever hope for.

"Are you all right?" He spoke with a slight English accent in a deep resonant baritone.

"Fine, thanks." Kerry found her balance, removed her hands, and backed away, shrugging off his hold on her. There was something achingly familiar about his touch, as if she belonged in his arms and he belonged in hers. But she was certain she'd never seen him before in her life.

"You're at the wrong place," she told him, kneeling to replace the hammer in her toolbox that sat on the ground. "The Leprechaun costume contest is across the street at Sir Plantsalot."

His gaze followed hers to the medieval themed garden nursery on the other side of the thoroughfare. The false front was shaped and painted like a castle complete with a turret at each end. The entrance and exit driveways were drawbridges over the drainage ditch "moat". Strands of colorful pennants ran from the tops of the turrets to the ground. Larger pennants fluttered in the breeze from poles in the cone-shaped tower roofs.

"I'm not a—" he began.

But Kerry didn't care what he was or wasn't. She slammed the toolbox shut, drowning out whatever he was saying. "They stole my idea. Somehow, they caught wind of the Leprechaun costume contest I was planning for St. Patrick's Day, and they stole it."

Kerry picked up the toolbox and brushed past him, once again all too aware of his physical presence. She couldn't understand her reaction, why her body was responding to him as if they were lovers.

Shaking her head, she pushed through the gate that led to the lawn and garden ornaments. The toolshed was in the back. When she reached it, she opened the door, but the darkness within was like a black abyss just waiting to swallow her up and crush her. She flipped the switch a couple of times, but no flare of light filled the small shed. The damn light bulb had blown again. Sweat broke out on her upper lip, and she set the toolbox just inside the threshold, pushing it farther in with her foot. Shutting the door, she turned around—only to collide with the Leprechaun again.

Once more she found herself in his embrace, and her body immediately switched from an unnatural fear to a natural arousal. Her heart raced and blood pounded through her. She didn't know why she was having such a disturbing physical reaction to him. Her hormones didn't normally go off the chart over every good-looking man she encountered.

Maybe because it had been too long since she'd been with a man, but she didn't have time to deal with it. Ever since Sir Plantsalot moved in across the street six months ago, with its extravagant display and double the area of her own nursery, she'd been concentrating on trying to keep the business afloat.

But it had been an uphill battle. She extricated herself from his arms.

"I told you, the contest is over there." She backed away from him with a toss of her head then looked him up and down again. "Tell you the truth, I don't think you have a very good chance of winning. You don't look like a Leprechaun. You're not wearing green."

"But I'm not—"

Kerry didn't wait to hear his response. She strode off toward the greenhouse. She had too much work to do without getting involved with a badly dressed Leprechaun…no matter how attracted to him she was.

"…a Leprechaun," Myghal finished to empty air.

He frowned as he watched her hurry down the path toward the transparent building filled with all kinds of plants. He'd never considered his Heart Match could possibly be in the Other Realm, the dimension where humans lived. It'd been a long time since he'd walked among humans. Their world was too noisy and flashy, their air too dirty. They were always rushing, yet they seemed to accomplish little.

And how was he supposed to carry a human woman back into Pixieland in the Faerie Realm when he was out of dust and wasn't sure he could get back himself?

But he found his gaze drawn to the way her hips swayed in the tight blue leggings she wore. No, they were called jeans, he suddenly remembered. He liked everything about her, from her red-gold hair to her crystal blue eyes to the sprinkling of freckles across her upturned nose. Twice, she had slammed into him, and twice, her generous breasts had pressed against his chest. He'd seen her nipples tighten under the form-fitting shirt she wore—T-shirt, it was called.

A dull ache began in his balls as his cock responded to…her. He didn't even know her name.

She didn't seem to want anything to do with him and that went against what the dust was supposed to do. His Heart

Match was supposed to instantly recognize him as her mate, as well. But she seemed to have other things on her mind. Like the contest across the street.

She disappeared through the door, and Myghal's gaze drifted over the statuary inside the fence. An army of garden gnomes—from small ones only as tall as a handspan to two in the back that were about the right size for Gnomes—was spread out over most of the area, along with bird baths, small benches, and flower pots. Too bad the Gnomes weren't real.

He smiled. No self-respecting Gnome would be caught in the clothing these wore. Red vests, blue trousers, yellow shirts, purple caps. Gnomes dressed in browns and tans and dark greens to blend in with the forest they lived in and the earth they worked in.

One of the two tall statues near the fence caught his eye. It looked suspiciously like a Troll... Myghal strolled through the stone army. No, not stone—concrete. The human words were coming back to him slowly. He wandered near the suspect statue. That one looked like a Troll because humans had no idea what Gnomes and Trolls really looked like. Just as they had no idea how evil Faeries could be or they wouldn't present them as children's playthings.

Satisfied that the statue was only human error, Myghal turned around and headed toward the building where she had gone. If it was what humans called St. Patrick's Day here, then he had only a few days before the Spring Equinox. Not much time to convince the human woman that he was Prince of the Pixies, she was destined to be his Princess, and discover a way to get them both back to Pixieland.

*****

Tredje, the Troll, sucked in a deep breath when the Pixie Prince disappeared into the building. He punched the Gnome next to him. "Do ye think the Pixie recognized us?"

Gomit grunted. "Here, now. I don't have to suffer that kind of abuse."

Tredje snarled. Neither of them was happy with the situation, and the other knew it. When the old Faerie Queen—the present King's great-grandmother—banished the Trolls to live with other assorted earth-based kin in the Other Realm, they had declared their independence from the Fae. Of course, the Fae still considered them in their service. Fortunately, the Fae rarely visited the Other Realm these days and seldom had need of Trolls.

But the Sprite messenger, tiny in both realms and able to pass from one to the other in a body of water as small as a dewdrop, had arrived a month ago and called on the Troll Thane and the Gnome General. Through its ability to locate Faerie Realm folk that all Sprites possessed, it had brought news that the Pixie Prince would soon pass into the Other Realm to go to his Heart Match. Sprites were also able to pass through the time continuum as well. This one had slipped through to see where the Prince had gone and who he had gone to, then it had brought the news into this realm before the Prince's escape actually happened in the Faerie Realm.

The Trolls and the Gnomes were to stop the Prince by any means necessary. It happened that Tredje lived across the way from where the Prince would land, and the General had chosen Gomit, so the two had been paired to carry out the Faerie King's mission. A sorrier warrior, Tredje had never seen. Still, a sorry Gnome warrior could beat the best Pixie any day. And with the help of a Troll, they'd soon be done with this assignment and Tredje could be back home under his bridge sipping dandelion wine in no time at all.

Gomit scratched behind his ear. "I don't know. He looked at you a long time, but I think we blend in well enough."

Tredje looked at the colorful clothes and little pointy hats he'd pilfered for them to wear to match the other Gnome statues. Pitiful, what humans thought of Gnomes.

"Aye, but Pixies have a sense about things, I'll give'em that," Tredje said and tugged his beard.

"Do we have a plan?"

Tredje sighed. They'd been over it dozens of times while waiting for the Prince to arrive, but the Gnome's short term memory was shorter than he was.

It would have been easier if they'd been able to snatch the woman before the Pixie showed up, but the Pixie's spell would have brought him to the exact spot where they would have hidden the woman, so it had to be done after he arrived. "We kidnap the woman until after the Equinox. With the woman out of the way, the Pixie won't be able to wed her and all will be well for King Norfe."

"True, true. But how do we get her?"

"We wait until dark. You know as well as I do that she stays here until past sunset. Then we grab her."

"And where did we say we'd hide her?"

Tredje sighed heavily. The Gnome was hopeless. "We'll take her back to me bridge across the street. The Pixie won't think to look right under his nose."

Chapter Three

Kerry was all too aware when the Leprechaun entered the greenhouse. She continued to trowel dirt, moving plants to bigger pots. She couldn't stand the thought of throwing out any plant and tried to keep them all until they sold. Or died. She really wasn't very good at running a nursery, something she'd always dreamed of doing. But her dreams had entailed actually working all day with the plants, not spending most of her time taking care of the business end.

Kerry had decided long ago what she really needed was a job as a gardener. Unfortunately, she didn't discover this until after she'd borrowed the money to open Cockleshells & Silverbells Nursery…well, the whimsical name had sounded good at the time.

She watched the Leprechaun out of the corner of her eye as he surveyed the rows of plants. Too bad he wasn't a real Leprechaun because she'd caught him twice. Inadvertently, but still she'd had her hands on him both times. He would have to give her his pot of gold, and she'd never have to worry about money again.

When he started moving the plants around, she stood and called out to him.

"Hey, is there something I can do for you?"

"The plants aren't happy. Coriander and dill should be together, but mint should never be near the parsley."

He sounded like he knew what he was talking about. And if re-organizing her plants kept him away from her, then all the better. Why he didn't just go across the street and enter the contest, she didn't know.

After a while, when she'd almost finished, she looked up. He'd moved nearly every plant in the herb section and had started on the flowers. But, she had to admit, the new arrangement looked—and even felt—more harmonious as she walked between the rows of herbs to stand beside him.

"You really do have a wonderful way with plants," Kerry said, not in the least jealous. Well, maybe a little. She had a green thumb and plants prospered under her care. But she didn't have any kind of sixth sense that let her just *know* which plants should be where.

"Where I come from, knowing about flowers and plants is natural," he said with a shrug.

"Where do you come from? You sound like you might be from England, but your accent's not quite like anything I've ever heard before." Then Kerry laughed. "Not that I hear very many English accents around here. Mostly what I hear is on TV or in the movies, and I imagine most of them are faked."

"England," he said as he stepped around her to move another pot of marigolds.

Kerry had the feeling he was just repeating the word, not really confirming that it was where he was from. When he didn't say anything else, she didn't pursue it. It wasn't any of her business anyway.

"My name's Kerry O'Neill. I own Cockleshells & Silverbells, and I wish I could afford to hire you. Although if I could hire anybody, it'd be a bookkeeper, so that I could spend all my time with the plants."

He straightened another pot and looked at her. His eyes were the lightest and loveliest shade of green she'd ever seen. Even the color of spring shoots was too dark. Misty green…like morning fog drifting across a forested mountain in summer…

Kerry shook her head. When did she become poetic again? There had been a period in her life when she could take the time to stop and smell the roses she loved to tend, and then describe the experience in poetry or prose, but she hadn't been able to do that in too long. Now, all her energy was spent in keeping her head above water.

"Kerry is a beautiful name. I'm Myghal," he said.

Strange name for a strange man.

"Thank you. Myghal is an unusual name."

"Not where I'm from."

"England?"

"England."

"Right." Kerry had the feeling he wasn't being entirely truthful with her, but he wasn't exactly lying either. He was…a puzzlement. "I'm sorry, but all I can offer for all your help is to share my lunch."

"You have a smudge." He raised his hand to her face, his fingers splayed across her cheek and jaw as his thumb wiped a spot at the point of her chin. Then the tip of his thumb slowly swiped across her bottom lip.

She had the sudden urge to share more than her lunch, like her bed. Desire, hot and sweet, swept through her at his touch. She just wanted to close her eyes and let him kiss her like he seemed to want to do. Maybe if she lost herself in a kiss and sex with a stranger, she wouldn't have to worry about the nursery or how to make the loan payment or anything else for a while. It would be nice not to have to think about anything except physical pleasure.

It would be over too soon, though, and the money problems would still exist. She sighed and backed up a step, tilting her head away from his hand. He took the hint and his arm dropped to his side.

"Let's get cleaned up and then we can eat." A quaver in her voice revealed how much he affected her.

She led the way to the sink, washed up, and left him to do the same. She hurried to her desk, set in a corner of the greenhouse behind a row of potted pampas grass. There was a smaller building in front, but she had felt suffocated and closed in when she tried to work there. One day she had simply dragged her desk and chair out into the greenhouse. Afterwards, much of her anxiety about doing paperwork had disappeared. Not all, but quite a bit. Being closed inside a tiny office with no window had just about sent her over the edge.

She pulled her lunch out of the mini-fridge and opened the first plastic bowl. Four boiled eggs. She hadn't had time to make a sandwich that morning. She lifted the lid on the other bowl to reveal pale green grapes. She split the bunch and dropped one in each bowl, then put two of the eggs in the other bowl. Two eggs and half a bunch of grapes would hold her until supper.

Myghal joined her as she opened a desk drawer. She kept salt and pepper shakers on hand, so she wouldn't have to remember to bring them from home if she needed them for her lunch. She motioned for Myghal to take a seat, then pushed aside papers and a handful of pens looking for the containers. She found the black pepper shaker easily enough, but the white saltshaker was nowhere to be found.

"I know it's got to be here somewhere," she muttered, rifling through the papers again. The drawer wasn't that big and it wasn't that cluttered. She should be able to find a four-inch-tall shaker.

"What are you searching for?"

She set the black shaker down with a solid thud. "All I have is pepper. I can't find the—"

She'd pulled the drawer out too far and it fell with a clatter, scattering pens and papers in all directions. Myghal helped her to gather them up. She still hadn't found the saltshaker. Where could she have put it? She'd never moved it from her desk before.

As Kerry reached in the refrigerator for something to drink, she thought she must be losing her mind. Her first set of plans for the Leprechaun contest had disappeared, too. She'd manage to recreate half of them when she saw the sign across the street at Sir Plantsalot announcing a Leprechaun costume contest.

She'd thrown them away in disgust, wondering if someone from Sir Plantsalot had pretended to be a customer and stolen her papers. Now, it seemed she might have mislaid them herself and the contest was an unhappy coincidence.

Chapter Four

Kerry brought out two bottles of water, her last, and made a mental note to add it to her grocery list.

"I usually have iced tea, but I was running late this morning and left it sitting on the kitchen counter. We'll have to drink water."

She pushed one bowl and a bottle of water toward him.

He plucked a couple of the grapes and popped them in his mouth. She had the urge to tell him he should eat the eggs first, but who was she to tell anyone how to eat their lunch? Even if it was her lunch.

"What was the sign you were putting up when I—when I arrived?" he asked as he ate a few more grapes.

Kerry chewed a bite of egg and swallowed, washing it down with water. "Posting the latest sale, trying to get rid of the shamrocks and Irish roses. I ordered more than I should have in anticipation of the Leprechaun costume contest bringing in crowds of people. It did, but not for me. Sir Plantsalot has had a booming business all week long. I've seen people over there that used to be my best customers. But that happened as soon as Sir Plantsalot moved in."

Myghal had started eating an egg. "Why do you think your customers abandoned you?"

"The ambiance. You can't compete with a castle. And they have a wider variety of stock at lower prices because they can buy in bulk. Even if I could afford to carry everything they do, I don't have the space. Their place is twice the size of mine." Kerry shook her head and sighed. "I was doing very well before they moved in six months ago. I was the only nursery in this part of the city and had built a nice clientele for only having been in business one year. But the first weekend they opened, my sales where half what they had been the week before. They've gone down ever since. I had to let go the one full-time employee and the two part-timers, and I had to give up my dream of hiring someone to keep the books so I could concentrate on working with the plants. Some weeks I don't break even. I guess you noticed that you've been here a few hours and not one customer has shown up. They're all over there, voting on the best Leprechaun costume."

Kerry stopped. She was surprised at how bitter she sounded. She shouldn't be going on and on about her problems.

"I'm sorry things aren't going well for you, Kerry," Myghal said. He sounded as if he were truly sorry and not just being polite.

"Thanks. I wish it could have worked out, too. The sign I put up slashed everything by fifty percent. I guess I need to change it to seventy-five percent now. I'm losing money, but I'd rather see the plants be sold than left to wither and die. Tomorrow, I'll give away a shamrock and an Irish rose with every purchase. If there are any purchases, that is."

It was time to change the subject. Talking about how her nursery had failed was depressing. "Lunch isn't much, but it's the only way I can thank you for what you did with the plants. How do you know which plants go where?"

"They tell me," he said with a mischievous smile. He bit into an egg, foregoing the pepper, and washed it down with a gulp of water.

She stopped chewing and pressed her lips together. She loved plants more than most people, and she often talked to them, but she had never even imagined that they talked back. She should have known better than to allow him to hang around. He was a stranger with a strange name and strange clothes, even for St. Paddy's Day. Maybe he'd got a head start on consuming green beer this morning.

He laughed, the corners of his eyes crinkling and his perfect white teeth shining. "I'm sorry, but the look on your face. I don't mean they talk to me, but they do communicate in their own way. It's hard to explain, but I can feel where they want to be."

"Of course, that's what you meant," Kerry said and ducked her head to pop in the last of the egg. "I wish I had that kind of affinity with plants. They flourish under my care, but I don't hear what they have to say."

"Then you're not listening," he said. "All plants have an area of energy around them that changes when they're happy or sick or dying."

"An aura?"

"Yes, like an aura. You have to listen to the energy, feel its changes. Only then can you know what the plant wants." Myghal rose, came around the desk, and stood behind her. He leaned over, his head close to hers and took her hand. Holding her palm about two inches from the nearest pampas grass plant, he whispered. "Close your eyes and listen, Kerry O'Neill."

Kerry grinned, but did as he said. She heard nothing except his deep, even breathing. She felt nothing except his arm along hers, his fingers entwined with hers. His breath brushed her cheek each time he exhaled. She couldn't concentrate with him so close. He was too much of a distraction and a temptation.

"Do you feel it?" He whispered again, a sexy, husky murmur of words that made her feel things, all right, but not what he had in mind. Or did he?

She opened her eyes and shook her head, turning to look at him. This close, she could see the tiny flecks of gold in his irises clearly enough to count them. His fingers stayed snugly with hers as he brought her hand back away from the pampas grass and rested it on the desk.

"If you practice, you'll understand what they have to tell you."

She nodded, unable to speak. She wanted him to kiss her, wanted to kiss him, but she couldn't bring herself to make the first move. She didn't have time for a man in her life as much as she wanted one and needed one…no, wanted *this* one—Myghal.

She wanted Myghal badly. So badly that her nipples burned and her skin prickled where he touched. She had been slightly aroused since bumping into him the first time. The sexual feelings had heated to a slow simmer when he'd cleaned the smudge from her chin. Now, it bubbled through her, causing her to dampen her panties and her clit to pulse with an intense ache she hadn't experienced in a long time, if ever, and never this quickly. If she didn't do something, she would regret it for the rest of her life.

Kerry took a chance. She kissed him.

*****

Tredje directed Gomit to stay with the Gnome statues. Gomit didn't object, just as Tredje suspected he wouldn't. In battle, Gnomes couldn't be stopped, but outside of full-scale war, they were the laziest of creatures. Taking up underground work after the Realm Wars had ceased, when there was no longer a need for an army of Gnomes, had softened the ugly blighters.

Turning his attention to the human woman, he'd noted her business wasn't very busy. Proudly, he'd also noticed a steady stream of human conveyances entering and leaving his castle across the way. That's what having a Troll reside beneath a bridge did for you! It also helped when the Troll stole the plans for a Leprechaun contest and stuffed them beneath your door. The contest would have brought in too many humans. He and the Gnome wouldn't have had the chance to capture the woman.

But back to the matter at hand. Aside from the Pixie—and Gomit and himself, of course—Tredje had yet to see another living soul enter the front gate this day. Not that the Pixie had entered by traditional human means. He'd popped into this dimension right behind where the woman stood after tacking a new sign across the old.

So, Tredje didn't try to conceal himself as he scurried across the loose gravel toward the building where the Prince and his intended Princess had entered. He did try to make as little noise as possible as he neared the transparent wall. The greenhouse was full of potted plants that fortunately obscured the outside view from the inside. Unfortunately, they obscured the inside view from the outside as well. Tredje couldn't see a thing.

He motioned for Gomit to join him. But either the Gnome was taking his statue act too seriously or he'd fallen asleep standing up. Tredje waved his arm in ever-widening arcs until Gomit finally saw him. Gomit trudged across the space between them, huffing for breath as he joined Tredje.

"We have to lure the woman out here somehow…" Tredje tapped his bearded chin as he looked around for inspiration. He espied the little hut in the back. The woman had gone to it to put up her tools earlier. Tredje had seen her flip the little switch that gave humans illumination, but no light had come on. And there was no window in the building. The perfect spot.

He poked Gomit. "There. That little hut. If we make some kind of noise out by the hut, she'll come running to see what it is. We'll trap her inside and tie her up. Then as soon as everything is quiet, we'll carry her to me bridge."

Gomit remained quiet, as he should, and Tredje grinned broadly. There was never anything wrong with a Troll's plans.

Then Gomit opened his mouth. "If we make a noise loud enough to bring the woman, won't the Pixie come, too?"

Tredje's grin turned to a snarl. Leave it to a Gnome to spoil a perfect Troll plan.

Tredje tapped his chin again. "We'll have to wait until the woman comes out to close for the night. She always inspects the grounds before leaving. We'll make a quieter noise, one she can hear but the Pixie can't. When she enters the hut to see what it is, we'll grab her then."

"But what if the Pixie comes with the woman to inspect the grounds before they leave?" Gomit whined, wringing his hands.

Tredje was ready with an answer. He poked Gomit in the chest and growled, "In that case, Gnome, you'll have the privilege of creating a diversion to get the Pixie out of the way."

Chapter Five

Myghal was taken by pleasant surprise when Kerry pressed her lips to his. He knew she found him a curiosity, but she hadn't seemed particularly attracted to him until this moment. He had begun to think he'd ruined everything by not reciting the entire incantation, and that the dust had landed him with Kerry at random. But as she deepened the kiss, sliding her lips over his, slipping her arm around his neck, he knew she was his perfect match, the other half of his heart. He could feel it the same way he could sense what the plants wanted.

His cock thought so, too—a painful, throbbing reminder that he'd been imprisoned at Castle Faer for two moons without female companionship of any kind. By the time Malthe and Sirrin had rescued him, even the female Faerie guards were starting to look good.

How would it be with Kerry? he wondered. Need always drove him. The physical need he had no control over, and the emotional need was just as uncontrollable but impossible to slake. While he always found physical release, he'd never found an emotional connection with any Pixie female he'd fucked. Would it be different with Kerry? Pixie lore said that coupling with the other half of his heart would be an experience like no other.

If this melding of lips and mingling of breaths were indications, then he didn't need to worry at all.

Kerry's other hand slid down his chest, brushing his nipple, and his sac tightened. He knelt, fitting himself between her legs, and rested his hands on her thighs. She drew in a deep, sudden breath.

Myghal pushed his tongue between her parted lips as his hands glided up her thighs. His thumbs met where the seams of the material came together and were sewn into a thick bump. He pressed in, rubbing in circles, and Kerry moaned into his mouth, her lips trembling against his. He continued the pressure and the circles until her hips thrust back and forth, rocking her clit into his thumbs in a constant rhythm.

He felt the tension build in her, felt her excitement escalate. Her breathing deepened and her lips went lax. She laid her head on his shoulder and put both arms around him. She was nearing her peak and he wanted to join her, to peel the jeans from her long legs and drive his cock into her hot wetness.

He shook and his knees grew weak at the mental image of fucking Kerry, but he managed to restrain himself. Kerry needed this as a gradual acceptance of their intimacy. If he tried to do more, the interruption might make her think twice about letting a stranger touch her like this, and she might refuse any further closeness. Without physical intimacy, he had little chance of convincing Kerry to travel to another dimension and marry him.

When her rhythm increased and little noises escaped her throat, Myghal knew it was almost time. He gentled the pressure of his thumbs, making her move into him harder. With only a few more strokes, her hips bucked and he felt her hands fist in the material of his tunic. She moaned, one long, low vibration that sounded like the sweetest music he'd ever heard and almost did him in, then her body went limp against him. He removed one hand and put his arm around her, caressing the long hank of hair down her back while his other thumb continued to massage the tender spot.

Gradually, her hands released his tunic, but she didn't move from his embrace. After a few moments, she cleared her throat.

"I-I'm sorry, I don't know what—"

"Shhh, don't be sorry," he said soothingly. "I only wanted to make you feel good."

She laughed, but it was a small sound and almost ended on a sob. She did pull away from him, then, wiping her eyes, but not meeting his. "It did feel good, Myghal. But I don't know why I let you do that. Especially here, in the middle of the day. Oh, my God, anybody could have walked in."

"But they didn't," he said and brushed strands of hair from her face. He placed a finger under her chin, compelling her to look at him. Her blue eyes were luminous with tears and her cheeks flushed with embarrassment. He was relieved to find no regret in her warm gaze.

She drew away from his touch and stood, a hand on her desk until she was steady. He was still kneeling and his face was now in an interesting location. If she were naked, he could have buried his tongue in her pussy easily. She seemed to suddenly become aware of this and her eyes grew wide. She stepped around and away from him.

He pushed himself to his feet with difficulty. His stiff cock made maneuvering a challenge if he didn't want to hurt himself. His weakened knees threatened to buckle, and, like Kerry, he used the desk for support until he was sure he could stand and walk.

"I have to go..." She waved in the general direction of the restroom. "I—" Then she kissed him, quickly, but with meaning. "I owe you one."

Then she was gone. He was almost in pain from the hard-on, but he grinned. He had Kerry's promise to take care of that problem. He just didn't know when.

Chapter Six

Out of embarrassment, Kerry spent the rest of the day putting as much distance between Myghal and herself as she could. He seemed to understand because he spent most of the afternoon outside, rearranging the plants out there. Every once in a while he caught her watching him, but he only smiled that incredibly sexy smile, all-knowing but not arrogant, as if they shared a secret no one else in the world could share.

She supposed that was true. No one else could know about what he'd done to her that afternoon in her office chair, that he'd given her the most intense orgasm she'd ever felt. Or perhaps it just seemed that way because it was him. Didn't sex seem better when it was with someone you felt an incredible connection to?

Not if you'd just met that someone a few hours ago.

But she had just met Myghal that morning, and she did feel an inexplicable connection to him, as if he were the missing piece in the jigsaw puzzle she called life.

All afternoon, she tried to reason with herself. She didn't really believe in love at first sight. That worked in old movies, fairy-tales, and romance novels, not in the real world. In the real world, there was so much to consider—backgrounds, religion, whether children were wanted, and a million other things she couldn't think of off-hand. Properly taking the time to get to know one another would reveal them.

Then she would look at Myghal and her heart would race. Every rational thought would dissolve in the heat of her desire for him. More than desire was impossible right now, but desire was enough.

Kerry had put up another sign announcing seventy-five percent off everything and business had picked up. There was a sporadic stream of customers in and out all afternoon and many of them actually bought something. She remained open until long after Sir Plantsalot had closed, hoping to catch people on their way home from work.

It was well past sunset and there hadn't been a customer for half an hour when she decided to call it a night. She asked Myghal to make sure all the lights were off in the front building and the greenhouse while she made sure everything was secured outside. When she finished, they could leave.

As she covered the grounds, she thought about Myghal. She hadn't thought much about anything else except him all day. A customer might distract her for a few moments, but as soon as she saw him across the lot, she would go all tingly and warm. It had been difficult to concentrate on selling plants. And became even more difficult when Kerry got the impression that Myghal expected to go home with her.

Well, she had practically promised him a hand-job.

She felt her face heat up in embarrassment…but her body heated up as well. By the size of the bulge in his britches when the tunic lay tight across his lap, she wouldn't be disappointed. As long as he knew how to use it.

She suspected he knew how to use it very well.

Kerry grinned at the prospect of experiencing mind-blowing sex later that night.

She'd come full circle and was standing in front of the toolshed when she remembered about the blown bulb. The grin faded away. She'd just have to do it tomorrow…in the light of day. So she could see how to screw it in. Yeah, that excuse worked every time.

She had started up the walkway toward the greenhouse where Myghal waited when she heard the noise. It sounded like a pitiful mewing coming from inside the shed. How could a kitten have gotten in there? She'd only been to the shed twice that day, when she'd changed the signs, and she hadn't seen a stray cat all day. She hesitated. The shed had its back to the nearest outside light, and she only had a penlight with her. The small beam of light would do little to dispel the darkness within the shed.

Kerry couldn't leave the kitten in the shed all night. It was probably cold and hungry. She could call Myghal to help her, but then she'd have to explain why she needed him to get a tiny kitten out of her own shed. Well, chances were, when she opened the door the kitten would run out and streak off into the night. Maybe she didn't need to get Myghal at all.

Turning on the penlight, she approached the shed. Her palms were already slick with sweat, even though the night air was chill enough for a heavy jacket. She put her hand on the doorknob, but her fingers just slid around it. She wiped her palm on her jeans and tried again. This time the knob turned.

She released it and gave the door a little push to open it wide. She waited, but no tiny ball of fluff shot out through the door. Then she heard the mewing again. It came from the back of the shed. The poor thing was probably too frightened to come out.

"Here, kitty, kitty, kitty," she called out softly and scratched the jamb, hoping to make an interesting enough noise so the kitten would investigate. "Come on, kitty, kitty, kitty."

Still no furball. The mewing sounded again from the farthest corner of the shed. Kerry gripped the penlight tighter. This was ridiculous. It was just a shed full of tools and one tiny kitten. All she had to do was walk to the back, flash the light around until she found the stray, pick it up, and leave. No big deal. Something anybody else could do without a second thought. Why was it making her heart pound and her upper lip break into a cold sweat?

"I can do this," she whispered.

She shone the narrow beam of light into the yawning maw of darkness inside the shed. Her breathing had turned to quick, shallow gasps. If she didn't get control of herself she would hyperventilate. She concentrated, taking deep breaths through her nose and out her mouth.

But the longer she stood there thinking about it, the worse it would get. She needed to plunge into the shed and get it over with. She'd just be in there for a few seconds, maybe a minute, and then she could come out into the open where the floodlights gave the night enough brightness that she didn't feel trapped.

Kerry drew in a deep breath, clutched the jamb, and put one foot up on the threshold. She waited a moment, but she hadn't begun to really panic yet, so she brought up her other foot.

Concentrate on saving the cat. "Come here, kitty, kitty, kitty," she called again.

More mewing, but it didn't seem to have moved away from the far corner.

Just do it.

With the beam of the penlight illuminating only a narrow strip of floor ahead of her, she took another deep breath and walked forward. Halfway across the shed, the door slammed shut behind her.

She stopped and screamed, a short sharp sound that seemed to be swallowed up by the darkness. She swung around, losing her bearings. Sweeping the penlight back and forth, she tried to find something that looked familiar, but panic was seizing her, clawing at her chest and throat. She thought she heard something scuttle to her left and jerked the penlight in that direction. The plastic housing slipped from her sweaty hand, rolling with a frightening clatter across the floor and under the shelving. Pitch blackness closed in on her, pressed into her skin from all sides, and stole the breath from her lungs. When something touched her arm, she dragged in a gulp of air and screamed as long and as loud as she could. The high-pitched sound of terror went on for an eternity.

Chapter Seven

The shouting of her name brought Kerry back to her senses. Myghal had somehow managed to get her out of the shed because she had space around her and she had air to breathe. She stopped screaming, although by that time the sound she was making was little more than a hoarse squawk. Her legs gave way and her body crumpled. She didn't lose consciousness, but it was as if every muscle in her body turned to jelly.

Myghal scooped her up and carried her into the greenhouse. He put her down in the chair at her desk, the one where he'd done such wonderful things to her body that afternoon. Sex seemed to be the last thing on his mind as he hovered over her, his face a frowning mask of worry.

She reached out and stroked a lock of his long, ash blond hair. "I'm all right now," she said. The words burned her throat, and she reached for the bottle of water she'd left on the desk at lunch.

Myghal got it for her, uncapped it and put it to her lips. She drank the few swallows that remained. He set the empty bottle aside and picked up his, letting her drink from it. She swallowed greedily, but wondered what he would think of her when she told him about her irrational fears.

It mattered a great deal—maybe too much, considering how short a time they'd known each other—what Myghal thought about her.

"Are you hurt?" he asked, his voice thick with concern. "Do you need something? More water? Should I find a healer?"

She shook her head, happy to be able to breathe normally. She should have known better than to go into that dark shed alone with only a feeble penlight to relieve the crushing blackness.

"I'm fine now," she assured him and sat up straight. Her muscles and bones no longer felt as unstable as gelatin.

"Are you sure?" Myghal held her hands in his. His touch was comforting. "Was someone out there?"

She shook her head again. "It's my own fault. I have claustrophobia. If I'm in a dark, enclosed place, I panic."

She stopped, waiting for him to laugh or look relieved that it was nothing more serious or drop her hands as if she were a silly person wasting his time. Different people had done all those things and more over the years. But Myghal didn't laugh, look relieved, or drop her hands. He waited patiently for her to continue.

"I shouldn't have gone into the shed knowing the bulb was blown."

"Why did you go in there?"

She grinned awkwardly. "I heard a noise that sounded like a kitten. I thought I could just open the door and the kitten would run out. When that didn't happen, I thought I could quickly go in, get the kitten, and get out before—before I panicked."

He squeezed her hands. "You didn't see or hear anything else?"

"Not really, but the door slammed shut by itself. It's never done that before. The door isn't hung square on the frame, so if left alone it'll slowly swing open, not shut." She thought a moment. "And right before I started screaming, I heard a scuffling sound and felt something touch my arm."

"It sounds like someone was in the shed." Myghal gave her hands another squeeze then he stood. "I'm going out there and look around."

"No, you don't have to do that," she protested.

"If someone was in there to hurt you, you need to call your guardsmen." He started toward the door.

"Wait, Myghal. You'll need a flashlight." Testing her legs before she stood up because she felt as shaky as she had when he'd brought her to orgasm earlier in the day, she found she could stand and walk. With Myghal following, she went to the supply shelf over the sink and got the heavy-duty flashlight.

He took it, but she had to show him how to turn it on and off.

"I'll be back soon," he said and kissed her as naturally as if they'd known each other forever and were madly in love.

She followed him to the door.

"Be careful," she called, locking the door behind him.

Kerry watched him hurry along the path to the toolshed and go inside. He left the door open and it stayed open. An ice water chill raced along her spine. Someone had been in the shed with her. She hoped whoever it was had gone and Myghal would be safe.

And what of Myghal? He was a stranger to her, yet she had allowed him to touch her intimately and was now depending upon his help. What if it was a scam? What if Myghal was working with someone else, the person who had been in the shed? To gain her confidence, Myghal was playing the gorgeous hunk protecting her from the bad man who was threatening her. But what could they possibly want? She had no money and had made that clear to Myghal…but he was still here.

Kerry had a feeling it was much more complicated than a scam and that Myghal was more than a con man looking to score—the way he was dressed but with no interest in the contest, he'd said healer instead of doctor and guardsmen instead of police, and he didn't know how to operate something as simple as a flashlight.

Who was he and where was he from?

*****

Against the better judgment of a tiny voice in the back of her mind warning her not to, Kerry took Myghal home with her. On the way there, she wondered a thousand times if she was doing the right thing. After all, a good-looking guy in a bad Leprechaun costume could easily be a serial killer. Weren't most serial killers handsome and charming? After all, who would trust an ugly fiend who actually *looked* like a murderer?

But what else could she do? She still owed the guy a hand-job.

She'd asked him where his car was. He'd said he didn't have one. She'd asked him where he lived, but he'd said he'd just arrived today and didn't have a place to stay. She could have interrogated him further, but she was simply afraid of what he might say, afraid his story would be too fantastic to believe.

Kerry went through the drive-through window of a fast food joint to get something for supper. He stared at the blinking lights and neon signs as if he'd never seen anything like them before. When she asked him what he wanted, he said he'd have the same thing she was having. He didn't offer to pay.

At home, while they ate at her small dining table, Kerry decided she might as well tell him the whole story. She had been pleased when he didn't ask what caused her claustrophobia. He seemed to accept it as part of her. Everybody else always asked why, and that was when she clammed up and shrugged if off, saying she'd always been that way. But it wasn't true.

She swallowed a bite of burger and cleared her throat.

"I dated this guy in high school. I was a freshman and he was a senior. He was the bad boy type, always getting into trouble, but I thought that made him more attractive. He had a temper, too. I didn't really know how bad it was until one day he thought I was flirting with another guy."

Kerry sucked up a big mouthful of chocolate shake, letting the creaminess melt in her mouth. Myghal didn't say anything, just watched her while he chewed on a french fry.

"Anyway, we were out at the old gravel pit. That's where we all hung out because the pit wasn't being used anymore. There were a couple of old dilapidated sheds where we stashed beer and stuff. He accused me of making a fool of him with this other boy and smacked me around—"

"He struck you?" Myghal's eyes blazed in anger, and his hands clenched into fists.

Kerry nodded. "Yeah, it was the first time—and the last. After he slapped me a few times, he shoved me in one of the sheds and left me there. The shock of him hitting me was almost enough to send me over the edge, but it was just after sundown and it was so dark. I screamed until my throat was raw and I couldn't make another sound. Then I just curled up into a ball in the middle of the floor. I didn't sleep, I just lay there all night with my eyes shut tight. It was mid-morning before anyone found me. Everyone was out looking for me, and a friend thought to check at the pit. My boyfriend said he'd only meant to leave me out there a couple of hours to teach me a lesson, but he'd gone off with his buddies, got drunk and forgot all about me."

Kerry crumpled up her wrappers and sucked the last of her shake.

"I never saw the guy again. He left town and I heard later that he'd gone to prison for a few years. Didn't surprise me. But ever since then I can't be in dark, confined places without screaming or curling up in a corner. Sometimes this house isn't big enough."

Myghal looked thoughtful. "Thank you for telling me, Kerry. I'm sorry you were treated so badly."

"Me, too. It only happened that once. I steer clear of bad boy types now. You never know what they'll do."

Of course, Kerry thought as they cleared off the table together, Myghal looked like a medieval bad boy with that long blond hair laced with tiny braids, the boots, leggings, and tunic. He didn't act tough, though. She squirted dishwashing liquid under the rush of water in the sink to wash up the few dishes she'd left from the night before. He was thoughtful and kind, and had seen to her pleasure before his own.

That reminded her...she owed him one.

Chapter Eight

When Kerry had washed the dishes and Myghal had rinsed them and set them to air dry, she turned to face him. She licked her lips and noticed his warm gaze on the action. She had done it as a stalling tactic because she didn't know what to say or how to begin.

If she didn't do something, the moment would be lost and she'd have to start all over later. She reached for his tunic and pulled the material up until the waistband of his leggings was exposed. The bulge was huge behind the criss-cross lacings, and Kerry felt guilty she'd waited so long to do this. He must have been uncomfortable all afternoon by the size of his hard-on. Slowly, she undid the tie and pulled the lace through the eyelets until the material parted and his cock was free.

Kerry dipped her hands in the dishwater again. Fingers dripping hot sudsy water, she wrapped both hands around his rigid length. Myghal groaned at her hot, slippery caress, and he thrust his hips into her grip, his cock sliding back and forth with ease. His hands went to her shoulders to hold them both steady

Remembering what he'd done to her at lunch and imagining what he must be feeling now stirred Kerry's blood. As her clit thrummed and desire coiled in her womb, she wished she could lead him by the cock into her bed and let him drive that hard shaft into her. But she'd promised to return the favor of a hand-job.

She put one hand into the water to re-lubricate. She entwined her fingers and folded her hands over his cock, placing her thumbs on top. He thrust into her makeshift channel, and she moved closer until the tip bumped into her belly.

While he pumped into her hands, Kerry's hips matched his rhythm and her clit burned for attention. Later, she told herself. This was just the beginning of a long, passionate night ahead of them.

His hands slid off her shoulders, tugged the T-shirt up until her bra was exposed. He dipped his fingers into the cups and scooped her breasts free. The touch of his warm flesh on her nipples sent currents of electricity shooting through her body. She closed her eyes, enjoying the sensations his touch intensified.

Kerry wanted more, so much more. She wanted to drop all their clothing, roll naked across her bed, entwining their limbs until it would be difficult for anyone to tell where one left off and the other began. She wanted him between her legs, deeply inside her, first increasing the pleasurable ache that ravaged her, then relieving it in a burst of heat that would spread from her center to her extremities.

Myghal's thumbs caressed her nipples, and he bent his head to suckle one, tonguing it until the peak was stiff and sensitized. His thumb took over, swirling in the wetness he'd left behind, as he placed his lips around the other, his tongue flicking and teasing.

Kerry tossed back her head and moaned. At the sound of her throaty expression of pleasure, Myghal's hip movements quickened into her hands. The soapy water had evaporated, but he provided enough natural lubrication for his cock to easily glide in and out of her hands.

Kerry knew when he neared release. His cock reached a higher degree of rigidity, and his thrusts were frenzied and deep, as if he could reach her sex from this awkward angle and through her layers of clothing. When he shuddered and his lips clamped tightly around her nipple, Kerry felt the orgasm ripple through his body and an echoing wave shuttled through her, too.

Gasping, Kerry put her arms around him, her hands slick with his semen, and held him close. She'd never had anything like that happen to her before. It hadn't been a true orgasm because her clit still ached, but it had been a release of some kind for her. A sympathy orgasm? She didn't know what else to call it, comparing it to the sympathy pains some men felt when their wives went into labor.

Their bodies were so in tune with one another, she'd literally experienced his pleasure. She couldn't imagine what would happen once they actually joined their bodies. They might explode. Or implode and take the universe with them, sucking creation into the black hole they'd left behind. She hoped not. She had a feeling she would want to fuck Myghal more than once.

Myghal released her nipple with a soft *plop* and straightened up. Neither of them was steady on their feet. Kerry reached over to grab the edge of the counter. She looked into his gold-flecked eyes and felt like she was looking into the mirror of her soul. Myghal smiled and swept a hand across her neck and into her hair, his thumb resting on her cheek and rubbing lightly.

She smiled back at him, unable to contain the sheer joy that bubbled up within her. "I hope that made you feel as good as you made me feel today at the nursery."

He nodded, as if he hadn't yet regained control of his voice.

"I don't understand what this incredible connection is that we have. I just know that everything feels so right."

He nodded again. "I'm glad you feel it, too."

She breathed. It wasn't her imagination. He felt the same force that drew them together like iron to a magnet. Physical lust didn't begin to encompass it all. She'd been physically attracted to other men, but had never felt compelled to act on it within hours of their meeting.

And none of the men she'd had in her life had ever admitted feeling anything like what was happening between her and Myghal. They had come into the relationship with the expectation that it would be temporary, drifting away after the newness wore off. She had, too, until now. This was different. This was more than a temporary fling with a stranger to keep the loneliness at bay.

She felt all this and they had yet to properly have sex.

Sex sounded like a good idea right then.

"The kitchen can wait," she murmured. "But the bedroom can't."

"Neither can I." He kissed her, a short kiss but as full of promise as a longer, deeper one. "Where is your bed chamber, Kerry O'Neill?"

"Down the hall, second door to the right."

She laughed as he picked her up and cradled her against him. She pressed her lips to his, working her mouth against his. This wasn't a quick kiss, but a lingering one that stirred a fire in their blood.

He laid her down in the center of her bed, kneeling beside her. She looked up at him, wishing she knew everything there was to know about him. It would be fun to discover all the little things as well as the big things about him, but she couldn't help wondering what it would have been like if they'd grown up together and been friends for years instead of only knowing each other for mere hours.

Myghal was a stranger. She couldn't lose sight of that fact, no matter how drawn to him she was.

Kerry sat up straight. "Are you clean?"

He frowned in puzzlement then looked down at himself. "You cleansed one part of me well, but I could use a bath."

She giggled. "No, I mean clean as in free of sexual diseases. As much as I want you and as close as I feel to you, we've only known each other today."

"Oh, I see. No, I have no diseases."

"Neither do I. And I'm on birth control, so we don't have to worry about pregnancy."

"That's good." But his response didn't sound relieved as most men's did. The crease deepened across his forehead. "You do want children, don't you, Kerry?"

It was an odd question coming from a man she'd known less than a day. She couldn't remember any of the men she'd seriously dated ever asking that question. "Sure, when the time is right and the man and I agree it's what we want. What about you?"

"Aye, I want enough children to fill a pala—a home."

He'd stumbled over a word. Had he been about to say palace? What an eccentric man Myghal was.

"Now, I'd like to take a bath."

She sighed. "Probably a good idea. We both worked up a sweat this afternoon at the nursery. But a shower would be quicker."

"A shower?" His eyes narrowed in concentration. "Oh, like a waterfall."

"Something like that. I'll throw your clothes in the washer, too." She scooted off the bed. Reluctantly. As much as she wanted him right that second, he needed a little time to recover from the hand-job in the kitchen. And after grubbing around in potting soil and fertilizer all day, a shower sounded like a great idea.

Chapter Nine

After showers and washing and drying Myghal's clothing, Kerry and Myghal returned to the bed. To Kerry, this was the culmination of all they'd been through together that day. They had satisfied each other's physical needs, but now was the time to fulfill her longing to be in his arms, to be one with him.

Kerry wished she understood where this driving passion came from because she'd never felt it with any other man. There had been men in her life that she'd merely wanted physically, some she'd felt close to, and a few she'd even thought she loved. Myghal had become an obsession, both physically and emotionally, and in less than twenty-four hours.

She was beginning to wonder if her feelings were healthy when Myghal ran a hand over her slowly, from breast to mound, and kissed the center of her belly, near her navel. She knew then she didn't care. Perhaps this one night and a hard, sweaty fuck would purge her of these unrealistic romantic notions.

"Myghal." She breathed his name as if it were her last.

He slid over her leg, bending it to make room for him. "Yes, Kerry?"

"I don't know. I feel so many things for you. I'm feeling too much and it doesn't make sense."

Myghal smiled and dipped below her line of vision. Kerry raised her head and watched him trail kisses from her belly button, across the slight round of her abdomen, to the dark red-gold patch. She squirmed in anticipation, waiting for the moment his tongue delved into the curls, and spread her legs.

Myghal placed his arms beneath her thighs, his hands on her hips, and settled down. He licked the curls first, teasing her, the tip of his tongue barely touching her clit. But each tender flick sent waves of pure pleasure through her. She wiggled and pushed forward, trying to catch his tongue, but he darted and dodged. He went farther down, caressing each soft fold in turn.

"Please, Myghal," she begged, trying to push her pussy into his face.

Myghal's grip tightened on her hipbones, and he thrust his tongue deeply into her channel, stroking up until his lips surrounded her clit. Her pelvis undulated against his mouth and her hips rose higher. When the moment came, it caught her off guard, vibrating through her like the deep pounding of a bass drum.

When the beats grew farther and farther apart, Kerry's back relaxed against the mattress. Myghal still nibbled at her pussy, helping to bring her down easy. A soft sigh left her lips. Her body surprised her. Myghal's continued caresses built up the thrumming tension again. She still wanted Myghal, wanted his cock inside of her, wanted to be even closer to him. Didn't want to ever let him go.

She writhed against him and he looked up at her. His hands slid around her as he gave her one last lick and moved up over her.

"Your nectar tastes like the honey made from the sweetest flowers."

His words made her toes curl. She'd never heard such poetry from a man, especially a man in her bed.

His chest glided across her stomach, but he stopped long enough to suckle one breast and then the other. She rubbed her pussy against him, not even sure which part of his body she touched. It didn't matter. She was connecting with Myghal and that was what drove her.

She ran her fingers through his long hair, drawing him up to her. He settled between her thighs, his hot cock cradled against her curls as she bent her legs and hugged his waist.

"We've waited long enough." She whispered the words between gasps for air. "I want you inside of me now, Myghal. Now."

"With the greatest of pleasure, Kerry O'Neill."

He gathered her to him, and the tip of his cock nudged her first. She quivered in anticipation and need when he pulled back. Then he thrust forward, hard, his cock sinking completely into her molten depths. She cried out and held him fast with her arms and legs, levering her hips side to side as if to seal him in, until they were fused together and could never be separated.

Tears filled her eyes and spilled from beneath her closed lids. How could she feel this oneness with him? She barely knew him, but they fit together like the two pieces that made the whole of a puzzle.

She hadn't locked him in, of course. He held onto her firmly and withdrew. She mimicked his movement, the friction of his rigid cock against her velvet walls creating a heat that infused her. Each thrust sent a wave that raged out of control and seared every nerve ending.

When the burst of pleasure was near, their movements grew frenzied, and Kerry felt a surge of energy surround them. It was almost as if she were feather-light and floating, as if her body touching Myghal's was the only contact she had with anything solid. Their lovemaking must have made her delusional because she even had the sensation of cooler air passing across her back, as if the mattress had disappeared or she'd left the warm surface behind.

Then she shattered into a million white-hot fragments, her spine bowing with the intensity. She lost sense of time and place and everything except Myghal's cock riding her fast into oblivion. Then his grip tightened on her, his back arched, and for a moment his body became as stiff as his cock had been. She felt his hot seed pump into her and bathe her channel, strengthening their unity. She had a part of Myghal within her. His semen would soak into her flesh, and he would truly become one with her. Their mystical connection was heightened by their physical union.

Kerry held him tightly. At the same time that Myghal's body went limp around her, she felt a little jolt as if something had bumped up against them. Her eyes flew open, but nothing seemed out of place. She flexed her shoulders and found the mattress solid beneath her again. She attributed it to the mystery of their bond.

Myghal rolled to his side, wrapping her in his arms, and Kerry snuggled against him.

*****

"Oh, my," Gomit whispered faintly and turned away from the window. Gomit had been standing watch around the corner of the human woman's dwelling, but had joined Tredje to report he'd seen nothing amiss. When he'd glanced through the glass, he lost his color and looked like he might faint. Tredje had never known Gnomes to be prudes, but Gomit was a weakling in many areas.

From his hiding place in the shrubbery, Tredje had watched the Prince and his intended Princess with interest. Perhaps the time had come to make a trip to the Thane's Golden Gate Bridge and purchase one of his daughters for a wife-slave. The thought of a Troll maid doing to him what the Prince had done to the human woman—lapping at her cunt with as much enthusiasm as a cat licking cream—made his cock ache.

He absently rubbed his stiff member through the silly blue Gnome trousers he still wore as a disguise. Tredje wondered how much of his cache of gold he'd have to relinquish for one of the Thane's daughters. Greedier than most Trolls, the Thane would want double or triple the going rate for a wife-slave. But to have one of the Thane's daughters as his own would raise his status in the Troll community. He had to weigh the matter carefully.

The coupling couple floated in the air, about halfway between the bed and the ceiling, in what Tredje knew to be the ultimate in Pixie pleasure. Levitation while fucking meant that the Prince had indeed found his Heart Match. Not that the Faeries doubted he had, but they might reward Tredje for the information. Who knew what tidbit the Faeries would find valuable?

The human woman's back arched. She had reached her peak, crying out her pleasure noisily while the Prince rammed into her again and again. Tredje stroked his cock briskly until he brought himself relief with a grunt, spurting his seed into the blue trousers. The Prince found his as well, and they landed on the mattress, lightly enough that neither was disturbed.

Tredje sighed. The urgent need to couple disappeared with his release. As usual, when lecherous thoughts prompted him to think about paying out good gold for a wife-slave, his own hand proved to be more than capable of taking care of the problem. No need to dip into his cache after all.

"We should go," the Gnome whispered from the other end of the row of bushes.

"We're here because your plan to capture the human woman in the hut failed," Tredje reminded him. The Gnome wouldn't dare disagree although they both knew it had been Tredje's idea. "We have to watch and seize any opportunity that arises to grab her tonight."

The Gnome snorted, then Tredje heard him draw in a deep breath. "The Prince won't leave her side until morning."

"More than likely, he won't leave her front." Tredje sniggered at his own joke. "But, aye, you're right. They'll be at it all night, fucking like rabbits."

"Aye," Gomit agreed. "And a goblet of dandelion wine beside the fire sounds good right now."

"That it does, that it does." Tredje contemplated the situation. They still had several days before the Equinox, and the Prince didn't seem to be in any hurry to find a way back to the Faerie Realm. Tredje suspected he had to convince the human woman to go with him first. By the way she seemed to enjoy his fucking, Tredje didn't think it would be too difficult for the Prince to talk her into it.

Tredje pulled at his beard. He would enjoy watching them fuck again and might even find relief once more, but the lure of dandelion wine was too great.

"Let's go home to me bridge and have some wine. Ye know, that's the best idea I've had all day," he said as they left their hiding place and disappeared into the night.

Chapter Ten

Kerry awoke to the wonder of warm and protective masculine arms around her just as they'd been when she fell asleep. Myghal. Just the thought of his name and what it invoked, all the feelings and sensations it stirred in her from merely one night, filled her with awe. For a long moment, she couldn't remember the last time she'd awakened in the arms of a man. And when she did finally recall the boyfriend from last year, she could barely remember what he looked like. She had certainly never felt like this.

It didn't matter that Myghal hadn't told her his last name. It didn't matter that she'd known him less than twenty-four hours. None of it mattered because she was falling for Myghal, falling hard, and nothing he could do or say would change what she felt for him.

She thought one night would rid her of the needs of her body, but it was so much more than that. None of it made sense, but she didn't think she'd ever get enough of him. While making love to him, she'd felt as if the mattress had vanished or that she was floating. A trick of passion, no doubt, but it had actually felt as if they'd risen into the air. For a few moments, she felt nothing beneath her and a cool rush of air passing over her back.

Kerry eased out of his arms and from the bed. He made a sound, a cross between a sigh and a moan and shifted position, burying his head deeper into the pillow until she could see only one of his closed eyes. She watched him with a fond smile. His long ash-blond hair lay in a tangle across his shoulders.

She reached out to touch him, to run her fingers over his arm, but stopped herself in time. She shouldn't wake him. If he woke up and smiled at her and looked at her with his sleepy bedroom eyes, she'd be too tempted to return to bed.

But before Kerry withdrew her hand, his eye blinked open and he reached for her, his fingers wrapping around her wrist. He tugged her toward him as he rolled onto his back. She resisted only a second because he did smile, and now both eyes were on her, inviting her. She moved with him until her body lay over his with only the sheet between them.

"Where are you going?" Myghal murmured as he planted kisses on her palm and the inside of her wrist.

The touches warmed her all over, especially the pit of her belly. When her clit began a rhythmic throb, she almost moaned. Instead, she bit her lip. Hard. A little pain would bring her to her senses.

"It's morning and I have a business to run."

He shook his head at her, and she felt his cock grow in length beneath her. She wanted nothing more than to yank the sheet away from him and repeat what they'd done the night before. Floating sensation and all.

"I have something better in mind."

Kerry laughed, a throaty sound because of her arousal. "I don't think it's your mind that's working right now."

He smiled again and Kerry melted. Then shook her head.

"Those plants can't sell themselves, and I have a loan payment to make." She kissed him lightly on the lips and tried to slip away from him, but he held her tightly.

"The plants will wait." He pulled her up until she straddled his body, balanced on her knees. "Turn around, Kerry."

"Myghal, I have to open the nursery," she protested, but her voice sounded weak.

"You will. In a little while," he promised. "Now, turn around."

The simmering heat that surrounded her clit wouldn't let her say no again. She did as he said, and while she was off of his body, he kicked the sheet to the foot of the bed. She straddled him again, this time facing away from him. In front of her, his cock stood tall, thick and rigid from its nest of light brown curls. She bent over, brushing her hair out of the way, and took the engorged head in her mouth.

Myghal's hands on her thighs guided her back until his mouth was on her pussy. His fingers slid up to her cheeks, rubbing and squeezing as he greedily licked and sucked the sensitized folds of flesh. Kerry pumped her hips, raking her clit against his tongue. How many times had Myghal brought her to orgasm since he'd walked into her life the day before? It might as well have been the first time because her body raged with need.

She lubricated his cock with her mouth, taking him deep into her throat and still didn't reach the base. She wrapped her fingers around his shaft, moving her hands and mouth up and down in tandem.

By the time they settled into a matching rhythm, Kerry tripped along the edge of passion and felt Myghal's cock grow even harder in her hands. One more stroke for each of them, and Kerry plummeted over at the same moment Myghal's hips thrust up hard. They both groaned with the release, hers a throaty sound because of Myghal's hot, tangy semen spilling into her mouth, and their bodies bent with the effort. She continued to milk his cock while she wriggled against his lips, drawing out the last bit of pleasure for both of them.

*****

Lazily, Myghal watched Kerry enter the bathroom and a few moments later heard the shower running. He imagined her beneath the running water, her hair drenched, her breasts and the red-glinted thatch of hair between her legs glistening wet. The enticing image he conjured made his exhausted cock stir against his thigh. He was tempted to join her in the shower, bend her over and fuck her from behind, but by the time he finished playing it out in his mind, the sound of the shower had stopped. Later, he promised himself.

As his Princess, she'd never have to worry about such mundane things as currency again. Her time would be filled with helping him run the princedom and, eventually, they'd share in raising their children. She could oversee the palace gardens and work with the plants as much as she liked.

Sitting up, he tried to ignore the building ache in his balls. If he still had any doubts the spell worked, this constant state of arousal while near her would have convinced him otherwise. That they'd levitated while coupling had been proof enough. A Pixie only levitated during sex without conscious thought when with his Heart Match.

He was already half in love with her. Just knowing they were destined for one another was enough to open his heart to her. His first task was to find a way back to the Faerie Realm. After that, he had to convince her of who he was and what they were to one another. It wouldn't be easy. Kerry was too practical, too grounded. And while Myghal understood the need for practicality and grounding in this magically bereft Other Realm, she would have to open her mind and imagination to all the possibilities to even begin to believe in him and his realm.

He had only a few days to accomplish everything.

When Kerry sailed through the bedroom, throwing him a smile along with his clean clothes, Myghal got up. He showered and dressed, but when he walked into the kitchen and Kerry giggled, he frowned. She kissed him quickly.

"I'm sorry, Myghal. What you're wearing was all right for yesterday. Everybody goes a little crazy and expects to see Leprechauns on St. Patrick's Day. Especially those of us of Irish descent." She poured coffee into two mugs. "But today is back to the real world, and you'll get more than a few strange looks if you go out in that get-up."

Myghal drew in a deep breath. "I'm not a Leprechaun."

"Oh." The grin fell from her lips as she set a plate holding a muffin in front of him. "Well, then why are you dressed like that?"

"I'm a Pixie," he said and carefully watched her reaction.

She frowned, as if thinking, and handed him a mug. "Are Pixies Irish?"

"No."

"Ah. Okay. Uh, sugar and creamer are here on the counter."

Suddenly, Myghal wasn't looking at Kerry. She was spooning tiny white crystals from a bowl into her coffee, and his attention was focused on the bowl. Could it possibly be…?

He waited until Kerry had turned her back before he stepped to the counter. Setting his mug aside, he stuck his finger into the bowl of precious crystals. He didn't feel the energy radiating from the matrices of the crystals, but that could be because he was in the Other Realm where too many other forms of energy contaminated every inch of space.

He touched a few of the crystals to his tongue. Sweetness saturated his taste buds and disappointment flooded through the rest of him. Although these crystals looked exactly like raw pixie dust, they weren't what he needed to return to the Faerie Realm.

"—won't be gone long," Kerry was saying as she walked toward the door. "The mall is just a few miles away. I'll be back before you know it with some clothes that won't get you arrested."

The door shut behind her and she was gone. Distracted by the crystals in the bowl, Myghal hadn't read her reaction. She could very well be going for help if she thought he was dangerously deranged.

Myghal poured his coffee down the drain and rinsed out his cup. They didn't have coffee in the Faerie Realm. They drank water, wine, and mead. They didn't have—what did she call it? Oh, yes. Sugar. Food in the Faerie Realm was sweetened with honey, but more often than not was eaten in its natural state.

Thinking of Kerry's confusion when he told her he was a Pixie, not a Leprechaun, he wondered if he should leave the house and stay out of sight until he knew if she returned alone or brought someone to take him away.

Myghal finally decided he would trust that the charmed dust knew what it was doing when it thrust him into Kerry's life and trust Kerry to recognize the connection between them even if she didn't know exactly what it was.

All he could do was wait and see.

Chapter Eleven

Kerry stood behind some tall potted plants, pretending to prune them. She wore gardening gloves and held a pair of shears, but she was really observing Myghal. He was busy rearranging the flower section and seemed happy doing so.

When she'd left the house, it had been her intention to go to the police and have Myghal carted away. But the more she thought about it, she knew she couldn't do it. She found herself going to the strip mall and buying jeans, shirts, and a jacket for him, paying out money she couldn't really afford.

She'd been pinching pennies until Lincoln squealed, as the saying went, for so long that it felt strange to walk into a shop and buy something new that didn't have to do with the nursery.

The guy just needed a chance to get back on his feet. As to why he thought he should dress like a Pixie instead of a Leprechaun for St. Patrick's Day, she didn't have a clue. He had that slight English accent, so maybe it was a tradition wherever he was from. A place where they had healers instead of doctors and guardsmen instead of police.

Calling things by different names and dressing like a Pixie wasn't enough to get him committed.

He'd certainly been a boon for business! Cars all but screeched to a halt and quickly turned into her driveway. Myghal had spent the morning working with the flower plants, rearranging them, watering them, repotting those that needed it. After lunch, he'd taken off his jacket and worked in his shirtsleeves in the unseasonably warm afternoon. With few exceptions, the drivers of the cars were female. Most held two or three.

The women would begin by strolling through the plants, but they invariably gravitated toward Myghal. As far as Kerry could tell, the women would strike up the conversations, but she couldn't help but notice that Myghal was almost as attentive to them as he was to her. Almost.

Many of them wandered away again, with smiles on their faces and plants in their arms. Myghal made sure each one left with a shamrock and an Irish rose. But one woman had been there longer than any of them. She was pretty in a dark, sultry way with a mane of black hair and long, lithe legs. She stayed close to Myghal even when others approached, as if staking out her property.

Several times, Kerry started to go out there but stopped herself. She'd never been the jealous type, and she didn't understand where this overwhelming need to claim him came from. Maybe the same place her feelings for him originated. Some place deep inside that no man had ever tapped before.

She told herself over and over there was no reason to be jealous. She hadn't seen him touch any of them intimately or lean close to whisper suggestively—not even the sultry brunette. Perhaps he was just being polite. Perhaps…

Kerry threw down the shears and yanked off her gloves.

Perhaps he was just being *more* polite to her. Free room and board and sex. What more could an itinerant alien ask for?

Kerry crossed the greenhouse to her desk in the corner. She had paperwork to do. Piles and piles of paperwork. And as grateful as she was for this day's little spurt in sales, it was too little, too late. She barely had enough to cover next month's expenses. What about the month after that? If Myghal could keep pulling them in in droves for the next six months, she *might* make it, but she had the feeling the novelty would wear off soon enough—especially if he didn't respond to their obvious advances.

What if he did?

Her suspicions provoked, she couldn't put *that* genie back in the bottle.

Both situations—financial and emotional—were hopeless. With one last bitter glance at Myghal and the black-haired woman standing almost close enough to touch, she dove into her paperwork.

*****

For a long time Kerry was aware of nothing except columns of numbers that were never big enough for incoming and too big for outgoing. Suddenly, she looked up to find Myghal staring at her from the edge of her office space. He smiled, and she almost melted. Then she remembered the brunette and looked out the tiny area of window not obscured by plants. The leggy woman was still out there, standing among the rose bushes, her arms crossed. She seemed impatient.

Kerry turned her gaze back to Myghal. "Your customer is waiting for you."

He shrugged. Was the movement too casual, as if he were only pretending not to care? Kerry shook herself mentally. It really wasn't in her nature to be overly suspicious. But a woman like *that* didn't hang around unless she was sure of a payoff.

"She won't buy anything, but she won't go away." He held up an empty bottle. "Do you have more?"

Kerry nodded and opened the mini-fridge. She handed him a full bottle of water from the six-pack she'd bought that morning. He uncapped it and took a long drink. Kerry couldn't help the thought that flitted through her mind—that she wished his lips were sucking on her clit instead of the water bottle. Her body grew warm, watching him, thinking about what he could do with those talented lips. It was all she could do not to sweep her desk clean, sprawl on her back, and spread her legs for him.

He wiped his mouth with the back of his hand. "Thank you. Here, water in bottles tastes much better than what pours from your…uh, spigots."

Kerry pushed aside the ledger she'd been working on. "You don't have bottled or running water where you come from?"

He slowly screwed the cap back on the bottle. He looked cornered, as if he searched for a way to answer her.

"No bottled water," he said at last.

But that didn't answer the second part of her question about running water. She didn't ask again. She wasn't sure she wanted to know. After all, a stream could be called running water.

Kerry jumped to her feet. She had to move, to get away from her corner. The transparent walls of the greenhouse were beginning to close in on her, and that wasn't good at all. She marched around the desk and headed for the door.

"I'm going to see if your friend wants anything."

Myghal caught up to her and stopped her before she'd gone another yard.

"She's not my friend. You're the only friend I have here."

She pulled loose from his hold on her arm. "Why is that? I don't understand where you're from, what you're doing here, or why I—"

Kerry broke off and bit her lip. She wasn't about to spill her guts to him about her feelings when she knew so little about him.

"You sound angry, Kerry O'Neill." Gently, he took her into his arms. "Have I done something wrong?"

She almost blurted out that everything was all wrong, but she went into his embrace instead. And that made everything all right. It felt right to be close to him, to hold him and be held by him, to make love with him until it seemed like they floated off the bed.

"I'm not angry. I'm—" But she was at a loss for words, unable to express all the emotions boiling over inside of her.

"You're what, Kerry? Fighting the urge to make love?"

She nodded. It wasn't all she was fighting, but sex with Myghal seemed to have taken over and become the most important. What was balancing the books and trying to find a way to save her business compared to fucking Myghal?

He kissed her, taking her breath and her tongue, sucking hard. The mock fucking set her clit afire and desire burning through her veins. He backed her up all the way to her office space, past the row of potted pampas grass, until the backs of her thighs hit the edge of her desk. Was he a mind reader?

His fingers fumbled with the snap and zipper of her jeans as his mouth continued to devour her. When he grunted in frustration, Kerry helped to unfasten her pants, then undid his as well. She reached in and pulled his cock free, the silky skin hot and hard. She stroked it repeatedly as Myghal's hand dove inside her panties, two fingers curling up inside her, the knuckle of his thumb pressed to her clit.

"I don't understand..." Kerry whispered, massaging his cock and leaning into his hand as his fingers fucked her. "I don't understand why I want you all the time."

His fingers delved even deeper. "We were meant for each other."

Chapter Twelve

Kerry believed in lust at first sight, but not love at first sight. He hadn't said anything about love, had he? But didn't "meant for each other" mean love, too?

His other hand slid inside her panties, leaving a hot trail across her cheeks as he peeled her underwear and jeans below her hips. She started to help him push them lower but he stayed her hand. Instead, he turned her around so that her backside was to him and bent her over the desk.

Questing fingers found her wet lips again, and his cock nudged her there. Arms resting on the desktop, she arched her spine, pushing her pelvis back and up to make his entrance easier. His hands slid beneath her blouse, over her stomach and ribs and under her bra until her breasts were in his palms, thumbs pinching her nipples against his forefingers.

Myghal rocked against her and his cock drove into her pussy. She increased the arch of her hips until his balls struck her clit with each thrust. He glided in and out in a smooth, fast rhythm, squeezing her nipples with each forward thrust. Kerry closed her eyes and enjoyed the building tension coiling in her womb. As her orgasm neared, her hips joined his pace, striving to make contact with his balls.

When the explosion came, surging warmly through her entire body, Kerry moaned with the intense pleasure. She rubbed her clit against his tight sac to prolong the sensation. Myghal's long thrusts turned into short, quick jabs until he ground his hips into her with a guttural groan. His hands tightened on her breasts, and she felt him spurt within her.

He collapsed across her, and all Kerry could hear was the sound of their breath coming in gasps. His deflated cock was still inside her. Kerry flexed her inner muscles around it. She wanted him to fuck her again and again, but she knew he needed time to recover and—

They were draped across her desk, once again where anyone could walk in and find them. The pampas grass plants afforded some privacy, but her corner didn't have a door. Why did all common sense take flight where Myghal was concerned?

"Myghal..." Kerry moved, and Myghal gave her nipples one last squeeze before he stood up. Kerry rose, too, straightening her bra and blouse and pulling up her jeans. She turned to face him. "We've got to stop doing this here. If someone walked in—"

Myghal swung her around. "Don't be ashamed of pleasure."

She shook her head. "I'm not. But it's something that should be private. For some reason, I can't keep my hands off of you."

"I'm glad," he said with a sensual grin that made her heart flip-flop in her chest. He kissed her. "I can't keep my hands off of you or my cock out of you." He took her hand and placed it on his crotch. "Already I want to fuck you again."

She squeezed his growing bulge. "Me, too. But we can't do this anymore."

He frowned when she took her hand away and peeked through the plants. The brunette was still there, impatiently pacing through the hardy evergreen shrubs. Several other customers wandered around.

"I'll give them each a shamrock and an Irish rose and send them on their way." His hand slid between her legs and rubbed her swollen, aching pussy. "Then I'll come back and lock the door so I can fuck you until you scream."

Kerry moaned, his promise and his touch stirring her desires again. She didn't know why she was constantly horny around this man. Perhaps it was an overreaction to the fact that she hadn't been laid in six months before Myghal walked into her life. Had it only been yesterday? It felt as if she'd known him forever. Even if she didn't know much about him.

"Oh, Myghal." Reluctantly, she pulled away from him. He was disappointed but didn't persist. "They're potential customers. They might buy something."

He nodded, touched her cheek, kissed her, and turned to leave. She almost called him back, the tingling in her clit insisting that she do so, but she bit her lip to keep from saying his name. She watched him cross the greenhouse and walk out the door…with the oddest premonition that she might never see him again.

*****

Kerry looked out the window one more time. The brunette smiled seductively when she saw Myghal emerge from the greenhouse. Kerry wondered what the brunette would think if she knew what Myghal had been doing in here. Several other women flocked to him, and he had a smile and a word for each of them.

All these women today…and yesterday, too, she suddenly realized. What she thought had been in response to her drastic sale prices might have actually been Myghal's magnetic presence. They seemed drawn to him even from as far away as the road. As if there were something…magical about him.

She shook her head. She needed to get her head out of the clouds and back into her books. Looking at the disarray on her desk, she shook her head again and ran a hand through her hair. How was she ever going to concentrate on bookkeeping when all she could think of was bending over the desk while Myghal fucked her from behind.

Kerry plopped down in her chair—a place that conjured up more images to distract her—and pulled the ledger toward her. She straightened up the stack of receipts and started going through them one at a time. Glancing up from time to time, she always saw the brunette hovering close to Myghal. Her mouth moved, but Kerry had no idea what she might be saying. Well, she had an idea, but she didn't *know*. That woman had been out there all afternoon. What else could she want except Myghal?

Kerry became absorbed in making columns of numbers balance, quite a while passed until she looked up for the last time before snapping the book shut. She rubbed her neck and stared out the window.

Shadows had lengthened considerably as the sun moved lower in the sky. She'd spent more time on the books than she meant to, but at least she'd done most of her work. She rested her elbows on the desk and rubbed her neck while gazing out across the rows and rows of potted shrubs.

She couldn't see anyone, not even Myghal. Perhaps she could close early and make up to him what she'd denied them earlier. Turning him down hadn't been easy for her, but he'd seemed really disappointed.

Kerry stood and walked outside her office area. Pushing leafy plants aside, she looked outside. From here, she had a good view of the parking area. No vehicles of any kind. So, the leggy brunette had finally given up. Kerry smiled triumphantly and turned away. She spent the better part of an hour straightening up the greenhouse.

When everything was put away, she wondered why Myghal hadn't come in. Surely he'd finished rearranging all the outside plants by now. She left the greenhouse and stood on the path to the toolshed, looking over her grounds, but Myghal was nowhere to be seen.

Kerry wondered if he could have possibly been hurt or sick and lying among the plants or statuary. She ran back inside for a flashlight and jacket. It was almost twilight and the air had cooled considerably.

By the time she'd searched between every row of shrubs and behind every stack of bags of mulch and fertilizer and even every corner of the front building and toolshed, night had fallen. Where could Myghal have gone?

The image of the leggy brunette with the seductive smile exploded in her mind.

Just a few hours ago, she would have sworn that Myghal was not the kind of man who would just walk out on her without a word. She hadn't thought he would walk out at all because there was a connection between them. She didn't understand it, but it was real. Even Myghal said he felt it.

But she'd looked everywhere on her property and hadn't found an injured or ill Myghal. He said he didn't know anybody else here. Where else could he have gone?

The only answer was with the brunette.

Kerry closed her eyes against the burn of unshed tears. She felt like an idiot, a gullible fool. Myghal had just appeared out of nowhere into her life. Why wouldn't he disappear just as easily? He'd never made her any promises. They'd known each other a little over twenty-four hours.

So why did it hurt so much?

With tears scalding her cheeks, Kerry ran inside long enough to grab her purse. She ran through the gates and locked them behind her. Behind the wheel of her car, she swiped tears away as she stabbed at the ignition.

Myghal was gone.

Chapter Thirteen

"Lady Kerry," the Gnome said with bowed head as he removed his cap. "I am Gomit, your humble servant."

Kerry stumbled back in surprise. She bumped into the side of the small front building. She blinked at the little man who was dressed just like the taller garden Gnome statues she had for sale.

Myghal leaving her must have cracked her mind. She'd spent a sleepless, restless night, her body enflamed with need and aching for Myghal. She'd come to work, hoping to find him here, that he'd wandered away for some reason and got lost but somehow found his way back again. But he hadn't been here when she arrived, her eyes red and swollen from weeping, and he didn't show up all day. She'd resigned herself to the fact that Myghal had gotten what he wanted until a better offer came along. Namely, the leggy brunette.

The day had dragged by. She'd been about to go home when the garden Gnome introduced himself to her. Kerry didn't know whether to scream or run. All she could manage was a whimper. The Gnome continued talking.

"'Tis regretful I am to inform you that his royal highness, Prince Myghal, has been captured by a despicable Troll."

"Wh-Wh—" Kerry clamped her lips together and swallowed hard. The little man dressed like a Gnome spoke English, and she heard every word he said, but none of it made sense. Servant, royalty, captured… Prince Myghal? "Wh-What are you t-talking about?" she was finally able to sputter. "Wh-Who are you?"

"Gomit, at your service. 'Tis a shock, I understand. Prince Myghal hadn't a chance to tell you everything, indeed. I—"

"Why are you calling him *prince*?" Kerry was surprised she was able to speak a whole sentence without stopping to catch her breath. "What is he prince of? And by captured, do you mean he's been kidnapped?"

"Aye, Lady Kerry."

"Oh." She breathed easy for the first time since she'd found Myghal gone. But she immediately tightened up again. She shouldn't feel relief. He hadn't left her, but had been kidnapped.

"'Tis sorry I am to admit my part in the deed, but my liege, General Gorgicz, instructed this worthless servant to play along with the Troll but to thwart him at the first opportunity."

"General Gorg— And a Troll." Kerry pressed against the brick.

The Gnome seemed harmless enough and subservient enough, but she had yet to wrap her mind around the fact that one of her Gnome statues had come to life. No, that was impossible. The Gnome just happened to look like the statues because…well, because he was a Gnome. And he was telling a wild tale about a man who might be a prince that she had just met and fallen head over heels in lust with two days ago.

What was she supposed to do? Stand here and listen to a Gnome? Yes, because he said Myghal had been kidnapped.

"'Tis a long story, Lady, and time is of the essence, if I understand the Prince's situation correctly. If you please, I'll tell you what I know."

Kerry drew in a deep, shaky breath. "It would please me greatly. If you'll come in the greenhouse, you can tell me all about it."

Gomit followed behind her, cap still in hand. She glanced back at him while she led the way, but he was doing nothing more than pumping his short legs to keep up with her. She slowed her walk the rest of the way.

Inside, she flipped on the lights. She went to her desk and fell into her chair. She hadn't realized how weak her legs were until that moment. She offered him the extra chair and he climbed into the seat.

"Maybe you should start at the beginning," Kerry suggested.

"'Twould take all night, I fear. Besides, some of it's not my place to tell. I'll be brief as I can. The Troll, Tredje, and I were sent to prevent Prince Myghal from taking y—"

"Prince?" Kerry interrupted. "Myghal never told me he was a prince. Prince of what?"

"Prince of Pixieland, a part of the Faerie Realm."

"Pixieland?" Kerry's tone rose in disbelief. "Myghal has to be over six feet tall. Trust me, there's nothing pixie about him."

Gomit's gnarled face split into a grin. "Aye, but his royal highness is indeed Prince of the Pixies. The old Prince, Myghal's father, died over three months ago. Myghal, being his only child, inherited the title. And the responsibilities. Unlike most royalty in your human realm, rulers actually rule their domains in the Faerie Realm."

"I see." Then Kerry shook her head. "No, I don't really see at all. I'm supposed to believe this, but if it were coming from someone other than one of my garden Gnomes, I'd have called the police already."

"Nay, Lady. Your humble servant isn't one of your statues come to life. My home is far away from here."

"Right. Okay. Let's get back to Myghal. You say he's been kidnapped. By a Troll." Kerry couldn't believe the words that were coming out of her mouth.

"Aye. The Faerie King sent word that Prince Myghal was to be stopped from bringing you to the Faerie Realm before the Equinox at all cost. Tredje tried once to kidnap you, but—"

"Tredje?"

"Aye. Tredje the Troll."

"Of course. And the Equinox is..." Kerry pulled her desk calendar closer. "Tomorrow. Why would Myghal need to take me to the Faerie Realm before the Equinox?"

Gomit squirmed in his seat and ducked his head. "I couldn't say, Lady. But the Gnomes and Trolls and some other Faerie Realm folk who live in your world are expected to do King Norfe's bidding even though we consider ourselves independent from the Faerie Realm."

The little Gnome's tale was getting more and more complicated, and Kerry's suspension of disbelief was wearing thin. This had to be some trick? But who would be playing it on her? And why? April Fool's was another two weeks away.

"I don't mean to be rude, but could you please not get into Mother Goose's political agendas." She said it with a smile, but she felt as if she was being had. Possibly by Myghal himself. He'd been dressed like a Leprechaun, after all. Strike that. In light of what Myghal had told her and Gomit had just confirmed, Myghal had been dressed like a Pixie. No wonder he'd had no interest in the contest across the street.

"Aye, Lady Kerry. As I said, instructions came from King Norfe to stop Prince Myghal from taking you into the Faerie Realm at all cost. The Trolls sent Tredje, and our leader, General Gorgicz, sent me. What the Trolls don't know is that we Gnomes have been in service to the Pixies since longer than any of us can remember. We are bound by honor to serve the Pixies before the Faeries. The allegiance goes back so far that even our Elders don't remember why, but we believe the Pixie Prince at that time did a great deed for the Gnomes, and we are obligated to repay the kindness until the end of time."

"I understand," Kerry said. The quiet dignity of the homely little Gnome touched her deeply.

"Then you understand why I joined with Tredje, just to upset his plans and help in my small way. I've managed to convince Tredje that I'm dim-witted and clumsy so he hasn't relied on me too much." Gomit sighed heavily. "I daresay a Pixie

Prince has helped them out a time or two, but Trolls have no honor."

While part of her found his tale ludicrous, another part of her was beginning to believe. The little man sitting in a chair in front of her was not merely a midget in a Gnome costume. His features were unlike anything she'd ever seen on a human being. Yellow eyes, nose, mouth, and jaw were smashed or out of alignment. And everything he said meshed with what she knew about Myghal—little as it was.

Now, she started to worry about Myghal. If the Faerie King commanded they stop Myghal at all cost, and if the Troll had no honor, this Tredje might kill Myghal.

He must have read the concern on her face because he smiled a little. "Tredje is too lazy to expend the energy to hurt the Prince and too vain to think his plan of holding him captive will fail. I can distract Tredje, but you'll have to free the Prince. The Troll mustn't know I've helped the Prince or I would do it myself. The Gnomes' honor-bound liege to the Pixies has to remain a secret in case another occasion should arise when our help is needed."

Kerry ran a hand through her hair. The surreal quality of the past few days since meeting Myghal had increased tenfold. "I thought all you fairy-tale type people had powers. Why couldn't Myghal just zap the Troll or something?"

Gomit shook his head. "It's not that easy in this realm. We Gnomes have never had any special powers. And here, the Pixies have almost no magic. The Prince is as vulnerable as any human. The Troll has a bit of limited magic. When he uses it, he has to take the time to recover his energy before he can use it again."

"All right." Obviously, there were rules that had never made it into any book of fairy-tales Kerry had ever read. "Where is the Troll holding him?"

"In Tredje's dwelling beneath the bridge across the street."

"At Sir Plantsalot? You mean, Trolls really do live under bridges?"

Gomit's eyes widened, showing how startlingly yellow the irises were. Not golden-yellow or amber-yellow, but bright buttercup-yellow. And now, Kerry realized, it was more than the unusual color. The pupils were vertically slitted, like the eyes of a reptile.

"Of course. Where else would Trolls live? Most are too lazy to do more than sleep in the rushes underneath. But Tredje has been uncommonly industrious in this case. He has excavated an extensive series of tunnels and chambers in the embankment between the two bridges. He says you must always go into his dwelling beneath the bridge marked 'enter' and leave beneath the bridge marked 'exit'. He's quite proud to have two bridges to himself, especially near a castle, even if it isn't real. Castles are quite a rarity in this country."

"Quite," Kerry said absently. Myghal held in an underground dwelling. The Troll was probably no bigger than Gomit, so the tunnels and chambers would be small and dark and suffocating. She broke into a sweat just thinking about it.

She couldn't... Could she? She had to be the one to save Myghal because no one else would believe the story, and Gomit had to preserve the secrecy of his allegiance to the Pixies. But how was she supposed to force herself into the cramped quarters of the Troll?

Chapter Fourteen

Kerry slipped on dark coveralls and strapped on a tool belt with an array of tools that could be used as weapons in case Tredje the Troll saw through Gomit's distraction and discovered what she was doing. She also carried a box cutter to release Myghal's bonds. Gomit had assured her that Myghal was bound with rope, not chains.

She checked the bright beam of the heavy-duty flashlight several times as they crossed the five lanes to Sir Plantsalot. By that time of night all businesses along the thoroughfare were closed and very little traffic moved along the street.

Gomit lead her to the exit bridge. Kerry watched as he quickly scrambled down the side of the drainage ditch. She glanced around to make sure no cars were coming and no one was lurking about then went after him.

The ditch was deeper than she was tall, so no one would be able to see what they were doing unless they were right on the side of the street or on the bridge above. Kerry switched on a small penlight as they moved into the shadows beneath the bridge.

"Tredje's sitting chamber is near the entrance," Gomit explained, keeping his voice low so it wouldn't carry on the night air. "He stays there all evening until he goes to bed. His bed chamber is about halfway between the entrance and the exit."

Kerry could already feel the sweat collecting on her upper lip and trickling down the small of her back even though she should have been comfortable or even a little chilled in the crisp night air. It was too dark beneath the bridge, among the scrubby weeds, and she was only able to tolerate it because Gomit was with her. What was she going to do when he left her alone? How was she supposed to crawl into that small opening and travel along the cramped tunnels without screaming?

"Wha—" Her mouth was dry, her tongue like a wad of cotton. She swallowed. "What if he decides to check on Myghal?"

Gomit thought a moment. "He might before he goes to bed, but you should have the Prince freed and both of you away from here by then. You'll need to move quickly."

Quickly. Kerry didn't think she could move at all. Already, she felt the pressure of the darkness. She could imagine the tunnel walls bearing down on her from all sides. Suddenly, her chest felt heavy and she gasped for air.

"Are you all right, Lady Kerry?" Gomit asked, his voice thick with concern.

She shook her head and closed her eyes. No, she was not all right. She was scared. More than scared, she was petrified.

"Is there anything I can do?"

She shook her head again. She had to save Myghal, but she didn't know how she was going to force herself to enter that tunnel where it was dark and small and closed in. Before she realized what she was doing, she had crawled out from beneath the bridge into the open. She rose to her knees and turned her face to the sky, breathing in deep gulps of air.

"I'm sorry, Lady Kerry," Gomit said close to her ear. "We don't have much time. If I don't return soon, Tredje will become suspicious. He might decide to look in on the Prince and make sure he hasn't escaped. Trolls are naturally distrustful and Tredje keeps a close watch on me. This is the first chance I've had to tell you about the Prince. Will you be able to free him?

Would she? She had to. Somehow, she would have to make herself enter the Troll's tunnel and find and free Myghal. Kerry swiped the back of her hand across her upper lip.

"I'll do it," she said.

Gomit sighed in relief. "I knew I could count on you, Lady. Give this to the Prince. He'll know what to do with it."

Gomit pressed a small, ridged bottle into her hand.

"Now, I must get back. Do you remember the way?"

Kerry nodded, then watched as Gomit trundled down the ditch toward the entrance bridge. Gomit had gone over the directions with her as she readied for the strangest adventure she would certainly ever have in her life. She had repeated them over and over until she had them memorized. Now, she went over them again in her head, but she realized it was a delaying tactic.

Myghal needed her. Why wasn't that enough to overcome this stupid, irrational fear of dark, enclosed places? Myghal had helped her through being locked in the toolshed. He'd told her that she was strong enough to defeat the fear whenever she was ready to do it. She had to be ready now.

Kerry got to her feet. She looked at the bottle that Gomit put in her hand. She stared at it in bewilderment. The bottle was the saltshaker from her desk in the greenhouse and had been missing a couple of days. Why would Gomit steal it? And how would it help Myghal?

With no answers, she tucked the saltshaker into the zippered pocket that held the box cutter and turned around. She used the penlight to find the opening again. The small hole looked to be nothing more than perhaps where dirt had been washed away. It was barely big enough for her to wriggle through. What would be on the other side?

"Take it one step at a time," she muttered and bent to go under the bridge again. "A ladder. Gomit said there would be a rope ladder fastened to a large root that protruded just under the hole."

Kerry forced one foot in front of the other until she was at the hole. She switched on the large flashlight and put the penlight away. The beam revealed a space that was barely large enough for her to enter. Sweeping the light down, she saw thick ropes knotted around a root bigger than her leg.

But the dark and enclosed space was too much and she had to close her eyes or run. She couldn't run. She had to do this to save Myghal.

Kerry took deep, even breaths, breathing in through her nose and out through her mouth. The tightness in her chest, that panicky, fluttery feeling, eased a little. She had to try again.

Slowly, she opened her eyes, keeping her breath even. She focused on the bright beam of light following the rope ladder until it reached the bottom. It looked to be about a ten-foot drop. She could climb down that far. Sure, she could. She just wasn't sure what would happen after that. Would she start shrieking until Tredje the Troll found her and did who-knew-what to her? Or would she just curl up into a little ball in the corner until Tredje and Gomit ran across her days later? Either could happen. She'd just been lucky that she'd screamed in the shed the day before. Otherwise, Myghal might never have found her and she'd still be there, huddled in the corner in the dark.

The dark, her enemy. Enclosed spaces, the bane of her existence. She faced both right now, but she had to overcome them to save Myghal. She took another slow, deep breath.

Holding on to the dirt above the hole, she put one leg, then the other through. Before she could think about it too much, she wiggled around until she was on her stomach, her legs dangling. She was barely holding on because one hand held the flashlight. There was no way in hell she was releasing the light, so she had to think of something and quick.

She managed to hold the light under her chin and rummage in the pocket on the tool belt until she found the bungee strap. She looped it around her neck and fastened the ends through the handle on the flashlight. She immediately lowered herself until one foot reached the root. She tested her weight, then put both feet on it when it held.

She gripped the dirt at the bottom of the hole and bent until she could feel the root with her other hand. She lowered one foot, taking a quick look with the flashlight to place the next step. In this way, she was able to move downward until she could hold the rope with both hands. She finished climbing down.

Keeping busy had kept her mind off of where she was.

But now she felt the walls of the tunnel pressing in on all sides. Faint light came through the hole at the top of the ladder. Up there was open space and air to breathe. Her throat threatened to close, and her chest tightened up again. All she had to do was scramble up the ladder and she would be able to breathe again.

"*Myghal,*" Kerry whispered and closed her eyes. She gripped a rung of the ladder and pressed her forehead against it. She had to focus on helping Myghal.

Once more she took deep even breaths until her heart was no longer racing in her chest. She had to save Myghal. It was extremely important for him to return to his realm before the Equinox on Tuesday. Even though she didn't have any idea why, if it was important to Myghal, then it was important to her. She couldn't save him if she allowed herself to dissolve into a puddle of neuroses or, worse, run away. He might forgive her, but she'd never be able to forgive herself.

All right, what was she supposed to do next? What had Gomit told her? She had to think a minute before she recalled his directions.

Stand at the bottom with the ladder at her back, then turn left.

Slowly and without opening her eyes, Kerry turned around until she could feel the knots of rope digging into her spine. She swung the flashlight up with her left hand and opened her eyes.

Dizziness swept over her, as if the tunnel was tilting one way and then the other. She had to close her eyes again or she might topple over or puke. Or both. Tears of frustration scalded them, but she refused to cry. She didn't have time. She had to free Myghal. She took a step, her hand pressed against the dirt to her left. She moved to the left a few more feet then tried to open her eyes again.

This time the dizziness wasn't enough to make her stomach churn. She angled the beam of the flashlight against the far wall to give the greatest area of light and tried not to think about the expanse of darkness surrounding her or how the ceiling lowered the farther she walked until she was nearly bent double. She finally had to drop to her hands and knees.

Kerry had never been in a situation where everything seemed to literally close in on her.

She focused her gaze on the circle of light cast by the flashlight, and concentrated on the directions Gomit had given her.

Taking a deep breath, Kerry reminded herself once again that she had to save Myghal. That thought alone gave her the courage to crawl forward.

Chapter Fifteen

Gomit called them doorways, but they were no more than arched openings cut in the dirt that led to either another tunnel or a chamber. When Kerry reached the doorway to the chamber where Myghal was being held—if she had followed the Gnome's directions correctly—she barely stuck her head in with the flashlight.

"Myghal?" Kerry whispered. According to Gomit, this part of the Troll's lair was far enough away from his sitting room that she didn't have to worry about making noise, but the tightness in her chest and throat didn't allow her to speak above a whisper. "Myghal, are you here?"

Kerry heard a grunt, then a scuffling sound. She flashed the beam of light all around the chamber. It was much larger than she'd expected, with almost as much floor space as her bedroom. The ceiling was, of course, no higher than the tunnel ceiling. She would still have to crawl to enter.

A bright reflection made her stop moving the flashlight. Unruly ash blond hair glittered in the beam. Myghal! He lay on his side, a rag secured in his mouth with a piece of cloth tied tightly around his head. She scuttled through the archway toward him.

His hands had been bound behind his back, and his feet tied together. Another rope, drawn through the rope between his hands, then through a metal loop fastened to a post buried solidly in the dirt, and the one between his feet ensured he couldn't move from the spot.

Kerry set the flashlight so that the beam illuminated them both, but didn't shine directly into their eyes. She untied the cloth around his mouth first and withdrew the rag between his lips.

He looked at her with such tender emotion while he worked his jaw that Kerry saw no need to ever tell him that she had doubted him and thought he'd gone off with the leggy brunette.

He grinned. "You know, don't you?"

Being with Myghal eased her anxiety, and the tightness in her chest and throat had relaxed, so she could speak normally.

"That Faeries and Gnomes and Trolls exist? Yes. That you're a Prince instead of a slightly eccentric Brit who doesn't know the difference between a Pixie and a Leprechaun? Yes." Kerry took a deep breath and grinned back. "That I think I might be falling in love with you? Yes to that, too."

"The feeling's mutual. Now, if you could get me loose, I'll show you how much."

Kerry unzipped a pocket and reached in. She felt the box cutter and the saltshaker and brought out both. Gomit had said the shaker would be important to Myghal. She began cutting the rope behind Myghal.

"As much as I'd love to right now, we won't have time to explore exactly how much. The Gnome, Gomit, said we needed to get out of here as quickly as possible. The Troll—I think his name is Tredje—would be checking on you before he goes to bed."

Myghal groaned as he straightened his legs.

"I'm not sure why. By the size of these tunnels, the Troll isn't much bigger than the Gnome. It seems to me you and I could handle him."

Myghal shook his arms to get circulation back into them. "Trolls are mean little bastards. They have magic all their own and no ethics to keep it in check. That's why the old Faerie Queen—and the Faeries aren't known for their morality, so you can imagine how bad the Trolls are—banished the Trolls to this realm. Their magic is severely limited here and keeps them where they can do the least amount of damage. But they still have control of some magic."

Kerry massaged his legs. "If the Faeries are the ones who banished the Trolls, why would a Troll help them prevent you from going back into your realm? Why would a Troll help a Faerie?"

"The Trolls are still in service to the Faeries and are required to do their bidding when called upon."

Kerry nodded. All of this was supposed to make perfect sense. She supposed it did…in some other dimension.

"How did they capture you?"

"When the last customer left--"

"The tall brunette?" Kerry couldn't help but ask.

He nodded. "She didn't seem to want to leave, but I finally made her understand it was closing time."

Kerry thought he sounded exasperated rather than flattered by the attention. She bit her lip to keep from grinning like an idiot.

Myghal stretched out one leg then the other. "They had strung rope across one of the walkways, and I tripped. I caught a glimpse of Tredje before he knocked me out. When I came to, I was here and all tied up."

"Gomit said you have to return to Pixieland by the Equinox. He didn't say why, though." Kerry's elation dissipated. She was afraid to hear the answer to her next question. She had a feeling it wasn't going to be an answer she liked. "When you go, you'll be gone for good, won't you?"

Myghal reached for her, placing a hand at her neck and drawing her closer. He kissed her, his lips possessing hers. Tears filled her eyes. *This is good-bye, isn't it?* One last burning kiss to carry with her the rest of her life. When they broke apart, gasping for breath, Myghal rested his head against hers.

Kerry didn't wait for his answer. She jerked away, knocking his hand aside. She tried to scramble back, but Myghal lunged for her. He caught her and they rolled together across the chamber floor. When they stopped, Myghal was on top, straddling her, pinning her to the dirt with her arms raised over her head.

"Let me go!" she said between gritted teeth as she struggled to get the big lug off of her. "What's the point? You're leaving and that's that."

"You didn't let me finish, love," Myghal said softly.

"What does it matter? What were you going to say? Something like—Hey, next time you're in the woods and find a pixie ring, wave and say hi."

She tried to wrench her arms free from his grip, but he was holding her too tightly.

"No, I was going to explain why I need to return to my realm by the Equinox…and why you'll be coming with me."

When the words sank in, Kerry froze. She could see his face by the beam of the flashlight, and he didn't look like he was teasing her.

"You— You want me to…visit?" she stammered. She never thought he would want her to go with him or that she would even be welcome in his realm.

"No, I want you to come with me and be my wife."

Kerry's mouth worked, but no sound came out. Had she heard him correctly? Was he asking her to marry him?

He slid his hands into hers as he spread his length over hers. She still held the saltshaker in one hand, and it was trapped between their palms as he entwined his fingers with hers.

"The truth is I have to be married by the Equinox for Pixieland to retain its independence from the Faeries. But," he murmured as his mouth came close to hers again, "you're the only woman I want for my Princess. Will you marry me, Kerry O'Neill?"

Chapter Sixteen

Marry him? Going from never seeing him again to marrying him gave her mental whiplash. She hadn't considered marriage. At all. They'd only known each other a few days. How could they even think about marriage?

He had to marry by the Equinox to save Pixieland…but she was the only woman he wanted to be his Princess. What should she do?

"I know everything is moving too fast." His heartfelt apology touched her. "I wish I had time to court you like you deserve. But I can promise you I'll do everything within my power to make you happy. The palace gardens will be yours to do with as you will. And we can visit this realm whenever you like."

"Gardens?"

He grinned. "The palace is surrounded by gardens, filled with every flower and herb imaginable—and some not imagined in this realm. We'll rule Pixieland together, but the gardens will be yours."

The thought of expansive gardens, a sea of colorful flowers and blooming herbs, tempted her. But a marriage couldn't survive on the promise of a garden alone.

"What— What will happen if I say no?"

"My heart will break," Myghal said. "If I don't marry, Pixieland will revert to the Faerie kingdom. The Faerie folk would invade, and the Faerie Guard would police us. We would wither under their rule. Are you saying no, Kerry? If you say no, I'll have to return to the Faerie realm and marry to save my princedom. I have to do this for my people. But I'll never forget you, Kerry, and I'll never love another, not even the one who would be my Princess. You are the other half of my heart."

Kerry's eyes filled with tears again, but this time because of what she felt for Myghal. If she never saw him again, her heart would break as well.

"Yes, I'll marry you."

"Are you sure, Kerry?" he asked, but he was smiling.

She nodded. "I'm not sure what I'm getting into, but I do know what I feel for you is real."

"Good." He kissed her again, a lingering fusion of their lips that left her breathless. When he pulled away, he touched her face. "We probably should get out of here before the Troll comes."

"Yes, we should."

Myghal helped her sit up. Only then did she remember the saltshaker. She handed it to him and showed him how to remove the top.

"Gomit said you would need this. But I can't imagine what you can do with salt."

He stuck his finger into the salt crystals and touched them to his tongue. He became more excited than when she'd agreed to marry him.

"Do you know what this is?" he asked incredulously.

"It's salt."

He laughed. "It's Pixie dust in its raw form."

"Salt is Pixie dust?"

"And Faerie dust. Pixieland supplies the Faeries with their dust. That's why King Norfe wants control over us, so he can control the dust. But what none of the Faeries or other folk know is that dust isn't mined in Pixieland. It comes from here, your realm."

"We supply you with Pixie dust?" Kerry had momentary visions of mining conglomerates shipping truckloads of salt to Pixieland.

"The Gnomes do. They were always soldiers, but after the Realm Wars ended, they started mining these crystals for us to use with our magic. The crystals have to be reconditioned and charmed, but—"

A thud reverberated through the tunnels, and Kerry heard a gruff voice shout, "On your feet, you clumsy git."

"The Troll is coming," she whispered anxiously. "Can you use the salt to get us out of here?"

"Not like this. I have to change the matrix and charm it. It will take a few moments. Can you keep the Troll distracted until it's done?"

"Sure," Kerry said, but she wasn't sure at all.

Myghal poured the salt into his palm and cupped his other hand over it. His face pinched in concentration, and a pale white light, growing stronger as she watched, glowed through his fingers.

Footsteps sounded just outside the doorway. She didn't know how to keep the Troll occupied, but blocking the doorway would be a start. She crawled forward and when she reached the opening, she looked up into a misshapen face—sunken muddy black eyes, a twisted bulbous nose, and a lipless slit for a mouth revealing mismatched and discolored teeth. It was the ugliest face she'd ever seen.

The Troll lifted his lantern. "Well, now, what have we here?" he growled.

"What do you want?" Kerry snapped.

"You're an intruder in me home and ye ask what I want?" He jerked his chin to indicate the chamber behind Kerry. "Gomit, get in there and see that the Pixie is still secured. I'll take care of the human."

The Troll reached out one stubby hand, aiming a blunt finger at her. She felt a pull behind her navel, then she was jerked through the doorway and slammed against the opposite tunnel wall.

Dazed, Kerry watch as Gomit, moving slowly, entered the tunnel. He glanced back at her, and she thought she saw him wink. Then the Troll was in her face, his lantern raised high.

"If ye weren't so damn ugly, I'd keep ye for my wife-slave after I send the Pixie Prince back to his own realm." His fetid breath washed over her and she gagged, shrinking back from him as far as she could. "But I can't stand the look of ye. I'll have to get rid of ye for knowing too much about me bridge."

Before she could tell him the feeling was mutual, sparkles in the air caught her eye. They glittered in the lantern light and floated down around the Troll. He gasped and his eyes widened when they came within his view. "What th—?"

Before he could finish the sentence, his body went stiff. Just as he started to topple over, Myghal plucked the lantern from his grasp, and the Troll fell with a solid thunk.

Myghal helped her to sit up. "He'll be all right. In a couple of days."

Kerry grinned. "What about Gomit?"

"I'm here, Lady Kerry." The little Gnome, not nearly as ugly when compared to the Troll, appeared in the doorway. "You'd both best be off now. Tredje had received a message by Sprite that more Trolls are on their way because the Thane isn't pleased with the way Tredje is handling the situation. They could arrive at any time."

"You're right, Sir Gomit." Myghal flashed him a smile. "I thank you, and all the Pixies thank you for your help."

Gomit bowed. "It's been a privilege and an honor to serve in my small way."

Myghal looked at her. "Are you ready to go with me into the Faerie Realm?"

"What about Gomit? Won't Tredje and the other Trolls think it's strange if Gomit isn't unconscious or something? I wouldn't want him to get in trouble."

"Never fear, Lady. The Prince has charmed a little dust for me."

Myghal laughed. "He'll be unconscious with bruises and cuts all over him, but without the pain. They'll think he put up a good fight."

Gomit leaned closer to Myghal. "An excellent choice, my liege. She cares about those who serve. The mark of a true Princess."

Kerry blushed, but Myghal nodded and clapped him on the back.

Once again, Kerry heard sounds—this time, loud voices ranting and raving—echo through the tunnels.

"It's time, my liege," Gomit whispered.

"Are you ready, Kerry? Transportation will feel strange, but it will be over almost instantaneously."

She nodded that she understood.

"Hold my hand. You'll experience complete darkness, but it will be over in a moment." He looked at her questioningly, as if asking if she'd be all right.

She nodded and did as he directed, intertwining her fingers firmly with his. Then he threw a bit of dust over them, and sparkles filled the air, each miniscule crystal shimmering and glinting in the lantern light. The crystals coalesced into a swirl that whipped around them both. Her bones felt loose and a sharp sensation sank to the pit of her stomach. Then all went dark.

Chapter Seventeen

Kerry walked along the path of rose-pink stone through the wildest part of the vast gardens that surrounded the Palace. Here, indigenous plants were allowed to flourish and overflow every available space. The garden was a riot of color and the air scented as sweetly as a perfumery with every plant in full bloom even though it was only the first day of spring.

Her wedding had been as magical as any childhood fantasy. Whisked away by Pixie dust to a land somewhere over the Rainbow—as good a description as any, as far as she was concerned—the wedding had taken place immediately. No one needed to fill out a form to get a license.

She wore a wedding dress straight out of a fairy-tale, a frothy confection of iridescent white, shimmering with every color of the rainbow whenever she moved. The longest points of the uneven handkerchief hem barely reached her ankles, the shortest her knees. She'd been crowned with a circlet of white and blue roses. And she'd already seen beds of blue roses, all shades from palest sky blue to deepest indigo.

Blue roses were a genetic impossibility in her world.

How strange that even as a child she'd never envisioned being swept off her feet by a prince and taken to his castle...er, palace. She had always pretended to slay the dragon, find the treasure, and save the kingdom...er, princedom. Yet, here she was, the only human—as far as she knew—to marry a prince and become a fairy princess...er, Pixie Princess.

She'd slain no dragons—Myghal said they lived deep in Wildwood, the dark and forbidding forest that separated Pixieland from the Faerie Kingdom—but by marrying a Prince she'd saved the princedom.

And the only treasure she ever wanted was Myghal.

Princess Kerry turned to find her husband, Prince Myghal, a few steps behind her. He was devastatingly handsome in fawn-colored leggings and a billowy-sleeved shirt made of the same soft-as-cotton but iridescent material as her gown. Their ceremony had been performed in a Pixie circle, witnessed by most of the good folk of Pixieland, and presided over by Chancellor Malthe. Myghal's friend Sirrin had served as his best man, and Sirrin's sister had acted as her maid of honor. They were called by different terms, but the meanings were the same.

At the conclusion, they'd been showered with a cloud of glittering, sparkling Pixie dust that had been charmed to bring them all kinds of good luck, good fortune, and bright blessings. Kerry had watched the sunlight play off the bits of crystal, knowing in its raw form it was simply salt mined from the earth in her realm by the Gnomes. That was a royal secret, of course.

While everyone had danced to wild Pixie music and drunk dandelion wine and honeymead, she and Myghal had slipped away to be alone. The gardens were empty. Everyone, including the gardeners, were celebrating the royal marriage and the saving of Pixieland.

"Are you happy?" Myghal asked as he caught up to her.

She nodded and melted into his arms. She was happy, satisfied, contented. This was an entirely different world, but she felt up to the challenge of trying to fit in and be a princess. With Myghal to help her, everything would turn out all right. He had said they could visit her realm any time she wanted. She had family and friends she needed to explain to…somehow.

"I wish Gomit could have been here. Without him, none of this would have happened."

"In time to save Pixieland," Myghal amended. "I would have made you my wife, regardless."

Kerry kissed him, a lip-searing kiss that aroused her. It had the same effect on Myghal. She felt his cock stir through their layers of clothing.

"Do you think he'll be all right? That the Trolls will believe his story?"

"In case you didn't notice, Trolls aren't the smartest of creatures. Tredje was typical. Mean and self-centered but dim. They'll believe Gomit because they believe Gnomes to be worthless."

"They wouldn't hurt him, would they?"

"No, because that would require effort. Even if they decided to, I have faith Gomit will talk them out of it. Gnomes are quite glib."

"It's a very good thing the Pixies did them a kindness in the past, so that Gomit was there to help us. He said no one really remembered because it happened so long ago. Do you know what the Pixies did for the Gnomes to win their allegiance?"

Myghal thought a moment. "Ah, yes, I remember the story. A Pixie Princess fell in love with a Gnome soldier."

Kerry stepped back, her eyes wide in disbelief. The Pixies were enough like humans that they could pass in her realm with no difficulty. But Gnomes, if they were all like Gomit, were quite different. "Are you sure about that?"

Myghal grinned. "Well, it's said he was uncommonly tall and handsome for a Gnome, and she was exceptionally short and plain for a Pixie. She was the youngest of a large brood of the Prince's offspring, and therefore not in line to inherit the princedom. And because she wasn't the most beauteous, to put it kindly, her father despaired of ever marrying her off and eagerly gave his blessing. The Gnomes, fearing the wrath of the Pixies over one of their kind having the audacity to ask for a Princess in marriage, were greatly relieved and swore their allegiance to the Pixies for forever and a day."

When Kerry had moved back, she'd stepped off the pink stone path and into a bed of wild mint. The tender leaves, warmed by the sun and crushed beneath her feet, released a cool crisp scent that wafted around them on the light breeze. She caught Myghal's hand and drew him into the center of the bed of mint and into her arms. Her hand slid down between their bodies and found the hard length of his cock. It swelled at her touch.

"You know, we have yet to consummate this marriage," Kerry whispered. "In my world, a marriage isn't a true marriage unless it's consummated."

"The same is true here." Myghal sounded as if he fought for breath, and his fingers skimmed the neckline of her bodice. "Our marriage won't be recognized as legitimate until we complete the union."

He plucked the intricately tied bow in the center and pulled the lacings free. When her breasts were exposed to his eager gaze, he cupped one, his caress as light as the breeze but strong enough to send a surge of hot pleasure speeding through her body, from nipple to clit in less than six seconds.

"You're saying...Pixieland is still in danger?" Kerry murmured between gasps for air. "Then we must sacrifice for the good of the princedom."

"Aye," Myghal agreed and swooped his head low to take the erect tip of one breast between his lips. "For the good of the prince and the princess as well."

Kerry laughed breathlessly. She found the lacings of his leggings and untied them. Dipping her hand inside, she wrapped her fingers around his thick cock and rubbed back and forth along its rigid length. With a deep sigh, Myghal tugged her gown until it was bunched at her waist. He went down on his knees and slid her gown and panties down at the same time. She stepped free of them and went down to her knees as well.

"I want you, now, Myghal."

"Your wish is my command, wife."

Kerry lay back as Myghal climbed between her thighs. He tugged at his leggings, freeing his cock, and thrust into her. Kerry rested her bent legs on his hips, matching the tempo of her hips to his. She opened her eyes. She wanted to see him, see her husband.

"I love you, Myghal."

He looked down at her, his green eyes darkened with passion. "I love you, Kerry O'Neill."

Their bodies moved and built momentum. Kerry held onto his shoulders and watched the reflection of his desire cross his face. With one hand, she reached down to crush more mint and fill the air with its scent…but her hand touched nothing.

She turned her head and her hands scrambled to hug Myghal closer. "We-We're floating!"

"Aye, we are." He spun them into an upright position, so that now Kerry sat on his lap but was still impaled by his cock. "Spontaneous levitation during sex only happens when the couple is meant for each other."

Although it defied the laws of physics, Myghal pumped into her without shooting them off into space. Tentatively, Kerry moved her hips, catching his rhythm again. When they continued to hover about a yard above the mint bed, she relaxed against him, her arms around his neck.

When the heat of their desire burst and soared through her, she knew without a doubt that Myghal was the other half of her heart, body, and soul. She would gladly pledge her love forever and a day to her prince of pleasure.

About the author:

Lani welcomes mail from readers. You can write to her c/o Ellora's Cave Publishing at 1056 Home Avenue, Akron OH 44310-3502.

Also by Lani Aames:

Desperate Hearts
Ellora's Cavemen: Tales From the Temple I anthology
Eternal Passion
Lusty Charms: Invictus
Things That Go Bump in the Night II anthology

Why an electronic book?

We live in the Information Age—an exciting time in the history of human civilization in which technology rules supreme and continues to progress in leaps and bounds every minute of every hour of every day. For a multitude of reasons, more and more avid literary fans are opting to purchase e-books instead of paperbacks. The question to those not yet initiated to the world of electronic reading is simply: *why?*

1. *Price.* An electronic title at Ellora's Cave Publishing and Cerridwen Press runs anywhere from 40-75% less than the cover price of the exact same title in paperback format. Why? Cold mathematics. It is less expensive to publish an e-book than it is to publish a paperback, so the savings are passed along to the consumer.
2. *Space.* Running out of room to house your paperback books? That is one worry you will never have with electronic novels. For a low one-time cost, you can purchase a handheld computer designed specifically for e-reading purposes. Many e-readers are larger than the average handheld, giving you plenty of screen room. Better yet, hundreds of titles can be stored within your new library—a single microchip. (Please note that Ellora's Cave and Cerridwen Press does not endorse any specific brands. You can check our website at www.ellorascave.com or

www.cerridwenpress.com for customer recommendations we make available to new consumers.)

3. *Mobility.* Because your new library now consists of only a microchip, your entire cache of books can be taken with you wherever you go.
4. *Personal preferences are accounted for.* Are the words you are currently reading too small? Too large? Too...**ANNOYING**? Paperback books cannot be modified according to personal preferences, but e-books can.
5. *Instant gratification.* Is it the middle of the night and all the bookstores are closed? Are you tired of waiting days—sometimes weeks—for online and offline bookstores to ship the novels you bought? Ellora's Cave Publishing sells instantaneous downloads 24 hours a day, 7 days a week, 365 days a year. Our e-book delivery system is 100% automated, meaning your order is filled as soon as you pay for it.

Those are a few of the top reasons why electronic novels are displacing paperbacks for many an avid reader. As always, Ellora's Cave and Cerridwen Press welcomes your questions and comments. We invite you to email us at service@ellorascave.com, service@cerridwenpress.com or write to us directly at: 1056 Home Ave. Akron OH 44310-3502.

Cerridwen, the Celtic Goddess of wisdom, was the muse who brought inspiration to storytellers and those in the creative arts. Cerridwen Press encompasses the best and most innovative stories in all genres of today's fiction. Visit our site and discover the newest titles by talented authors who still get inspired - much like the ancient storytellers did, once upon a time.

ELLORA'S CAVE
ROMANTICA PUBLISHING

Printed in the United States
39342LVS00001B/241-258

9 781419 952364